I Can See
the Rain Is Gone

I Can See Clearly Now the Rain Is Gone

George Korankye

First edition
Published in Great Britain
By Mirage Publishing 2009

First published in paperback 2009

A CIP catalogue record for this book
is available from the British Library.

ISBN: 978-1-902578-48-4

Mirage Publishing
PO Box 161
Gateshead
NE8 1WY
Great Britain

Printed and bound in Great Britain by

Book Printing UK
Remus House, Coltsfoot Drive, Woodston, Peterborough, PE2 9JX

Papers used in the production of this book are from sustainable
forests, thus reducing environmental depletion.

'A Jade is useless before it is processed; a man is good for nothing until he is educated'
Chinese proverb

Dedicated to all Diagnostic and Therapeutic Radiographers worldwide. Radiographers, at times in traumatic situations, are confronted with unimaginable horror, resulting in emotional and psychological problems. Yet they are not deterred and continue to work discreetly in the background. I hope this book helps educate the public not only of their training, but also of the care and dignity which form an essential part of all their work.

'Tell me and I'll forget. Show me, and I may not remember. Involve me, and I'll understand'
Native American proverb

Contents

Introduction

'There are no hands so gentle as those that have known adversity'

The above anonymous quotation forms the underlying principle of this book. The book is intended to show the diverse roles radiographers play even in major traumatic incidents. But it accomplishes this in a 'gentle' sympathetic manner. Many people outside of the hospital environment are ignorant of radiographers. A member of the public in response to a pre-amble of the book by the Edinburgh *Evening News* commented 'What does a person who takes pictures of bones know about trauma?'[1]

Turn on any TV programme, read any medical thriller/fiction and you will find numerous medical characters like doctors, nurses, psychologists - not radiographers. The reader's response is thus symptomatic of this attitude. This is the first 'faction' book with a radiographer as the main character.

The SCoR is trying to address the public's perception of radiographers, hence the inception of Radiographer of the Year Competition in November annually. Radiographers are involved in nearly 90 percent of diagnostic and therapeutic procedures. For example, the

---

[1] Writer tells how medics coped with Dunblane horror at http://edinburghnews.scotsman.com/latestnews/Writer-tells-how-medics-coped.5438025.jp Retrieved July 2009

book mentions a dialogue between two ambulance men. They discuss famous TV and media medical characters. Josh, Charlie Fairhead and Harry represent paramedics, nurses and consultants in the BBC TV drama *Casualty*. George Clooney's Dr Ross in NBC's *ER* has made this character universal. Doctor Jones of ITV's *This Morning* is a household name. There is no similar recognition of radiographers.

The book, although fictional, will hopefully help educate the public in the duties of radiographers. Diagnostic Radiographers are involved in: Ultrasound, CT and MRI scans, Nuclear Medicine, Bone Density, Endoscopies, Cardiac surgery and Dental examinations.

In the operating theatre, they are necessary for urology and orthopaedic procedures. Forensic Radiography is another branch unknown to the public. On an educational note, archaeologists, historians and anthropologists have utilized their diagnostic skills in finding more about our ancestors by x-raying mummies,[2] tombs, etc without opening caskets. Unknown to the public are radiographers who undertake research in universities and non academic facilities.

Then there are the Therapeutic Radiographers who play an important role in cancer diagnosis. The recent fall in some cancers[3] has led to the profile of some medics being raised, but not radiographers. However, most cancer patients will come into contact with a Therapeutic

---

[2] Ancient Egyptians unwrapped: CT scans reveal shrouded secrets of 2,000-year-old mummies www.dailymail.co.uk/sciencetech/article-1195045/Ancient-Egyptians-unwrapped-CT-scans-reveal-secrets-beneath-bandages-2-000-year-old-mummies.html Retrieved July 2009

[3] Dramatic drop in deaths from most common cancers http://info.cancerresearchuk.org/news/archive/pressreleases/2009/july/drop-in-deaths-common-cancers Retrieved July 2009

Radiographer who will be an integral part of their treatment and care.

With so much negative publicity relating to the health service, this book shows a different aspect of the NHS. In spite of MRSA, C DIFF, rising litigation, a few incompetent doctors, etc, there are individuals and professions, some prominent, others working tirelessly without fanfare in the background, who feel and care deeply about those they meet.

When a major incident occurs such as Lockerbie (Scotland), 9/11 (US), the July 2005 atrocities (London), the bombings in Mumbai, Spain or any country worldwide, radiographers will be involved in the medical chain.

Once all efforts to save a life have been completed, a radiographer's role goes on. They may have to x-ray a dead body to provide forensic information for pathologists, coroners or the police. These individuals are therefore not immune to the emotional and psychological scars their patients undergo.

Radiographers do not just take pictures of bones they see traumatic situations daily.

Enjoy the book and I hope once you've read it with an open unbiased mind you will have a different concept of radiographers. And who knows, perhaps one day children will grow up not playing *doctors and nurses*, but *doctors, nurses and radiographers*! Oh and lastly, why not listen to the song *I Can See Clearly Now* by Johnny Nash, it portrays the whole sentiments of this book.

'They who love most are least valued'
English proverb

Acknowledgements

'Words have no wings but they can fly many thousands of miles'
Korean proverb

In writing this book there is always the possibility that I may miss someone. If so, please forgive me. Thanks Richard for the idea for the book. You too Mr Robin Mckinlay, the anaesthetist, for being helpful. 'A teacher is better than two books,' German proverb. I haven't forgotten your profession and the ethical dilemmas you too face. Mrs Kavanagh A/E Consultant, thanks for your constructive criticism and advice. Gerry, Tricia, and Kevin the radiographers, thanks. John the porter, I have listened to you and tried to convey how you and your colleagues felt. As you said: 'there were grown men crying their eyes out' that day. Thanks for the wonderful insight you provided me. June the cleaner, I haven't overlooked your 'mob', thanks. Colin, thanks for the information about the role of A/E nurses. Kevin at orthopaedics, thanks for pointing me in the right direction too. All at work i.e. Jenni, Gillian, Laura et al who provided me with feedback, thanks! Then of course, Mr Smith and Mr Teahan the consultants, thanks for the wonderful insight you both provided. Oh by the way, Mr Smith, enjoy your retirement in November 2009.

However my thanks go to my 'ruthless' copy-editor, Johnny at Mirage. No I didn't mean that, honestly I appreciated your 'tactful' remarks. Your comments were invaluable. If it were not for you inputs the story would not have flowed so easily. Yes I do go on a bit. My wife-Sharon - and Anne-Marie at Queen Margaret University have already said that. As the Irish say 'A friend's eye is a good mirror.' My thanks too to Gemma Fraser and the Editor of the Edinburgh *Evening News* for giving me such a balanced coverage even before the book became published. The feedback from your readers provided valuable information about the lack of information the public have of radiographers. 'The wise adapt themselves to circumstances, as water moulds itself to the pitcher.' Chinese proverb. I hope I've addressed some of the points raised. Thanks to Anne Brown of Kippen for her editing and constructive criticism.

Thanks too to Warner Chappell and Johnny Nash for allowing me to use the title and lyrics of the song *I Can See Clearly Now* (the rain is gone) in the book.

Finally thanks to Steve at Mirage for having faith in me and encouraging me to write another book although I had given up the idea. You are right 'Worrying never did anyone any good'. And when I worried about critics you quoted Machiavelli 'Hatred is gained as much by good works as by evil.' To those who have played a lesser part and who I have inadvertently missed I repeat, thank you!

'He who does not thank for little will not thank for much'
Estonian proverb

I Can See Clearly Now the Rain Is Gone

I can see clearly now the rain is gone
I can see all obstacles in my way
Gone are the dark clouds that had me blind
It's gonna be a bright (bright), bright (bright)
Sun-shiny day.

I think I can make it now, the pain is gone
All of the bad feelings have disappeared
Here is that rainbow I've been prayin' for
It's gonna be a bright (bright), bright (bright)
Sun-shiny day.

Look all around, there's nothin' but blue skies
Look straight ahead, nothin' but blue skies.

I can see clearly now the rain is gone
I can see all obstacles in my way
Gone are the dark clouds that had me blind
It's gonna be a bright (bright), bright (bright)
Sun-shiny day.

Legal Disclaimer

Although this book is based on actual facts and events. Incidents, events, conversations, characters and timelines have been changed for dramatic purposes. Characters are entirely fictitious. Any resemblance to real people, living or dead, is entirely coincidental and is not intended to depict any actual person or event.

This book inspired by and based on some true events, however, has been fictionalized and all persons appearing in this work are fictitious.

The characters and the events in this book constitute an artistic invention and have been used only for the creation of the story. They do not represent any particular person and do not reflect events from this person's life. The characters and places have been changed and do not reflect on the identities of actual people and places.

The author has fictionalized conversations and deeds, they do not necessarily reflect events that may or may not have happened.

Although some aspects of this story may remind you of the Dunblane incident, this story and its characters are fictional and the events and actions portrayed do not reflect the actions of any principals involved in that incident.

Chapter 1

The Accident and Emergency Department of Bonnyholly Hospital waited with bated breath. Dealing with traumatic situations was routine and yet no one had ever experienced, or anticipated, what was about to unfold. In the distance, wailing sirens were initially barely audible. As they drew nearer, the sound grew in intensity and the atmosphere of the hospital became electric.

Like foghorns, the clamour made some think of the Sirens of Greek mythology which drew the sailors onto the rocks; sirens of destruction. A few of the gathered staff sniffled uncomfortably, and noiseless tears, faintly coloured by mascara, trickled down their cheeks; others remained silent. Most could not contain their emotions and appeared visibly shaken, their chests heaving as they tried to control themselves. Then there were those who stood twirling their thumbs nervously in a circular motion. The rest, with downcast eyes, gazed thoughtfully at the ground, perhaps expecting the floor to offer some words of wisdom, condolence or encouragement. Gulps of air as loud as thunder could be heard in the silent atmosphere, and occasionally the phlegmatic staccato of the clearing of throats, feet shuffled about nervously, like footballers waiting for the referee to blow his whistle for the final of the local derby. All eyes had that glazed concentrated stare. The adrenalin in the air was reminiscent of two pugilists facing each other with high octave energy and bare fists ready to pounce on their opponent and beat them to a pulp.

Even jovial Mark Walker, the radiographer, known for cheering patients with his wit and banter, knew this was not an appropriate time for any banality. Everyone had a premonition this would be a day to remember. A day that would be indelibly printed, indeed etched on their minds forever. It was a day when they were all going to experience the truthfulness of Robert Burns' words 'Man's inhumanity to man makes countless thousands moan'. Some would recover; some wouldn't; sadly one would end up the same way as the victims they were about to treat – dead, because of the sheer stress of being a witness to unimaginable horror. Hands that habitually delivered care and comfort to the injured and dying would deal their possessor a cruel blow. Some would not be able to return to work. A few would become physiological wrecks as they turned to drinking to ease their tortured guilt-ridden minds.

The victims' families would blame the police for their supposed incompetence and cover-up. Questions would be raised in the media by the public and in Parliament, triggering a full-scale public enquiry. The despicable act would leave no one unscathed as it spread its tentacles far and wide. The news of the outrage would reach around the world. It might be said the victims would be the lucky ones; the survivors ironically, and tragically, becoming the victims. How cruel events can turn a day of joy into one of such sorrow.

Rising like a phoenix out of the sadness will be the deed of one group of people. This small band is involved in over ninety per cent of all diagnostic procedures. Their role is mostly unknown by the public, their profession largely ignored, seldom on any news channel, or in newspapers, books, comic strips, or films and no famous actor is noted for playing that role. They are virtually unheard of, except to other medical professionals but they will emerge as heroes from this tragedy. Without their skills, reliable diagnostic information would have been difficult to obtain, and their work continues when everyone else goes home.

After this day, their occupation will finally be recognized by the government who, in appreciation of their tireless commitment, will allocate a special day in November to them; even the Queen will pay them a surprise visit because of a chance remark she reads in the media. Out of the ashes of despair on this day will grow the recognition of this humble group of workers. So, who are these people? The answer lies in this story.

Bonnyholly lay in a picturesque location. Its inhabitants had been drawn from all corners of the United Kingdom. Many of its residents were the fifth and sixth generation, many others incomers. This mixture of people from all parts was reflected in the accents, words and language they used. Bonnyholly had a unique dialect of its own with a mingling of Scots and English.

In the hospital, the siren voices were growing ever louder, ever closer. At first, it sounded as if there was only one ambulance but as the ominous sound came nearer, it was evident there were two or more and eventually no-one bothered to count. The cacophony grew as ambulance and police sirens intermingled, rather like those usually heard on television programmes, and added urgency to the situation. It was a bit like an orchestra coming to a crescendo in a grand finale of, perhaps, the *Last Night of the Proms*, but there the similarity ended. The Proms always concluded with a joyful rendition of a famous song. There would be no joyful conclusion that day.

The few minutes before the arrival of the ambulances seemed like an eternity. The hospital stood in eerie silence awaiting its unwilling guests, the passengers in that ambulance convoy whose condition was so far unknown and could only be guessed at. Some of those waiting wished those blasted drivers would turn off their desperate sirens. They could not. They had to keep them on, to say to other vehicles 'Get out of the way. Make room for me. A life is at stake here.'

Whom were these ambulances bringing to Bonnyholly Hospital? They were defenceless little children. They knew that much; they knew something terrible had happened at the Primary School. It couldn't just be one child with the number of sirens that were approaching. So what had those poor children done to deserve such a fate? These weren't some victims from a drunken brawl on a Saturday night, or football fans caught up in pitched battles in the city centre after a derby match - nor were they victims of drink or drugs. They were just innocent little children.

How cruel the Greek Goddesses the Moirae: Clotho who spun the thread of life; those infernal Goddesses who were supposed to determine each one's fate. How cruel you are Clotho, to spin so short a length for a poor child. What wrong has she done to you? You did not know her, or live with her. For nine months you knew nothing of the pain of childbirth or the sleepless nights, the changing of nappies. Ignorant also were you of the feelings aroused by her first smile, her 'drunken' first walk and the joy those unforgettable first words – 'mama', 'dada' - gave to her parents.

And now heartless Lachesis, who determined the

length of life, how hated you must be to spin such a small length of five years for such a beloved child. Her heartbroken parents did not get a chance to say goodbye. For them, there would be no teenage tantrums, walking down the aisle to the accompaniment of the 'Wedding March'. You have robbed them of grandchildren too. Cursed you be for all eternity, cruel, cruel Lachesis, devoid of any children, may your name be for ever reviled.

And finally you, Atropos, who cut the thread of life; may your memory too be odious to any parent for your cruelty. Accursed be all you goddesses, may no one name their children in your honour because of your vindictiveness, for your lack of compassion on that frightful day. Do you know what you all in your wisdom conspired for those innocent children? Were you aware what havoc you were reaping? Would you have been so cruel if it had been your own children? Did you have a perverse enjoyment seeing those small lifeless limbs resembling polished marble marionettes lying so still and lifeless? Even the beauty of the Three Graces did not match those children in their motionless state. Was this all an act of jealousy because you envied those poor, poor humans who possessed things you could not have or were unable to replicate – their children, their offspring?

The silence was broken by the radio.

'Ambulance one here. We're five minutes from base. We've three victims on board. All three's condition is critical. Over.'

'Ambulance one, we receive you,' said base, 'have all staff on standby. Over and out.'

No sooner had ambulance one finished than ambulance two radioed in a similar message. The staff could hear the sombre voices of the crews through the radio speakers. In the background between those fateful words heard on the radios was the bleeping of machines on standby at the hospital. It was as if even inanimate objects knew what lay ahead. Their constant flashing lights gave the impression they could not, today, of all days, malfunction. When ambulance three radioed in, it seemed to the staff, their premonition of something truly dreadful was coming true. With the report of ambulance four, they were in no doubt that this was no ordinary trauma situation they were dealing with. Some knew a little of what to expect but others who had been working that day and were not tuned into the hospital radio were unaware of what lay ahead. Everyone had all kinds of scenarios running through their heads but they were to find to their cost how mistaken they had all been and how their expectations fell far short of the actual situation.

With the ambulance crews a few minutes away, Mark, the Superintendent Radiographer, decided to remind his staff briefly of what lay ahead. Mrs Rose McLeish, the Accident and Emergency Consultant, did the same. All departments had carefully rehearsed what to do in this sort of situation. But practice is one thing; reality presents different and often, very difficult challenges.

The minutes before the arrival of the first ambulance ticked slowly away. Four minutes to go. Mrs McLeish paced up and down the corridor nervously and as if to find something to keep her mind occupied, started examining her staff. Like a general inspecting his troops, she straightened collars, brushed off cotton wool fluff from Anne Stuart, one of the Accident and Emergency team's hair. They all looked polished in their uniforms except for the green plastic splash aprons, providing them with protective shields just as the Americans had planned for their proposed Star Wars project, which had attracted so much media attention. The addition of these barriers to their everyday uniforms was proof they were expecting blood and bodily fluids in copious quantities. At the end of this day and of their gruesome duties, those aprons would have been changed so many times that the hospital would have to send for additional supplies. Rose McLeish even went as far as switching the defibrillators and all the monitors off and on. It was as if she was pleading with them not to fail, not to let her down. She focused on the brand new machines recently delivered. She began mentally to speak to them in a way reminiscent of the chariot race in the film *Ben-Hur*, where Charlton Heston is seen affectionately conversing and simultaneously stroking the faces of his regal horses. He also appears to be pleading with his horses not to fail him in his final act of revenge against the Roman tribune Messalla, who had dealt so treacherously with his family.

Rose found herself playing a similar role. Passing Critcare, the machine with all its dials zeroed, she almost willed it to ensure its dials would rise - 'whatever you do, please don't remain in this inactive state once the casualties get here.' She was constantly amazed at the advancement of technology. Critcare was like a trusted slave, a bodyguard given the duty to protect its master at any cost. It could monitor blood pressure, temperature, the ratio of oxygen to carbon dioxide in the blood-stats, and it had the ability to literally revive a person. Incorporated in its casing was a defibrillator capable of restarting a heart.

If any machine could look after these children it was this one. If machines possessed feelings, Critcare would be in a class of its own. Rose McLeish was the only person with the power to deactivate it and without her acquiescence, it would function until its power source was terminated. She blushed slightly as she furtively placed an affectionate pat on the machine, hoping no one had noticed her eccentric behaviour. She silently wondered if the machines knew what great tasks would be expected of them. For an uncanny moment, the screens appeared to her to light up and then suddenly fade. She dismissed this as a figment of her imagination.

The gleaming new machines were no illusion though. They had replaced the 'old faithfuls' that very week. In a blessed coincidence of timing, the hospital had received some unexpected funding from the Scottish Government. Health Secretary Shonead Armstrong had paid a formal visit to the hospital earlier in the week.

How it annoyed Rose to see management pulling out all the stops to impress her. The estate department had been pulled off all jobs and given the task of repainting the corridors. Pictures drawn by local school children had been acquired and now graced those same corridors. Special flowers had been ordered, or to be precise, had been loaned from the local garden centre, to add colour and touch of flamboyance to the A&E wing, and, she supposed, in other areas too.

The whole scenario looked so false. She wondered whom they were trying to impress, and why. She had been fighting tirelessly for so long to have some of the old machines replaced but had been told that there was no money available, yet just prior to the visit of the Health Secretary, financial support had somehow been found.

Those machines were now displayed in all their pristine glory to Mrs Armstrong, who heaped praise on the management for such efficiency and for managing to keep up to date with the latest technology and all within budget. Rose remembered the Health Secretary's words.

'Bonnyholly Hospital is what we hope all Scottish hospitals should aspire to. Your management skills and patient care are second to none. The statistics you presented to me show you're using your funding to look after the staff and patients in a caring and professional manner. We are happy to support excellence, so well done all of you.'

Rose smiled wryly and thought to herself 'Why don't any of these ministers ever turn up unannounced without all the fanfare and ballyhoo? Then they would see the real hospital, not this sanitized environment specially manufactured to please them.'

Her views were endorsed by the removal and return of the flowers to the garden centre once the minister's visit was over. The gossip in the staff duty room was this was to recoup some of the cash needed for the air conditioning unit for the board-room. When Rose enquired why the plant life was suddenly deemed unsuitable for the hospital, she was told that it was to avoid contaminating the patients or, as it was put in hospital language, it was primarily to do with infection control. 'Infection control my ...' she checked herself before she could utter any profanity.

As the four minutes ticked slowly away, she continued her inspection, going through in her mind all the checklists. Had the waiting rooms all been cleared; had non-essential patients either been redirected to Bonnythistle, the satellite hospital, or been told to return another day? Next, she examined the resuscitation room, which her staff had abbreviated to *resus*. Were the resus trolleys in good condition, covered with crisp white Irish linen and the corners neatly tucked in around all the edges? Were the emergency cupboards all fully stocked with no essential drugs missing? She knew her trusted colleague Anne Noble (Anne with an e as she always reminded her) had done this.

Rose McLeish had absolute confidence in Anne as her track record was excellent and the A&E Consultant felt a professional affection for her. She had mentored her from her early days when, lacking in know-how and confidence, she had made mistakes. Her initial assessment, that Anne had potential and with a bit of coaching, mentoring and nurturing would be a suitable candidate for her to hand on the batten of leadership one day, had proved amazingly accurate. She had always been a strong advocate of delegation, and believed this showed an individual was competent and trustworthy. She only intervened if she felt there were glaring shortcomings which would interfere with either patient care or the team working spirit. If she had to offer personal assistance or comment, she ensured any advice was always constructive, intended to empower and enable someone, not tear them down. She always bore in mind a famous author saying 'correction does much but encouragement does more.' The words continued to be her philosophy. Even if things were drastically wrong and needed firm handling, if possible, she tried to encourage her staff. But at this particular moment she rechecked her resus trolleys herself, not because of a lack of trust, but because she was nervous. She knew Anne would leave nothing to chance, but she just had to make sure. A little sneaky peek, she thought to herself, would do no harm nor ruffle any feathers. Sheepishly she went around all the emergency resus trolleys, again opening them surreptitiously and noting their contents, and ensuring herself that everything was exactly as it should be.

In an undertone, she asked Anne if haematology had been informed. Anne gave her the thumbs up. She ticked this fact off her mental checklist. Were all the operating theatres free and had the surgeons been warned? She had to have confidence that this had been done, because it was too late to phone the theatre co-ordinator to check. Everyone knew what to do in a major incident. She had to trust her colleagues.

She glanced at the chalkboard, now wiped clean. There was no provision for names. Each patient would be assigned a number. Names would be added later. The important thing was to deal with the patient first. How different this was from her daily routine. Then, she wouldn't deal with a number. She would call a patient by his/her name, assess them, then diagnose and treat their condition. There was no time for that today and the indignity of individuals being rendered a number particularly vexed her. She was well aware many of the casualties would not survive the journey to the hospital. She knew some would actually die under her care. It was dreadful enough to be the brutal victim of a total stranger, but to suffer the ignominy of being treated in a hospital as a number, she felt, was an extreme affront to such young lives. But, she reflected, she wasn't there to make moral decisions; her duty was to care, stabilize and do the best she could for the children that chance had thrust under her supervision. She vowed silently that she would do all that she could.

Rose McLeish was fifty-four. To have attained the position of a female consultant in a male-dominated environment had been, to put it mildly, hard work. She'd spent six years at university, followed by eight years tutelage under sometimes harsh and ruthless superiors. After an extremely unpleasant episode when a male consultant stripped her of her dignity by chastising her in front of members of the public, she had vowed that she would never in her life treat others in a similar way. She was determined she wouldn't cause anyone to feel as she had that day, although secretly, with hindsight, she knew she had benefited from that dressing down in front of others. It was the catalyst for her development into a caring, and fair consultant who treated all, irrespective of her feelings about them, with compassion, dignity and respect.

She approved of a recent television programme *The Hospital* which she felt fully epitomized the dilemma many doctors faced in A&E, trying to treat all individuals without making moral judgements. At times, she had wondered at the self-inflicted injuries of many of the young she treated, asking herself why they behaved in such a way. Why was there the need for all these excesses, which were placing unimaginable strains on the National Health Service?

She remembered her own salad days, the drinking in the student union bars, the free love that accompanied those binges and the price some of her friends had paid. Some had dropped out of university; others had suffered repercussions that, even thirty years later, hurt her to remember. She mused that perhaps those good old days were not so good at all and maybe things had not really changed. Would today's young in later life also see their past as 'good old days'? She reflected that it wasn't only the young that engaged in destructive behaviour, but many of the older generation also did it these days.

Rose McLeish shook herself out of her reverie and laughed inwardly. She sounded like one of the psychiatric patients she'd treated recently. She thought this was what paranoia must feel like. She knew everything was in order, and yet she had this inexplicable desire to check and re-check things. It was like some poor individuals who can't relax on holiday because they constantly worry about the house, if they'd cancelled the milk, and turned off the lights, or whether they'd left the fridge switched on or off. All her concentration now had to be on team work, with each member playing his or her important part in what lay ahead. Remember TEAM, she told herself – Together Everyone Achieves More, knowing failure to apply that maxim would jeopardize patient care.

The clock was ticking the minutes away to the arrival of the first ambulance. Suddenly, on the scene appeared Tony Prescott, the bed manager with his clipboard. Everyone knew Tony; he was always running around A&E like a headless chicken. There were never enough beds in the hospital to suit his requirements. At times, he had to shuffle patients between wards to accommodate urgent cases. He would certainly be faced with challenges today. The special children's ward was full and doctors and consultants were busily assessing cases to see who could be sent home to recuperate. The dilemma was to ensure the specialist care the children required would not be compromised by discharging them prematurely. There might be bed spaces in other wards but it was imperative that children be kept in the ward specially dedicated to their requirements. Their needs were unquestionably different. Catheters, for example, were of a different calibre from those used by adults.

Tony knew that if children were accommodated in adult wings, there could be logistical problems like getting the right equipment and medicines to them. Children's medicines required different dosage and meticulous measurements were necessary to reduce toxicity. Tony appeared to be happy with his preparation; he too now could do nothing but wait and see. He was part of the team and he had to ensure his other professionals were also on the same wavelength. He was confident they were. He now stood at the ready with his clipboard, resembling a time and motion man at a factory who was assessing the competency of the workers.

Superintendent Radiographer Mark was also going through his final checks. It never ceased to amaze him the pivotal role radiographers play in such cases. Many people are aware of nurses, doctors, ambulance crews, paramedics and surgeons. The role of the breakdown man who is employed by the AA is better known than that of a radiographer, who is sometimes referred to as an x-ray nurse. Most people think of radiographers as people who go behind a screen to take pictures of bones. 'If only life was as simple as that,' Mark thought, knowing that the majority of people need the services of radiographers at some stage during their lifetime and yet few actually understood what exactly they do. Many people are sent for chest x-rays, and examining teeth and lower limbs comes fairly high in their work. Mark's thoughts went back to a recent conversation he had with a patient.

'I've always wondered,' Jennifer Hughes had enquired, during her chest x-ray, 'why I've to stand with my back to the x-ray machine and can you also please explain why I have to hug this chest stand and when you say so, I then have to take a deep breath and hold it?'

Mark was taken slightly aback; usually, patients just present themselves for x-ray with no questions asked. Jennifer Hughes had said all this without taking in a breath. Mark rather wished he'd taken the opportunity to x-ray her chest at that moment.

'Well,' he said, rather pleased to be asked a thought-provoking question. 'You know, you've made my day. It's good when a patient is interested in what a radiographer does. So many people just don't know what we do. Let me explain. Firstly, I ask you to hug the chest stand because of the position of the heart. You see, your heart, if you were facing the x-ray camera, won't show its true size, it'll be magnified. The same will happen to your pulmonary bits, all the big veins, and arteries coming out of your heart. But that's not all; it helps to show the central regions of the lungs better. Radiographers are also making sure the radiation dose patients get is kept as low as possible, so, by having your back to the x-ray camera, the areas that are sensitive to radiation like your thyroid and breast receive less radiation.'

'I see, but what about this taking a deep breath in, and then this metal thing you put on the cassette that has a big R on it' asked his patient.

'I was coming to that, Mrs Hughes.'

'Oh sorry,' she said.

'Not to worry,' said Mark reassuringly, 'you see, by breathing in and holding your breath for a few seconds, your diaphragm moves south and so we can see more of your lungs. After all, that's why you're having your lungs examined.'

'I hope you don't consider me a nuisance – and I promise I'll keep ma gob shut after this - but why do I either have to hug this chest stand or, as some of your colleagues say, put the back of my hands on my hips and roll my shoulders forwards? And you haven't answered the big R question, either.'

'Let me assure you, Mrs Hughes, you're not being a nuisance at all. I know I speak for all my colleagues in radiography when I say we welcome questions and wish more patients were like you. You see, your scapulae, as we in the medical profession call them, or your shoulder blades as you call them, are also in the lung area, so it doesn't matter which position the radiographer gets you to take. The main reason is to move those shoulders blades out of the way of the lungs.'

'So what you're telling me is you want to get as a big a picture of the lungs as you can, as well as keeping the radiation dose as low as possible and all the instructions you give me helps you do that.'

'That's one hundred per cent correct, Mrs Hughes.'

'And the big R?'

'The big R is what we call a marker. You see, the body has two sides, right and left. We put the marker on so that anyone who looks at the pictures a radiographer has taken knows which side it refers to. So the big R means that is your right side.'

'Oh that's interesting, but what would happen if you didn't put a marker on?'

'Well there could be dire consequences for the patient. I mean the worse that could happen is, for example, the patient might need to have something done on the left leg and the surgeon operates on the right one.'

'I didn't know there's so much skill involved in your profession.'

'Glad you realize that,' said Mark 'but you know it's not just skill, it's also patient care,' he added.

'What do you mean?'

'Well, imagine the waiting room is absolutely choc-a-bloc; it's not unusual for radiographers to miss their tea break so patients can be looked after. And then at times we are Agony Aunts.'

'Agony Aunts?' Jennifer was perplexed.

'Yes. Everyone coming to a hospital is not in fine fettle. Some start to pour their hearts out to us. Even if the waiting room is full, you just can't shoo them out, you have to listen. But it's not all doom and gloom, occasionally we get a sweetie from an old lady's bag which has been in there a while. Someone always brightens our day.'

'Well I hope you have a nice day and I hope you manage to get a tea break, you certainly deserve it.'

'Thank you, Mrs Hughes. I knew that was coming.'

'How?'

'I'm a radiographer aren't I, I can see right through you,' said Mark with a wry smile.

Jennifer smiled back. 'Thanks again,' she said as she left.

Mark brought his thoughts back to today. It would prove to be an important one for radiographers. Without their expert and technical skills, metal objects in the body couldn't be detected. Today the vital questions might be, *has a bullet lodged in a vital organ and how carefully must an A&E doctor or surgeon proceed in extricating it*? Only x-rays could provide the answers.

Mark's team of radiographers would have to work with many constraints in a trauma setting. They would have to take diagnostic images without, if possible, exacerbating the condition of the patients. They would have to think about so many things, such as if any of the patients were wearing a cervical collar, which couldn't be removed in case this led to paralysis - and possibly disciplinary action. They must work quickly, deftly, silently and carefully. At the same time, they might have to deal with a screaming, confused patient in a cramped resus bay. Their patients may have had pain relief but some trauma situations are so debilitating, that diagnostic images are impossible without some kind of movement causing anguished cries irrespective of the amount of analgesia administered.

Mark listened to the approaching sirens. He envisaged

the media praise for the noble effort of his team. Now the public would come to see his profession in a different light. How wrong he was. The noble efforts of his team would be largely ignored by the press and the broadcast media. Doctors, nurses and management would all give heroic details of how they saved children that day. There would be no mention of any of Mark's team; no interviews on television for them; no radio announcements. No one would say how, without CT, or x-rays, diagnosis would be impossible and certainly no one would know of the eerie moment when a silent solitary radiographer would be sent to the mortuary in the bowels of the hospital to x–ray small limp lifeless bodies for forensic records. His only companion would be his trusted portable x-ray machine and his duty would not be to establish the time of death, but to find any bullets that were still lodged in that small body, so pathologists could record the number of bullets embedded in that once vibrant little life who now lay still and silent.

Like the A&E Consultant Rose McLeish, Mark moved to inspect his troops and his equipment. He too went to the resus room to inspect the trolleys. He thought it was probable that the patients could not be moved and he was grateful that manufacturers anticipated this possibility and incorporated in their trolleys a mechanism whereby an x-ray cassette could be placed under a person's body. The cassettes fitted into a mechanical device, which could be slid to any position under the patient. Mark inspected each device to ensure it was moving freely and none were jamming. Satisfied all was in order in the resus room, he repeated the checks on the trolleys in the corridors awaiting their occupants.

Mark knew what might lie in store, but he was worried. Not for himself but for Fatima, the new young graduate straight from university. He wondered how she would cope being thrown into the deep end. Was it right to subject such an inexperienced mind to such horrors so early in her career? Would it be an act of kindness to send her home?

It was a dilemma. All his staff was needed; he couldn't afford to lose anyone as he was unsure exactly what to expect. To send her home would deplete his numbers; to let her remain risked affecting her deeply and perhaps permanently. It might influence her view of children and motherhood to such an extent that she would decide not have children herself, children that could potentially be subject to such unspeakable horrors as the children now nearing the hospital had undergone. Mark knew the odds against such a traumatic reoccurrence in Bonnyholly were almost inestimable, but he also knew there was still the possibility his actions could have devastating effects for Fatima. He pondered long and hard on whether to send her home or not. He had been through some very touchy situations in his life and was aware of what to expect - but was his young graduate?

Chapter 2

Mark was in a quandary, and in the brief moment before the mayhem began, he remembered why he became a radiographer. He had initially wanted to be a physiotherapist, but failed at interview stage. Looking back now, he was glad that he did not fulfil that first ambition. He recalled how different things were when he went to Bonnyholly College. In those days, there was no emphasis on research methods, quantitative or qualitative analysis, samplings and so on. These were for hoity-toity folk, those who went to Cambridge or Oxford or aspired to be professors. The emphasis was on-the-job training, two weeks college followed by two weeks placement. What he learned at college he immediately put into practice. There was no three months holiday during the summer as trainee radiographers get now. Instead, he went to work in a hospital during the summer holidays.

He wondered how the current crop of graduates would have coped with not only the tutors but the senior staff. Back then, it was a case of 'yes, sir', 'no, madam'. No first names were used for senior staff, and there was certainly no disrespect or back chat from juniors or trainees. In addition, he had to know everything about electricity. His training included the workings of generators, capacitors (not the flux type which had been made famous because of the film *Back to the Future*), step up and step down transformers, A/C and D/C currents, and everything else. Manually setting exposures meant there was very little leeway if he got things wrong. Give a patient too much and your film came out too dark, too little and no detail appeared. He remembered standing at the processor waiting with bated breath, literally biting his finger nails to see if his setting parameters had been correct while hoping his superintendent would not appear to peer over his shoulder. He thought about the difference these days. Computers, he lamented, had taken the skills out of radiography, doing the thinking with minimal input from the operator. All the radiographer had to do in many cases was press a button, and the computer did the rest.

Mark thought the advances in thirty years had been little short of astonishing. Back then, darkroom technicians, who later developed darkroom disease, were mostly responsible for processing films in the darkroom. But when on-call or in an operating theatre, the radiographer was responsible for developing his images - without a computer - which meant knowing about the chemistry of photography. So Mark not only had to have a working knowledge of fixers and developers, but also the skills of correcting any deficiencies in any of these chemicals and knowing when they were out of sync. He had become quite adept at it. He remembered having to do this at times with a short-tempered and impatient surgeon, with very little communication skills, who was harassing him to get on with it so he could proceed with the next step in his operation. He also remembered how in awe some of his friends were of their seniors and there being such a culture of fear, that instead of admitting a mistake had been made about an image, it was not unusual for staff to take home old radiographs.

He had fond memories, too, of his wife teasingly saying 'you're just a glorified photographer.' It seemed that even in the good old days the role of the radiographer was little understood.

Mark's mind returned to Fatima. In his training days, he and most of his friends and fellow students were white and most were women. Fatima was a Scottish Muslim, evidence in itself of how the face of radiography had altered. He mused how modern day radiographers were not only multicultural, they were also multi-faith, certainly multi-gender and definitely multitalented. The rainbow nation tagline adopted by South Africa could well describe the makeup of British Radiographers. Fatima was a second generation Asian, born in Glasgow after her family were deported from Uganda in the seventies. She had a Scottish accent and had qualified from Queen Margaret University with a First Class Honours Degree in Diagnostic Radiography. Mark had high hopes for her as she had a caring nature, was soft spoken, a rarity for a Glaswegian, patient and kind. Suddenly, Mark realized he had resolved his dilemma about sending Fatima home.

The answer had come in response to an interview question. He remembered how one of the reasons given for him being successful in his first application for a job was that he answered correctly a question about his perception of his strengths and weaknesses.

Donatello Bellascolie, one of the two interviewers, had asked in a formal professional voice:

'What would you say are your strengths and weaknesses?'

Mark's first thought was to launch into a declaration of all his strengths. He was a good student, had never missed any of his placements and worked hard. He was witty and tolerant of every view and opinion. He didn't intend to mention his weaknesses, thinking that to admit he had any would show he was not of strong character. But pausing for reflection made him realize that not having any weakness was an admission that he did not actually know himself. If he was unaware of any deficiencies in his nature, then he couldn't be trusted, as he would be unsure how he would react when circumstances which called for in-depth knowledge of himself arose. For example, if he was too proud to ask for help, he could attempt an examination that was out of his depth and thus put patients at additional radiation risks, all because he didn't want to look foolish.

Instead of denying any weaknesses, Mark answered honestly.

'My strength is, I've been told by those I've worked with, that I'm a caring person and I treat all my patients with dignity, even those hard to please. When examining patients, I don't see them as a number, I see people coming to a hospital because they are sick. So I try to personalize patients. I look at young ones as my siblings and older, more mature ones I visualize as my mum, dad, aunties or other relatives. This means that whoever I treat, I always have time to be patient and kind to them.'

He could see by the twinkle in Donatello's eye, he had answered partly correctly. Clair Londis, the other interviewer, took up the questioning.

'And your weaknesses?'

'I feel at times that my strength can also become my weakness,' Mark answered.

'What do you mean by that?' asked Donatello.

'Well I feel that being kind can be carried too far. If I'm too involved with the patients and too considerate, I could take the job home with me. I wouldn't be able to switch off when faced with traumatic situations. This would pose problems for my family as I would be constantly revisiting in my mind what had happened that day. The solution I've found is to get involved in other things, or take up hobbies that will refocus my mind on a completely different topic. I love reading, and very much enjoy going for walks, which I find very therapeutic as there's nothing better than smelling the fresh air after a long hard day cooped up indoors.'

Satisfied with his honest appraisal, Clair nodded, and Donatello ticked off a section on his interview form, and then they continued with his interview.

Recalling this had provided the answer to his current problem. There was no doubt in Mark's mind that a caring person would be an asset in a few minutes' time. The situation would soon resemble a battlefield. The victims would not be hardened soldiers, but defenceless children. Following in their wake would be their devastated parents, unsure of what was happening. The dreaded call to come to the hospital would be enough to trigger panic attacks in many of them.

The media, as always, would be hungry for news. So traumatic were the events that all radio stations were already intercepting their daily routine broadcasts with constant updates of the unfolding tragedy. It would be impossible to either obtain, or impose a news blackout in order to protect the children's anguished parents. It was imperative they should be consoled and cared for, while their children were being treated. They shouldn't be allowed to interfere with procedures because the last thing some of the medical team needed were screaming parents clogging the corridors and making examinations impossible.

Someone had to be part of the care team and Mark thought of Fatima. He felt that putting her in the front line in the resus room where the children would initially be taken would prove too costly to her in the long term. One alternative was to leave her in the processing room to insert the x-ray cassettes into the computer reader. But the nearness of the resus room to the computer readers meant parents could gather in the corridors separating these rooms. So Mark decided to put Fatima in charge of keeping the corridors clear. She would be involved, but he hoped she would be shielded from the full impact of what was now almost upon them. He congratulated himself on what he believed was the right decision.

Murphy's Law was to play a perverse role that fatal day and upset the apple cart. The words of Robert Burns 'The best laid schemes of mice and men gang aft agley' were to be proved true in Mark's case. Circumstances beyond his control developed, which Mark blamed himself for ever. No amount of counselling would convince him his decision was made with Fatima's best interest at heart, and at times, just as a person can be in the right place at the right time, they can also invariably be in the wrong place at the wrong time. Fatima's strengths were to prove her weakness.

Chapter 3

The radio crackled into life again.

'Ambulance crew here. Three minutes from base. Three occupants on board. GCS are ….' Vital statistics were relayed followed by 'Stand by. Over.'

'Received you, over and out,' was the response from base.

In the ambulance was Fred Kavanagh the Technician, along with Paramedic David McPherson who was looking forward to retirement later that year. They had worked together well as a team. Whenever the two were paired there was always good banter between them. Fred found some of his colleagues difficult to get on with, they were on different wavelengths so to speak, but not so David. He enjoyed the older man's company and how he passed on good tips and experiences. He couldn't remember them ever arguing. They had experienced being spat on, threatened with knives, coshes, broken bottles, had stones thrown at them, and even on many occasions having to change their uniforms because of people, especially drunks, being sick all over them.

There wasn't a situation they hadn't dealt with. Included in their CVs was experience of dealing with every medical emergency from heart attacks, strokes, impalements, to severed limbs from road traffic accidents, and of course childbirths. The number of grateful women who had named their children after

David would have bankrupted him had he been the birth father and had to pay maintenance money. They had indeed had their sad and lighter moments. Now, for the first time in their working relationship, there was a slight feeling of tension between the two men. With Fred driving, David bellowed from the back of the ambulance.

'For goodness sake, Fred, can ye nae git the finger oot?' said David who originally hailed from Aberdeen. His north-east accent had become diluted because of living and working all over the country and was stronger when he was angry.

'The Queen's Scottish is whit I speak, an oniebodie that dinnae understaund me is an eejit, a richt bawheid,' he would say jokingly. Sometimes, Fred quipped, he needed an interpreter. No-one was joking now.

'I'm going as fast as I can. Some dafties won't get out of the way. What'd you want me to do - run into the back of them or run them over?' replied Fred. He was English born and bred, but his time living in Scotland had not affected his accent. Occasionally though, he would incorporate one or two words from David's vocabulary of 'Queen's Scottish', a sure sign the man had influenced him.

'Are ye on some sort o go slaw the day? Did ye git oot o the wrang side o the bed? Can ye nae see we need tae git tae the hospital quickly. You've a polis convoy - for crying out loud keep up wi them.'

Fred was about to answer but he kept silent, knowing the strain his partner was under in the back of the ambulance. Only a few hours earlier, David had been discussing how he looked forward to retirement and spending more time with his grandchildren. He had talked eagerly about all kinds of 'bonding holidays' as he put it.

'Ye ken, Fred, I'm no just gaunae sit at hame an vegetate. I'm gaunae keep in fine fettle. And dae ye ken whit I'm gaunae dae, Fred?' he said.

'And what are you going to do?' Fred asked.

'I'm gaunae git up ivverie morning, drive tae ma dochter's hoose and tak wee David tae primary school. Efter aw, I'm used tae getting up so there'll be nae problem.'

As he mentioned 'wee David,' Fred could not resist a little joke.

'You know, David, I hope that your wife knows about all the wee Davids that you've given your name to.'

'Jealousy will git ye nae place,' said David, 'If ye can retire wi a bairn named efter you, Fred, that's a great privilege.'

'Aye you're right there, David,' said Fred.

They smiled at each other, Fred catching David's eye through the mirror.

The fact that there were three 'young Davids' in the back of the ambulance was making Fred more sympathetic to the cries for more speed from his mate. Then an anguished roar came from behind him.

'Help ma boab, Fred, I think I'm losing one,' said David, panicking.

'What'd you mean?' said Fred, horrified.

'His hairt, Fred, it's stapped for goodness sake. Fred, whit shall I dae!' David's voice was becoming hysterical.

'Have you given him adrenalin?' Fred knew this was a preposterous question, downright silly in fact. It was a case of teaching your granny to suck eggs, because someone with David's depth of experience would follow the correct procedure automatically. Fred's reaction was partly due to frustration, he had to say something, anything, to keep his partner focussed.

'Of coorse I've din that, ye daft bam-pot. Dae ye think I'm thick or something? Dae ye think I've been doing this job aw thae years an will nae dae such a basic simple thing? If ye cannae come up wi oniething mair constructive just shut yer gob and keep driving for goodness sake, and leave the thinking tae me, eh?'

David's voice was really raised now. Fred looked in the rear view mirror and witnessed a scene he would never forget. His mate had appeared to give up. He was staring at a lifeless body and holding his head in his hands.

'What's the matter?'

'I think I've lost him,' David said in a monotone.

'What's his stats, BP, and pulse?' asked Fred sharply.

The silent machine answered that question.

'David, *ABC*,' Fred shouted from the front of the ambulance. ABC was the method followed by any competent first aider trying to help an injured person. A was checking the airway; B was ensuring that no obstacles were restricting breathing and finally C stood for circulation. So if an airway was blocked, the logical thing to do was clear it either by physical or mechanical means such as a suction pump, then progress to the other steps.

Fred wanted to keep yelling out to David but he knew this was not the time for recriminations. There were two more cases in the ambulance. They usually carried only two people, but because of the number of casualties, they had been assigned three. If he couldn't get David to pull himself together, it would be three corpses arriving at Bonnyholly Hospital. Fred was getting desperate; he could not pull over by the road-side and relieve David of his duties, as this would jeopardize the rest of the patients. Ruling that option out, he could, as he perversely thought, make his partner feel guilty by saying 'Pull yourself together man. Are you a man or a mouse? Are you going to fall to pieces at this critical stage?' but he refrained from such an approach.

For the first time in his life, Fred realized how out of touch with reality he was. He lived by the principle of work hard, play hard. His job had made him see first hand the futility of life. Living for the day and enjoying life now was his main purpose. After all, judging by his job, you didn't know what tomorrow would bring. He had no paternal feelings either and was definitely not ready for any commitments. So it was very difficult for him to empathise with David. Looking back now, he realized how selfish he had been at times. He remembered one of his 'many flings' telling him she was pregnant. Fred's immediate response was cutting.

'I told you I wasn't ready to settle down. You do what you want to do, but I don't want to be saddled with any brats at this stage in my life. I want to enjoy life and live it to the full. After all, I'm only young once.' His relationship with Joanne finished that week and he never did find out what she did about the situation. Could he be a father? Would some 'brat' suddenly turn up his door one day, or would it be the Child Support Agency instead? In that moment of reflection, Fred began to understand how David felt. Instead of being angry with him, a tinge of jealousy enveloped his very being. His colleague had a quality he did not. In spite of all the carnage they had both witnessed, it had not made David bitter or devalue life.

Looking in his rear view mirror, he now said in a low soothing voice;

'Dave, imagine if those were your young grandsons what would you do?'

For the first time in their working lives together, he called him *Dave* not David. As soon as he said it, there was a reaction. David, who was by now visibly crying, and not attempting any form of resuscitation, appeared to be jolted out of his inertia. It was a critical moment as Fred, keeping his eyes on the traffic ahead, constantly glanced in his rear view mirror to see what was happening in the back.

Slowly, like the mythical phoenix, David began rising from his stupor. It was like watching one of those slow motion replays on television where every millionth of a second of the action is captured in meticulous detail.

David had two other children in his care and he was determined he was not going to let them die if he could help it. He didn't know their names. Incident Control had not given them any, this was neither important nor was it part of the procedure for dealing with a major incident. They were assigned numbers at the trauma scene by The Forward Medical Incident Officer, a practice reminiscent of the concentration camps when inmates were dehumanized by assigning them numbers. This was not the intention; giving patients wrist bands with numbers on them was more for reasons of speed. Trying to establish the name of an individual, especially in an unconscious state, would take valuable time away from concentrating on the job in hand - the saving of life.

'I'm sae sairy that I dinnae ken yer name, son. You are nae a number tae me. I ken ye understand,' said David. To a stranger listening, it might seem that David was experiencing a mental breakdown.

With number one lifeless, David's immediate reaction would have been to attempt CPR. This was basic procedure as far as he was concerned. But a look at the wounds told him this would have been a waste of time.

For the first time in his life, he felt he was playing God. Now, as never before in his life, he had the power of life and death in his hands. If he attempted to revive number one, he would have to forsake numbers two and three. He looked at the serene figure of number one, the slow trickle of blood oozing from his mouth and ears, then finally the silent monitors. Experience told him this was not a good sign. There was the possibility of brain damage of some sort, especially if blood was coming out of these orifices.

The only way of establishing his fears were not groundless was to x-ray number one. He often had an admiration for those professionals who had worked without any fanfare or publicity in the NHS since its inception. To keep his mind active, he changed the subject of conversation. From the back of the ambulance he spoke to Fred.

'Dae ye ken, Fred, one way o' confirming ma suspicions aboot number one is by x-ray?'

Fred was a bit astonished by this change of tack. But he decided to humour his pal if this would make him more useful to numbers two and three. He replied:

'I think you're right; what examinations will they do?'

'I'm no an expert, Fred, but I think either a CAT or MRI scans. Although I dinnae think they will put the poor little blighter through an MRI machine,' he replied.

'Why not?'

'I've a mate who works in MRI and he told me if you've anything metallic inside you they can nae pit ye intae an MRI. That's because MRI works by using powerful magnets. Dae ye ken some bawheid yince took a fire extinguisher intae an MRI room and it flew at thirty miles an hour intae the scanner and wrecked it? There's nae way they'll be pitting the poor guy intae an MRI machine.'

'You know,' said Fred, 'those radiographers do some job eh? Look at all the drunks we and the other lads take into Bonnyholly Hospital on a Friday or Saturday and they poor radiographers have to x-ray most of them. We ship them there and leave them. They must deal with stabbings, broken bones, road traffic accidents, and even attempted suicides just like we do. One radiographer told me that they have x-rayed people who have stuck things up every orifice in their body.'

'Awa wi ye, yer pulling ma leg,' said David.

'No, I'm not,' replied Fred seriously.

'Come to think o' it, they must be the unsung heroes o' the medical profession. Think o' it tae David Beckham, he's made the metatarsal a household name. But how did they doctors find oot he had broken his metatarsal?' said David.

'How?' asked Fred.

'Simple, by x-raying the bloke o' course. I'll bet ye he was greetin. Let's be honest, Fred, how many Joe Bloggs ken the names o' the bones in their feet, but because o' Davie Beckham, every Tom, Dick, Harry and Mary kens where the metatarsal is.'

'Come to think of it, I think you're right, David.'

'Aren't I ayeways,' quipped David and continued.

'We all ken aboot physios because o' footballers. Folk ken o' cruciate ligament injuries in the knee, but dae ye ken hoo it is diagnosed, Freddie, ma lad? By MRI I tell you, and whae are the first tae spot it? Aye, radiographers. But how monie radiographers dae ye know aboot? That BBC programme *Casualty* has made the Charge Nurse Charlie Fairhead, and Josh, the paramedic and that Dr - what-do-you-call-him again – Harry Harper, aw famous. In ivverie medical programme and film documentary you'll ayeways see doctors, nurses, even us paramedics in lead roles. Some o' these characters hae become household names, just like those in *Casualty*. I dinnae ken o' one where there's a radiographer in the leading role. Dae ye? Gae on, let's play a quiz. Whit's a famous telly or film doctor?' asked David.

'Doctor Findlay,' replied Fred, trying to keep David in a lighter mood.

'Aye but ye forgot the "Casebook",' said David sarcastically, then for good measure added 'blimey, Fred, how old are ye? You've been watching too much o' that vintage telly. How about a mere modern yin?'

'George Clooney.'

'That's mair like it. Whaur did you see him?' asked David.

'In *ER*.'

'Ye're absolutely richt. A bet ye cannae name a TV paramedic though,' David said softly.

'Now that's really, really difficult, I'm racking my brains. Come on, David, give a helping hand.' Fred said and then as if to keep the banter going said jokingly,

'Could it be Josh?'

'Which programme then, you smarty pants?'

'*Casualty*.'

'OK then. A famous consultant?'

'Harry thingamabob….'

'Name the TV drama?'

'*Casualty* again.'

'How abbot a well known doctor.'

'Dr Hilary Jones of TV's *Good Morning* programme.'

'Now, how aboot a famous radiographer, or a programme that featured radiographers.'

'Well, err…'

'Come on... come on we have nae got all day.'

'Hold on, didnae the BBC have that Irish guy, what's his name him with the Irish lilt and wise crack. It was Nis-something or was it Nes-something like that and didn't his name rhyme with some cereal?'

'Oh, I ken who ye mean, it was James Nesbitt when he played the radiographer Joe Keyes.'

'Spot on. What year was it?' said Fred.

'A think aboot the year 2004 and it was in twa pairts,' said David showing off his TV knowledge. 'But let's be honest, it was nae to show aff the work of radiographers, it's just a drama aboot a man who didnae intervene in a possible abduction and the sad consequences o' his actions. It's jist that he worked in a hospital as a radiographer. And hoo monie o' thae six odd million folk gawking at that drama kent the roles radiographers play?'

'How did you know over six million watched it?'

'I read it somewhere. Am I ever wrang?' said David.

Both men smiled.

'Ye ken, I know this isn't scientific, but I bet ye more people in their life will come into contact with a radiographer than with a doctor or nurse. Ye only see a nurse when you are admitted to a hospital, but you see a radiographer all the time.'

'What do you mean?'

The change of conversation had had the desired effect. David's mood had changed; he had regained his composure. It was as if he had been like a marathon runner who had gone through the proverbial wall and acquired his second wind. He would only become irritable and glum again once he knew the name and the circumstances of number one's birth.

'Come on, Fred, let's do oor best for these poor little blighters.'

Saving numbers two and three took on a new urgency. When number two arrested, the euphemism for stopping breathing, there was to be no repetition of the previous inability to act. Immediately, as if by instinct, David sprang into action like a coiled snake releasing its powerful muscles with dexterity with a possible meal in view. Without a thought, ABC came into play and ensured number two did not end in a similar state to number one. The final proof of David's recovery was the application of Entonox pain relief once number two was revived.

As if recognising what had happened, the police escorts increased their speed. Darting in and out of the traffic, the ambulance, with its fragile incumbents, was making steady progress. Fred kept his eyes glued to the mirrors, first his rear view one to reassure himself David's recovery was indeed permanent, and then he checked his wing mirror to make sure he could see no obstacles. To his surprise, there seemed to be a car closely following them. Was this one of those ambulance chasers, he thought to himself. This had been a bugbear of both men. It annoyed them how some people would use blaring sirens, which automatically cleared roads as an excuse for speeding, knowing there was little chance of them being apprehended. Then again, Fred thought, this may not be ambulance chasers but perhaps parents of the small occupants. He dismissed this idea as ridiculous. It would have been impossible for the parents to know their children were being taken to hospital, because once they had heard of the disaster, their initial call would be to the school to establish whether their child or children were involved in the episode; their initial action would be to go straight there to try and find out for themselves.

Much later, the death of the child in the overcrowded

ambulance led to a revamp of the service. The authorities came to realize the strain of trying to save more than one life at a time was unfair to paramedics. A public enquiry would establish that, irrespective of the tragic scenes that awaited the Incident Controller, only one major trauma patient should be carried in an ambulance at a time; in exceptional cases two, but with this proviso - the second victim's injuries should be minor, not major and life-threatening. This legacy of change would become a fitting tribute to number one, a child that was dearly loved and whose birth had brought so much joy to his parents Graham and Danielle Darling.

Chapter 4

Graham and Danielle Darling had said goodbye to their treasured son that historic morning, not dreaming he would never return. Living in a rural picturesque part of Scotland, a favourite haunt of tourists, the notion of their child meeting a brutal death was not something they had ever considered. This was something that happened elsewhere, in one of those inner city ghettos where knives and gun crime abound, and gangs run rampant. This culture of violence was repeatedly reported by the tabloid press and often featured in violent TV and film dramas.

Graham and Danielle were happy with their lives. Their son had been a late one, who was not only a surprise, but one they never thought they would have. They'd tried so hard to have children. These days, snuggling together on the living room sofa, they would often recall the manuals they'd read about conceiving, how they'd tried some of the suggestions from books and from friends that in retrospect now made them blush with embarrassment. They'd eventually decided on IVF on the NHS and had exhausted the amount of cycles Danielle was entitled to, without the success they had so desperately hoped for. But Danielle had stayed positive despite all the disappointing results. Graham loved her optimistic approach to life. She was always either humming or singing and her favourite game with him would be 'guess what song I'm humming'. Then if he got it right, she'd tell him to name the singer, and finally the year the song had come out. At times he had been frustrated trying to remember, but whatever song she picked always had some personal meaning attached to it.

A caring and observant husband, Graham knew how desperate Danielle was to have a child, the heartache behind her cheerfulness. He assumed, rightly or wrongly, that the singing masked her inner turmoil. In a supreme effort to make his wife happy, he decided to re-mortgage their house, the home they both loved.

The day Danielle found herself pregnant was indeed a thrilling one. Graham knew by her face something was different, but he could not quite tell what it was. Coming home after a hard day at the office, he was greeted by a strange but delightful aroma, one which immediately conjured up special memories. Danielle's seductive perfume was very difficult to resist, it immediately invigorated him, and if that wasn't enough, his eye caught sight of the treat spread enticingly on the dining room table - his special meal. The icing on the cake was the romantic music, their wedding song, playing in the background. Chris de Burgh's *Lady in Red* always pulled at his heart strings, no matter how often he heard it. For him, it meant Danielle. He started to hum the tune.

His first impulse was to take her in his arms and, holding her close, dance in the living room just as they'd done on their wedding day … ah, that first dance in front of everyone … he remembered every detail, but he checked himself.

His first thought was 'What's she up to? Oh no - it must be our anniversary and I've forgotten it.' But no, if he'd forgotten their anniversary, it would have been the silent look that would have welcomed him, not this romantic scene. There was something afoot. What on earth had he missed? He thought perhaps she'd bought a new dress or made some extravagant purchase, or maybe her hormones were to blame for the strange mood.

'Darling, I have something to tell you,' said Danielle.

'Have you forgotten my first name?' he joked.

'Darling,' thought Graham, thinking this was a bit strange. It always amused him when he was watching those old American TV shows and the husband would come in after a day at work and say 'Darling, I'm home.' It wasn't an endearment he and Danielle used often.

He plonked himself on the settee, absolutely shattered from driving in blistering heat on the motorway, stuck in bumper-to-bumper traffic.

'Ok what's up? What've you done? Go on; let me have it on the chin. Confession is good for the soul,' he said.

One of the things Danielle most loved about Graham was that he never seemed to get rattled easily; he was always considerate of her feelings, with no taking the mickey either privately, or publicly. She couldn't ever remember him treating her unkindly or humiliating her by his words or actions. She recalled a lovely anniversary card she'd received the year before, together with a beautiful bouquet of flowers delivered to the door. Graham had designed the card himself on a special website, and the words were especially touching.

Dear Danielle,

I know this is another year that your, no - our dreams haven't been realized, yet, but I want to encourage you to be patient and let nature take its course naturally. I'm the happiest man on this planet because I met you and am loved by you. An old Chinese proverb says 'To love someone deeply gives you strength. Being loved by someone deeply gives you courage'. The years we've spent together so far have been wonderful. I know we've had our disappointments, but I wouldn't have chosen anyone else to spend the rest of my life with. Jane Austen got it right in 'Sense and Sensibility'. She wrote 'It is not time or opportunity that is to determine intimacy: it is disposition alone. Seven years would not be sufficient to make some people acquainted with each other and seven days are more than enough for others.' These last seven years have indeed felt like seven days.

I want to remind you of the words of Sweeny too. 'A wedding anniversary is the celebration of love, trust, partnership, tolerance and tenacity. The order varies for any given year'. My beloved Danielle, you have and continue to face your challenges so bravely. Which of the above qualities have you needed? All of them! My mum says an anniversary is a time to celebrate the joys of today, the memories of yesterday and the hopes of tomorrow – I agree. Whenever you feel down, just remember this Swedish proverb 'Shared joy is double joy. Shared sorrow is half sorrow'. So happy anniversary, my love. The thing you most want could happen this year. Oh and finally, finally remember 'true love stories never have endings.' I love you always and forever –

Your husband Graham.

Ps hope you like the card I made especially for you.

Danielle had kept that card, and many others Graham had given her in a drawer in their bedroom. Those cards seem to have a healing effect, and whenever she felt slightly depressed, all she had to do was go upstairs, look at some of his loving words and she would feel better.

They had worked hard together to ensure there was always communication between them. Graham's mnemonic for a successful marriage was what he called the *Three Cs*. Communication, Cooperation and Consideration. He felt that, irrespective of the problem, good communication equals, or results in a good relationship, regardless of the circumstances.

Now Danielle steered him to the table, sat him down and just looked at him. For a few minutes all she did was smile, a smile as wide as a Cheshire cat's. Graham knew it couldn't be because he had forgotten their anniversary. Her radiant look confirmed his suspicions. What was she trying to say? No wonder some author had written the famous book about women being from a different planet. Maybe she's booked that holiday in the Bahamas, he thought, and he reminded himself she'd been saving up every penny, picking up loose change, and even opening up a special savings account. He gave up trying to work it out.

'Go on, put me out of my misery.'

'You know how I haven't been feeling well lately?'

'Err yes, I think I noticed something wasn't right, mind you it's just now and then, it's not every day, is it?' He was trying to be tactful, not wanting to put his foot in it if his assumptions were wrong. 'I put it down to your usual women's problems, or maybe you're just letting things get you down. I've told you, Danielle; just let things take their course naturally. Do you know some big wigs in the medical profession believe that if you're too stressed nothing will happen?'

'Well, Graham, I think you'll need to start decorating.'

'Oh for Pete's sake, Danielle, give us a break, I've just finished the living room and the bathroom, and I'll do the bedroom as soon as I get time. I'm fairly whacked when I come home. Is this what this special dinner is about? I thought for a moment I had forgotten our anniversary.'

'No that's not for a while yet,' she said.

'Anyway,' continued Danielle, 'forget that, what I meant is you'll have to start decorating the spare room.'

'Oh! Your mum isn't coming to stay, is she?'

'No, no, no it is because ....'

'Thank goodness,' he said, not even giving her a chance to finish her sentence.

Danielle paused deliberately to make sure she'd get Graham's full attention. As if by design at that precise moment, their favourite song by Chris de Burgh finished with the final words whispered by the singer '... I love you ...'

'Graham, I did a test and you're finally going to get your wish. You're going to be a dad - a dad - a big daddy ....'

After a moment's stunned silence in which his smile broadened to match hers, Graham jumped up from the table.

'Ya beauty,' he shouted, gathering Danielle into his arms. He wanted to pick up the phone to tell his mum, his aunties, his best friend Archie. Fleetingly, he thought 'I'll put an advert in the local paper telling the village of my wife's pregnancy.' He could feel his heart pounding and his chest heaving. Tears pricked his eyes.

'Danielle, are you sure?'

'Of course I am,' came the slightly hurt response as she drew back from his embrace.

'These things can be wrong, you know. Remember a while back at Bonnyholly Hospital when the hospital got a bad batch of those pregnancy kits, and many people were disappointed? Are you really sure, I mean positive? I know what it'll do to you – to both of us - if it's a false result.'

Danielle was beginning to lose her joyful outlook and in frustration blurted out:

'For once in your life, can't you be happy for me? Don't you know how I feel? You've never listened to me. You're only interested in *your* feelings, how about thinking about *me* for once.'

As she said this, Danielle knew her outburst was quite unwarranted and far from truth. Graham had shown exactly the opposite reaction. She felt guilty, and cursed herself inwardly for hurting the man she loved so dearly. Graham sensed her body language and acted swiftly to calm her. He took her right hand gently between his two hands and then spoke quietly, to take the heat out of the situation.

'It's just that I want us to be sure. Murphy's Law can apply in many cases, that's all. Come on, let's enjoy our meal, then put on one of your slushy girlie movies, and we'll sit with a bottle of wine and just chill out eh? In the morning you can phone the surgery to make an appointment to see the midwife for a test, and if the test is *then* positive, I'll decorate the room for you. I promise. Just be patient, please, Danielle.'

'I'll skip the wine though, just in case,' she said.

Still clutching her hand, he reached over and gave her an affectionate cuddle, and kissed her gently. Danielle blushed a little at his show of affection. How she loved his forgiving nature and the way he lived up to his principles by applying the second of his three Cs, consideration. He was the most considerate man she'd ever met. Sorry for her outburst, she spoke softly,

'I'm really sorry, I didn't mean what I said.'

'That's OK, dear, we're both under a bit of pressure. Come on now, let's enjoy the meal.'

Their relationship was back on an even keel, proving true Johnston's words 'An apology is the superglue of life, it can repair almost anything'.

The next day, Danielle phoned the surgery and made an appointment for her test, and when she got there, and the pregnancy was confirmed, the midwife gave her a book called *Ready Steady Baby*. All the information they both needed about her pregnancy was in it and they eagerly read every page.

The day of Danielle's thirteen-week test at Bonnyholly Hospital soon arrived. It was a new state-of-the-art hospital, equipped with all mod cons and built under the government's Private Finance Initiative scheme. The politics involved in its construction had caused many arguments in the pubs and clubs, and amongst all social classes in the district. Some felt it was a waste of money, some thought other services would suffer, and some, that the personal touch so much an integral part of a hospital atmosphere, would now be consigned to history.

What could not be ignored was the spectacular building set in a picturesque part of Scotland. The site had been specially chosen for the beautiful surroundings as much as for its strategic location. Built in a valley plain, the area had been carefully landscaped to enhance its environment. Artificial lakes filled with water plants were a major feature, with trees, shrubs and flowers of every colour imaginable to complement them. A specially constructed waterfall splashed down over the rocks, fed from streams and rivers flowing from the local hills. Frogs and toads had already made their homes in or around the water, and their croaking calls could be heard day and night. Swathes of lush green grass added an elegant carpet to the landscape, and were manicured to perfection by professionals with a passionate love for their work.

The possibility of flooding hadn't been overlooked by the engineers who created this oasis outside the hospital.

The lakes had an overflow system which fed surplus water into a reservoir, which in turn diverted excess water into the main river further down the valley. Fountains in each of the lakes sent their sparkling spray into the air at synchronized intervals, giving an impression of exquisite dancers performing to the watery music.

When the light was right, the mountains were reflected in the lakes giving the effect of a mirage. Subdued lighting was carefully hidden under some plants so as not to unduly upset any watery inhabitants. Footpaths had been paved with specially coated non-slip surfaces, and running parallel to the paths were neatly trimmed hedges. Mature and majestic trees which were already on the plot had been preserved, and had been specifically included into the hospital surroundings by the architects to provide living quarters for the many different species of birds in the area. Many patients swore that the birdsong and the cascading waterfall together with the cheerful croaking of the amphibians helped them relax and feel better. Because of its location in a valley, patients, in the wards which had been designed to overlook the grounds, were treated to a breath-taking panorama in all seasons, especially when the sun was setting or the moon was shining in all its resplendent glory.

Dotted in conspicuous places approaching the hospital were bronze statues of famous individuals who had contributed to the advancement of medicine. Sir Godfrey Hounsfield, Nobel prize-winning inventor of the CT or CAT scanner, which revolutionized medical imaging, was commemorated there, along with the Polish-born physicist Marie Curie, the winner of two Nobel awards and the pioneer of radiography.

During the summer months, the hills were covered

with plants, bracken, heather, and rough grass. Ironically, the Scottish weather, which was a constant bone of discontent amongst native Scots and visitors alike, was responsible for the beauty of landscape they were so proud of. In autumn, the seasonal reds, yellows and browns of the leaves were astounding in their variety. Views from the hospital were breath-taking, awe-inspiring and therapeutic. To the north stood the majestic Ochil Munros known locally as the 'big yins'. They then appeared to give birth to the less regal Skean Dhui range dubbed the 'wee yins' in the west. Looking east were seven mountains of varying sizes which rose and fell and appeared to resemble elephants linked to each other; the trunk of one wound round the tail of the next. Finally, to the south was a single mountain rising to a staggering fourteen thousand feet, permanently covered in snow and shrouded in clouds. At various times of the year, the cloud formation would descend to reveal its snow-capped peak projecting through a circle of cloud, giving the impression the mountain was wearing a regal tiara. No wonder it was called 'the Mither o' Aal Mountains.'

The whole range from the vantage point of a patient or visitor seemed to embrace the hospital in a protective hug. In winter, the whole scene changed. The surrounding mountains were covered in snow and ice, and the lush green grass became a virginal white as it succumbed to being patted on its head when the snow fell.

Graham and Danielle approached Bonnyholly Hospital Outpatients Department with apprehension. They each had mixed emotions, fear and excitement. With trepidation and nervous footsteps, they gingerly approached the x-ray department. The walk down the long hospital corridor to the department seemed like an eternity. Sign-posts pointed them in the right direction. Being new, there were a number of innovative features built into the design to make the hospital experience less intimidating. A yellow line on the floor with the instructions 'follow line to x-ray department' ensured they would not get lost.

They took it slowly where others might have hurried to get it all over with as soon as possible. It was sluggish for Danielle because of the myriad of questions bombarding her brain, some illogical, others understandable because she had waited so long for this momentous occasion. The couple passed porters, with their dark blue trousers and toning light blue shirts and ties; cleaners in their regimental green were also scuttling around to ensure the hospital kept its well-deserved accolade of the Cleanest Hospital in Scotland Award.

Doctors were dashing from ward to ward, and there were countless nurses, showing their level of seniority by the varying colour of their tunics. The young couple were not alone in their slow pace reminiscent of a tortoise. Old men, mothers in different states of pregnancy, and the wounded, limping painfully to A&E, were just as slow, and visitors meandered along as if they had all the time in the world. The whole journey was surreal, scurrying hospital workers for all the world like busy soldier ants, while some of the visitors and patients would have put a sloth to shame. Graham and Danielle finally arrived at the x-ray department and booked themselves in.

Linda Baintrope, the sonographer who would carry out the ultra-sound procedure, eventually called them in. She carefully checked her details to ensure she had the correct person for the examination, then laying Danielle on the examination table she began to explain the procedure.

'This is an ultrasound machine,' she told them. 'It

works by using sound waves to make pictures of your baby. It was developed from sonar during the war. Sometimes you can't see a full outline so I'll explain what to look for, and what you'll see.'

Before she started, she asked the obligatory question.

'Do you have anything to ask me before I start?'

'Yes,' said Graham, 'why are we in the x-ray department if it's sound that makes the pictures. Where do x-rays fit in?'

'That's a good question, Graham - may I call you that?' he nodded, allowing Linda to continue.

'Graham, many people don't understand what radiographers do. I'm actually trained as a radiographer and can go into the general rooms to take x-rays of broken bones and other things. A sonographer is a radiographer who's done more training to do this kind of examination. They've got to have a postgraduate certificate and pass a competency test and they can also report their findings. You see, when a radiographer takes a film, he can't report it. It goes to a radiologist – that's a doctor - who makes an official report, but the Government, facing a skills shortage, realized they had a pool of qualified professionals they just weren't using.'

'So what did they do?' asked Graham.

'Well,' continued Linda 'they brought in what's called Agenda for Change, and decided to give radiographers the chance to report their films. So, now, specially trained radiographers undertake a similar role to me, of reporting their findings. In some hospitals they're called Advanced Practitioners, in others, Reporting Radiographers. The radiographers in these roles are so skilled their success rate is equal to that of radiologists. It's given radiographers a much better career ladder – something to aim for.'

'That's interesting. I suppose there was resistance.' said Danielle.

'Obviously, initially some radiologists felt it would cost them their jobs, so they were a bit reluctant to accept us, but now, as they've seen their load lightened, many of them have welcomed the radiographers and are willing to train and mentor them. Here, in this department, Contricia is being trained and once she passes all her competency tests this year, she'll be a Reporting Radiographer.'

'Are there any future plans and proposals for your lot?' Graham asked, fascinated.

'Yes, quite a lot,' replied Linda.

'There are plans afoot to protect the name *sonographer*, just as the name *radiographer* is a protected title. You can't just call yourself a radiographer, you have to have undergone training, be fully competent and be registered with the Health Professions Council. Like any other professional body, this council has the power to either discipline or remove radiographers who do not come up to scratch.'

'Oh I see,' said Graham, 'how many radiographers are there in Britain?'

'I think about 25,000, but of course that includes those who are on maternity leave.' Linda replied.

The mention of maternity leave brought a wink from Linda which was returned by Danielle. That was what Linda liked about her job, even though she had been employed for years; the joy of proud parents seeing their baby's first scan always lifted her spirits. If she'd had a bad night with her children or husband, and irrespective of what happened at home, once she turned on the machine and was engaged in what is called gynaecological exams, finding a live and growing baby always made her day.

'Do you like your job, and is that all you do, looking for babies?' Graham asked her.

'Well, no. As you know, ultrasound is not as dangerous as x-rays, so the first port of call for many is ultrasound if at all possible. We've portable ultrasound machines in A&E to diagnose other conditions.'

'Like what?' he asked. Patiently Linda replied.

'It can be used for kidneys, and gall stones examinations, and for muscles, and you can use it to examine the liver, which makes me pretty sad at times. Cirrhosis of the liver can be seen effectively using this machine, and it upsets me when I see young people who've failed to take care of themselves and indulged in heavy drinking, suffering this kind of condition. I always look at them and feel a kind of compassion, because I think to myself that could be my son, or daughter, or if it is an older person, I see my mum, dad, or other relative. You'll know as well as I do that in Scotland we've a particularly bad drinking culture and my colleagues and I see the results first hand.'

'So just like every job you have your good and bad days then?' said Danielle.

'That's absolutely right. But I don't get up in the morning and wish I wasn't going to work today. I'm fortunate to have a job I love doing.'

'You know, that's interesting,' said Graham. 'My wife likes a lot of reading and Chinese sayings and you've just reminded me of one of those.'

'Which one?' asked Danielle.

'Choose a job you love and you'll never work a day in your life,' he answered.

'Easy peasy,' said Danielle, 'that's Confucius.'

The mention of drink and its consequences suddenly

elicited a defensive reaction from Danielle.

'Well, if things are fine, I'll certainly not be drinking during my pregnancy.' she said.

Linda noticed her reaction and moved swiftly to reassure her.

'To be honest, Danielle, there are so many conflicting findings, you'd be changing your habits daily if you tried to stick to all the advice you read or hear. The key is moderation, just be sensible. There are definite no-nos obviously, like illicit drugs, but even prescription ones can sometimes be dangerous to the unborn baby. With foods and things of that nature the jury is still out, so just be reasonable. Listen to the advice from your midwife, OK?'

Danielle smiled then nodded in agreement.

Linda asked Danielle to pull her top up then applied gel to her tummy.

Graham was curious. 'What's that for?' he asked.

'Well in a nutshell, it's to make sure the probe has good contact between your partner's skin and the object I'm trying to examine, in this case your baby. Sound does not travel very well through the air.'

With a circular motion Linda began to make sweeps across Danielle's stomach. She could see by the increase in the movements of her abdomen that Danielle's pulse had increased in anticipation of what was happening. Was there a baby there, was it dead or alive, or was this just a false positive as it is known in the medical profession? Many questions raced through Danielle's mind. She felt tense and apprehensive. Then Linda turned the monitor round to face her.

'Look, there's your future bundle of joy.'

'Is it all right? Is the baby alive?' Danielle's voice trembled with excitement.

'Oh I wouldn't worry about that, he – or she - is fine,' said Linda.

'How can you tell?'

'By the movement.'

'Even at this early stage?' Danielle was surprised.

'Yes,' said Linda reassuringly.

Danielle wanted to shout out. She thought of all those childless years, all the efforts of trying to conceive, some of the silly suggestions which would not have been out of place in a developing country. She remembered some well meaning book even suggesting certain foods could determine the sex of a child. 'How absurd,' she thought, 'sex is determined at conception, but when you're desperate you'll try, and believe anything!'

'Can you tell me the sex?' she asked.

'I could later on, but firstly it is unethical, and secondly, I could be wrong, and anyway judging by your body language, I'm sure that's immaterial,' Linda told her.

'You're so right,' said Graham who had felt a bit left out of the conversation, and it was his baby too.

With the special tools on her machine, Linda began measuring the foetus.

'I'd say the baby will be due in November according to my calculations.'

'That's about right,' confirmed Danielle, then added, 'Linda, are there any abnormalities … can things go wrong … can you see anything?'

Linda knew from experience, after the euphoria of the confirmation of a living being inside the mother, the next obvious question inevitably related to abnormalities. Every parent wanted to be sure their baby was all right.

With tact and empathy, she reassured them with answers based not just on her experience, and research findings, but also on the images currently being viewed.

'Obviously this is your first scan. When you come back for your second one, I'll be able to see a clearer picture, and give you a more accurate answer. But hey, stop worrying, just enjoy this moment eh?'

Graham then began to tell her how difficult it'd been for them to be where they were now. Once again, this was a moment for Linda to savour. It never failed to amaze her, the tricks Mother Nature played. Some women in a drunken night of passion ended up pregnant immediately, and would decide not to continue with their pregnancy, and yet, paradoxically, others in a stable relationship would try for years to be in that person's shoes. She could never understand why nature didn't just balance things out. Anyway this subject was too deep for her.

'See you for your next scan,' she said as Danielle adjusted her clothes.

'Oh, when will that be?'

'It'll be at twenty weeks,' Linda told her, then added 'haven't you forgotten something?'

'What?'

'This,' said Linda and with a press of a button on the machine a whirring noise started, followed by cutting sound. Linda then handed a scanned photo to the mother-to-be.

'Oh thank you. We're so excited we completely forgot his pic …' said Danielle.

Graham interrupted. 'Just a minute dear, it could be *her* not *his*' he reminded her.

'We're so excited we forgot *his or her* first picture?' she said.

The Darlings left the hospital on an indescribably high note. This pinnacle of happiness would be dwarfed only by the birth of their son.

As they walked to their car, Graham grabbed Danielle's hand and stood still gazing at the spectacular scenery that surrounded the hospital. 'Just look at those hills and the gardens. Aren't they pretty?'

'They are, but look at the Mother of all Mountains, talk about the wow factor.'

The mountain had decided to show off its glory after a sudden downpour. The cloud formation, like a diadem, had descended to reveal the snow-capped peak. The final touch was the sudden appearance of a rainbow which seemed to begin at the mountain range and end with its hidden pot of gold in the central lake of the hospital.

'Oh my, it's as if someone had just dropped a giant polo mint onto the mountain and it got stuck on the peak,' said Danielle in wonderment.

'What a wonderful description. I couldn't put it any better,' said Graham encouragingly. 'Or perhaps one of those crazy students has just climbed up there and put a giant traffic cone on top of the mountain.' They both laughed uncontrollably.

Danielle was ecstatic. The wonderful news she'd just been given and the scene of breath-taking beauty she was gazing at made everything absolutely perfect. She burst into song, and what could be more appropriate for that moment than Louis Armstrong's *What a wonderful world.*

Patients passing the happy couple smiled, pleased to see a pair so happy. Graham and Danielle went home to prepare for the birth of their son. Their preparations included painting the spare bedroom, and turning it into a nursery for their new arrival. They had not even started thinking of names. All they could think about was looking forward to the happy event.

I Can See Clearly Now the Rain Is Gone

A few days after the journey to the hospital, Danielle asked Graham if he'd thought of any names yet.

'No, not yet, we'll cross that bridge when we get to it' he replied in his usual pragmatic manner.

'Guess what, how about this?' and she started to hum a song. 'What's the song, singer and year,' she asked excitedly.

'Easy peasy,' he said, 'that's *Angie*, The Rolling Stones, 1972.'

'A tad on the sad side, don't you think?' she said.

'But I like the name,' said Graham slightly aggrieved.

'OK, how about this then?' Danielle pursed her lips and whistled another song.

'Easy peasy again. *Clair*, Gilbert O'Sullivan, 1972 again. I must admit I do like that name.'

'That's lovely, I do too,' she said.

'Aren't you forgetting one thing?' he asked her.

'What?' her brow began to furl.

'Go back to the question you asked Linda.'

'What question are you talking about; you saw how excited I was. I asked loads of questions?'

Graham laughed, 'You sounded a tad like your mamee.' It was Graham's turn to turn the tables. 'Guess singer, song and year.'

'Och don't be daft, Graham,' Danielle said, grabbing a cushion and throwing it affectionately towards him.

'OK, I'll tell you. You asked her about the sex of the baby. She told you she wouldn't answer. Remember why?'

'Because it wouldn't be ethical and ...' Graham interrupted her.

'Well so far we've only thought about girls' names, aren't we forgetting an important point?'

Graham then started singing *Na, Na, Na, Na Na Na,*

Na, Na Na, and told Danielle to guess the song, singer and year.

'*Hey Jude*, Beatles 1968, that's easy.'

Suddenly the penny dropped.

'Of course. Our baby could be a boy.'

'And what'll we call him?'

'Jude?'

'Maybe. Or perhaps ….' Graham restarted his new-found musical skills. Danielle stopped him, jokingly putting her fingers in her ears.

'Not that song you're humming anyway. No son of mine is going to be called *Crazy Horse* after the Osmond's song. Don't be daft, Graham.'

'See what I mean now? Just like your ma. Let's be patient. When the time comes we'll find a name and the name we finally choose will mean something, not just for our baby, but for us too,' Graham said.

'I nearly threw another cushion at you, for insulting my mother and imagining our son being called Crazy Horse, Darling,' Danielle said, laughing.

The months passed in anticipation, till the day the ambulance received an emergency call from control and raced to the Darlings' home. Her contractions had started and were now evenly spaced. Graham was taking no chances and insisted on her being taken into Bonnyholly Maternity Unit. In transit her waters broke causing the crewmen Fred and David to speed up. David held one of Danielle's hands, and Graham the other, whilst at the same time getting her to inhale Entonox to ease the pain. Staff were waiting with a trolley and quickly wheeled her into the delivery room. The result of all the drama was a healthy baby boy.

In the meantime, David had got his mop and bucket out and cleaned out the ambulance. He was used to it, but this time he did it gladly as it meant another successful mission, unlike some of the other bodily fluids deposited there on other occasions. A few days later, David was sitting thoughtfully in his ambulance. He turned to Fred.

'Ye ken, I've been thinking aboot that couple? While ye was driving we blethered aboot the hard times they've haud. I tell you something, Fred, that child is gaunae be smothered wi luve. He will nae ken whit's hit him. I bet ye he'll hae a lovely room, and as yon red heid Cilla Black wad sae 'a lora, lora, cuddles ...' Ah hope they dinnae spoil him. You ken ma guidwife Louise luves making cards, I'm gaunae ask her to mak a special ane for them.'

A few days later, David sent a card made by his wife to Graham and Danielle. On the front were the words:

'To Graham and Danielle. A baby boy born 22/04/1996 3.00 am weight 8lbs 5oz.'

Louise had pulled out all the stops to make a card that even she felt was special because of the circumstances surrounding the boy's birth. Taking an A4 card she folded it neatly into A5. With the expertise of an artist, she overlaid the card with a backing paper of blue stripes. Looking at it critically, she felt something was missing; it needed an eye-catching decoration. Rummaging through her drawer, a layer of mirror-board caught her eye and she knew that was exactly what was needed. It gave the plain paper an instant glow, and reflected the different colours in the room. Then came her 'Pièce de résistance'. She managed to fashion a teddy bear into layers and attach it to a pram. The result was the 3D effect of the image rising cleverly from the card. The smiling teddy, she had to admit, looked rather cute. If only she knew the name of the boy, she could have engraved it onto the teddy. Still, she felt something was missing. The final touches were simple but delightful. Silver ribbons were glued round the card and then with meticulous care she applied gold and silver lettering in an elegant font. The card was indeed stunning and on the mantelpiece, changed colour at different angles because of the mirror board effect.

Inside was a quotation from the poem by Diane Loomans *If I had my Child to Raise over again*, the one about spending more time with a child and doing the fun things together.

Louise had written a warm message inside.

Dear Graham and Danielle,

We hope you like this card and will keep it as a memento of the birth of your son. We know how much you've both awaited the arrival of your bundle of joy and we know you will make time to spend with him and have fun together. He'll always remember those times because 'Each day of our lives we make deposits in the memory banks of our children'.

Remember, 'children need your PRESENCE more than your PRESENTS'. Time spent with your baby will pay rich dividends later on in the future. If you build a good relationship with him, when he gets to his difficult teenage years, there'll be no generation gap. There's no doubt about it 'what's done to children they will do to society.'

As we said above, don't equate bountiful and expensive presents as an expression of your love. Sometimes, the poorest man leaves his children the richest heritage.

Love your wee boy, cherish him as we know you will

do. We know the sacrifices you've made and we hope you will be a very happy family. 'Love is the condition in which the happiness of another person is essential to you.' 'Love is above all the gift of oneself.'

We hope you like the quotations we've gleaned from several authors we've come across over the years. Their thoughtful sayings have been helpful to us in rearing our own children. The least we could do is pass them on to you.

With our love, from David and Louise McPherson.

Graham and Danielle were particularly touched by the card. They hadn't yet thought of a name for their new arrival, and the card made them decide what they would call him. He would be *David.*

None of them realized at the time the impact that card and its words were going to have on their lives.

David was later to learn that the patient called unceremoniously number one was, in fact, the child of Graham and Danielle. By a trick of nature he had played a part in his birth, and also his death. The realisation of that fact was to have a terrible effect, not only on David, but simultaneously shattering Graham and Danielle. The crime, perpetrated by a madman, was starting to have a ripple effect. Like a pebble dropped in a lake, its waves would begin to have shocking consequences not just for one individual, but for whole families, communities, and even a nation.

Chapter 5

Ambulance number one arrived at Bonnyholly Hospital with blazing sirens and flashing blue lights. Fred stopped with care so as not to exacerbate the condition of his patients. He ran round to the rear of the ambulance, flung the doors open and helped David rush their small charges to resus. The priority was number two. The automatic doors designed to keep heat in the buildings were disabled and left open to ensure a smooth and fast entry. The emergency staff were all prepared, ready and waiting in their respective places.

'GCS ....'

Fred relayed in meticulous detail the statistics needed to ensure those delicate, precious children entrusted to him were properly looked after. Very quickly, number two was taken into resus bay one, number three to bay two and number one to bay three.

Once the death of number one was confirmed, the porter, John, was called to take him to the mortuary. David stood beside his trolley, refusing to let go of the small white hand.

'I'm sae sairie, son,' he whispered, 'I'll nivver forget ye. Ye were aye a wee battler.' Tears trickled down his cheeks from his faded blue eyes. Fred approached him.

'David, we've got to go, there's more to come in. Control wants to know our time of arrival at Bonnyholly School.'

David turned round to Fred, his eyes bleak and perspiration matting his greying hair a little, as he struggled to control his emotions in the middle of this nightmare.

'I'll nae be lang, Fred,' he said.

The porter intervened.

'I've got to take this one into the mortuary. The space is needed for others.'

As he spoke, the second ambulance arrived.

David then turned to the porter and spoke in a husky, faltering voice.

'Err … can I come wi' ye?'

'David,' said Fred, 'you're not thinking straight, we've got to go. NOW!' He raised his voice to emphasize the last word.

'Look, Fred, I'll only be a minute. Ah just want to say my goodbyes.'

'David,' said Fred lowering his voice, 'there'll be time for that later on. Let's get going.'

But he realized it was futile to argue with his old buddy, and decided to allow David the few minutes he wanted.

The porter brought the trolley specially modified for bodies. He placed number one's limp frame on it. Gone was the trickle of blood; instead he looked peaceful and serene. Just before the porter covered the boy with the PVC cover, David looked down at the dead child.

'Ah hope you didnae suffer, son. Ah hope ye'll be happy wherever ye are. At least yer pain is over for now.'

As he spoke those words, he thought about young David's parents. Any suffering was over for their son; theirs was just about to begin. There would be the investigations, funerals, inquiries, reports and inevitably the conspiracy theories that always seemed to follow such outrages. For the parents, the agonies of this dreadful day and the pain of loss would remain forever.

David knew some people thought time was a great healer, quoting sayings such as 'They are not dead who live in the hearts they leave behind' or 'Death ends a life, not a relationship.' But he wondered if time could really heal, or any parent forget a child they had never seen grow up to achieve their full potential. The sight of a mother pushing a pram and cooing happily at her baby; the sound of children playing tig or skipping about in the street would all bring back the agony of loss. Even if the parents were blessed with other children, the one that wasn't there would leave a space, an un-fillable hole in their lives.

John the porter pulled the cover over number one, then reversed the trolley out of resus bay three. David held the doors open for him and headed towards the mortuary, passing Fatima in the corridor. She was clutching a pile of x-ray cassettes. In the corridor David turned to John.

'Dae ye mind if I push the trolley?'

'Why? It's my job. Why not just get back to your ambulance eh?' said John, not understanding why David wanted to do this. David turned and glanced at the porter. His stare was piercing but compassionate; it seemed to be pleading with him. John remained silent. The look David gave him was enough; he could feel the man's pain. He handed him the trolley and spoke quietly.

'Did you know him?' John was expecting to hear David say 'yes.'

But he didn't. 'Nae,' he said.

'You must have been very close,' John continued, unable to believe that someone without some sort of a relationship or bond would show such a fatherly interest in a total stranger.

'You know,' continued David, 'the moment he died I felt something snapped inside me. It was if I did ken him. I ken he is only a number noo, but I have a feeling I should ken him.'

John had had this kind of conversation with people on several occasions. He could count the number of bodies he had taken into the bowels of the hospital, and yet there was something different about these two, he couldn't put his finger on it. They seemed to be related. How, he wasn't sure, but there was definitely some kind of bond between them. John was later to find out his intuition had been right.

After their brief conversation, John dropped to the rear of the trolley and allowed David to push. It felt a bit like a funeral cortege he thought, especially with David walking so slowly, as if to the sombre strains of a funeral march. David could almost hear the slow beat played by a pipe band, and it brought some comfort as he gently began to hum the music playing in his head. Following behind, John interpreted the humming as groaning.

'They must know each other,' John repeated to himself, 'they surely must know each other.'

At the mortuary, John decided to give the man his privacy and stood back near the door. In a final act of parting, David opened the PVC covers, brushed a stray strand of hair from number one's ashen face and held the boy's now cool hands for the last time. The coldness sent a chill down his spine. There was no way back now; the lad had gone, and David knew the time had come to say his goodbyes.

'I ken that I dinnae ken ye, wee man, but I look on ye like ma wee grandson David. Ye ken I was kind of looking forward to retirement and playing wi him. He's aboot the same age as ye. The funny thing is that there was a wee laddie so like ye that was born aboot five years ago here. I think his parents named him efter me. Onieway ah want ye to ken laddie, ye're a braw looking lad, an ye were a wee battler. I'm gaunae miss ye. Tak care, hae tae rush noo. Ye ken that man Fred will be gaun bananas.' David broke down and wept. Collecting himself he continued more formally, as if the audience wouldn't understand his broad accent.

'Do you know what I'm going to do young man? I'm going to concentrate on what's important in life. I'm going to strive everyday to be kind, generous and loving. I'm going to keep death right here, so that anytime I even think about getting angry at anyone I'll see death and I'll remember you. I am so sorry I couldn't save you. If I could drop dead right now, I'd be the happiest man alive. I guess that's how death works. It doesn't matter if we're ready or not. It just happens. Death can sneak up on you like a silent kitten, surprising you with its touch; at other times death stomps in the front door, unwanted and unannounced, and makes its noisy way to your seat on the sofa. Death isn't the greatest loss in life. The greatest loss is what dies inside us while we live. The dead can't cry out for justice; it is a duty of us, the living, to do so for them.'

At the door, John could hear David's sobs as he tried to control the despair that threatened to overwhelm him. The scene touched him deeply. Here was a man who he was sure had passed through many traumatic situations and yet seemed to have met one he could not cope with, an obstacle which appeared to defeat him, his Waterloo.

David finally realized he was putting other lives at risk by delaying so long. There were other children caught up in this disaster, waiting to be brought to the hospital. He pulled his hand away, closed the covers, wiped his face and headed towards the waiting ambulance. Fred had the engine running and said nothing, just glanced with compassion at his friend. David got into the front seat.

'OK, Fred, let's go. What are ye waiting fir?'

Fred gripped David's hand briefly.

'OK. If you're sure you're OK, Dave.'

And as if to emphasize he was getting back to normal, David turned to Fred.

'And keep yer hauns to yerself. I'm *A* happily mairied man. And dinnae forget that in a hurry.'

They smiled at each other with affection and drove off, heading back to Bonnyholly School to pick up more casualties or would it be fatalities? They were soon to find out.

Chapter 6

Bonnyholly Primary School was in stark contrast to the hospital. Because of its dilapidated state, consultations were in progress and various firms had been approached by the council to gauge their interest in a possible PFI contract. The ballyhoo that accompanied the building of the hospital resulted in the council giving serious consideration as to whether it could finance the project from its own budget. However its legal department had informed them that failure to implement the Government's PFI initiative could be illegal and result in financial penalties. The council decided to seek further clarification of the current legislation. The school had been constructed during the Victoria era. The solid stone-built walls and strong cupboards were important features that would shield the children in their hour of need.

The school had an assembly hall, a gymnasium, and a swimming pool which had been added later to the building. In all other aspects it resembled any other modern day primary school. It had seven classes for P1 to P7, accommodating six hundred pupils ranging from five to twelve years old. The staff consisted of a head-teacher and deputy head, five auxiliaries who chaperoned children with reading difficulties, thirty teachers, three probationers and a specially appointed music teacher. In some classrooms, the stone fireplaces had been left so that the children could learn about the past. The area where the school was located was similar to the hospital. It still boasted playing fields, which had flood-lighting for evening games, and which were carpeted with artificial grass. The local council said real grass was too expensive to maintain, and replaced it with Astro Turf in a cost-cutting exercise.

Arriving back at Bonnyholly Primary School, the scene Fred and David encountered was beyond belief. A police escort was needed to guide them to the scene of the crime. Distraught parents had gathered en masse, not knowing if their child was alive or dead. This was in stark contrast to their first visit to the school, only a short time ago.

When Bonnyholly Hospital received the emergency call, the immediate response was to establish the severity of what they were dealing with. When the hospital switchboard received the call, it was relayed to the Hospital Medical Co-ordinator Stuart Mctavish, whose job was to establish its authenticity. He dialled Police Headquarters and spoke to Chief Constable Fiona Mctaggart. He then activated Code Red, which meant a major incident protocol had to be initiated. He immediately contacted Senior Nurse Sophia Gloag; Senior Emergency Physician Fraser Montgomery; Dr Mohamed Hussein, the Senior Manager, and the Risk Management Team Leader, Susan McCletchy.

Stuart McTavish reacted with disbelief although he wasn't naïve and knew these kinds of atrocities happened from time to time. They had systems in place to deal with major incidents, but living near a chemical works, he expected anything on this scale that he had to deal with, would be a chemical incident. But after his call to the Chief Constable, his worst fears were more than realized.

He knew he had to act methodically. A man in his 60s,

he had been in his position for ten years, having worked hard to get where he was. He tried to keep a cool head. He turned to his rota to find out who was on duty in A&E and was relieved to discover Rose McLeish was consultant that day. If anyone could cope with a major incident, she could. Even if it had been her day off he would have called her in, and he was so glad that she wasn't on holiday. He dialled the internal number for her department, identifying himself and asking to speak to Mrs McLeish.

'I'll get her for you, sir,' answered the voice on the receiving end.

'Thank you,' he said. He always tried to be polite to whoever was at the other end of the phone. It must be a generation thing, he thought to himself. Although he commanded a high position as far as the world was concerned, he never forgot his humble routes. His mother had brought up ten children on her own, after years in a violent relationship had led to divorce, and Stuart well remembered the stigma attached to divorce during his youth.

Mrs McLeish came on the phone.

'Stuart, how are you? I was expecting you to call,' she said. 'We heard the news on the hospital radio.'

'I think it's pretty bad,' said Stuart.

'Do they have any idea of the numbers involved?' she asked.

'Not yet. Rose, can you institute the major accident protocols at your end please?'

'I'm onto it,' she replied.

'Before you go, let me brief you on *METHANE*.'

This was the acronym for major incidents procedure. M stood for Major incident, stand by all departments; then E, the Exact location of the incident, which they knew was Bonnyholly Primary School; T was the Type of incident - in this case fatal shootings; H alerted the teams to ascertain any possible Hazards the staff should be aware of; A reminded them that Access routes to and from the location had to be clearly understood and once that was established, N stood for the Number and type of expected casualties which had to be determined, and all they knew at the moment was that a large number of young children had been shot. Finally E underlined the importance of establishing which of the Emergency services were currently on the scene.

After this brief explanation of METHANE, Stuart asked Rose McLeish if she thought her staff would be able to cope.

'Because ... I think ... it's going to be … err ….' he couldn't finish the sentence and as he searched for the right words she interrupted him.

'To be honest, the answer is I don't know, Stuart. I know we've practiced these drills and procedures before. But drills are one thing, a situation like this is quite another. I'm confident most of my staff can handle rough Saturday nights with drunks, stabbings - those sorts of things. But, Stuart, these are usually with adults and they've become hardened to them. Occasionally one or two have dealt with NAI's.'

Non Accidental Injuries usually involved minors, and they were always upsetting, but were generally few and far between. All staff had been full briefed in child protection, it was mandatory in their training.

Rose McLeish was worried.

'Stuart, we've a double whammy here. Firstly, the numbers you say are coming, and secondly the age group is very disturbing. You know as well as I do that most of my staff are women, and many of them have kids of their own. We've one or two men in the department, but they're mostly fathers themselves and they'll nearly all react in some way. If it was one or two children, then I'd say with confidence they'd take things in their stride, but, Stuart, you're talking of double figures here. And am I right in assuming all the injuries are gunshot wounds?'

'That's right, Rose.'

'And is it also true that quite a number, and I mean a large number, are dead?'

'Yes.'

'What's the average age of these casualties?'

There was a brief silence. If they hadn't already discussed the makeup of the A&E staff, the answer would have been instantaneous. Stuart paused. Rose rephrased the question.

'Did you say the casualties are from Bonnyholly Primary School?'

'Yes.'

'What year are we talking about? Primary One, Two, Three? What year, Stuart?'

'I don't have the exact year, it could be a mixture.'

She knew Stuart was trying to dodge the question.

'Stuart, will you give me the information I need. I can't prepare my staff if I don't have all the facts. What's the matter with you?'

Stuart replied like a boy caught lying.

'They're the youngest in the school, I think they're all about five years old.'

'Five years old!' she repeated in disbelief. 'Tell me you're joking, Stuart.'

'I'm not, Rose. I wish I was. I've been in touch with the Chief Constable and believe me, I'm serious. Deadly serious.'

'This is Scotland, isn't it?' said Rose, 'it's not some

developing world country where the kids go about willy-nilly with guns. We're living in Scotland, Stuart, things like that don't happen here. Do they?'

'Rose,' he said, 'have you forgotten Lockerbie? You know I was at Lockerbie when that Pan-Am plane blew up.'

'I didn't know that.' She was surprised at the sudden revelation.

'Well it's not a thing I discuss very often. But I was looking at the rota and there's a man in the x-ray department here who I worked with at the time.'

'Oh, who was that?'

'Mark, the Superintendent Radiographer, was there. You can have a quiet word with him before things get out of hand. I can assure you, Rose, think of your worst nightmare and then double it. In Mark's case, a lot of forensic radiography took place, but he also had to x-ray burns and blast victims to look for anything embedded in the bodies.'

'I suppose, without the help of the radiographers at Lockerbie, A&E in Crayford Hospital would have been struggling?'

Stuart agreed, and told her he had every confidence in her and her team, as well as reassuring her that a veteran with years of experience was in charge in x-ray that day, and would ensure that the best person was assigned to each job.

'All the best, Rose, and as I said, have a wee chat with Mark before the mayhem begins. And, Rose,' Stuart paused deliberately as if he was about to ask a personal question.

'Do you have children?'

'Yes I do.'

'Well, I know I said this earlier but you'll need to have

blinkers on today. I'm not being a scaremonger but I've been there, bought the tee-shirt and handed it back. Whatever you do, don't remember the faces of any of these children. Do not, I repeat do not, feel any affection for them. I know it may sound callous but if you do, you'll never be able to treat them. You'll freeze. You may treat one, but after the third or fourth, you'll be overcome with emotion. Blank out their faces, Rose, it's the only way you'll manage to care for them. The A&E Consultant at Lockerbie reacted quite badly so I'm forewarning you.'

Rose now understood why Stuart had found it so difficult to state the ages of the casualties, and she felt compassion for him having to deal with his second major disaster. She had always thought of him as a rather cold, unfeeling man. But now she had an idea of the torture he must have experienced and he went up in her estimation.

'Thanks for confiding in me, Stuart,' she said.

'That's all right. I know what some people feel about me. I'm not as tough as old boots as they make me out to be,' he replied.

What Stuart hadn't told her was that he was the Duty Consultant on the day of the Lockerbie bomb. He had eventually returned to work after a period of recuperation, but what he had witnessed stopped him applying for any medical roles that required a hands-on contact with patients. Bonnyholly had been a means of escape, and having a nice cosy office was his salvation. Even now he was glad protocols meant he had to be a co-ordinator and not get involved with individual patient management. He could not bring himself to face a similar situation again. He was afraid he would never recover if he did.

After their conversation, Rose McLeish was pensive.

Stuart had certainly given her food for thought. For some reason, the words of Dwight Eisenhower came into her mind. 'There's no tragedy in life like the death of a child. Things never get back to the way they were.' Her favourite lecturer at university had often quoted those words, and another of her tutors told his students regularly that 'The death of a child is the single most traumatic event in medicine. To lose a child is to lose a piece of yourself.'

Was this about to be tested, she wondered. She had originally wanted to specialize in paediatrics, but gravitated to trauma because of the variety of work she would be able to do. She had become an A&E Consultant by default. Now, after all these years, her wish for variety was going to be granted in a manner she had never anticipated or wished for. She made her way towards the x-ray department to speak to Mark.

Chapter 7

At the school, the police had set up a cordon to keep the terrified parents back. The full horror of what had happened was slowly beginning to unfold.

John McLean, an ordinary citizen with a personal gripe against society in general, had decided to wreak vengeance on a community for blackening his name. Why he chose that particular school was to be the subject of exhaustive police investigations, and lengthy research by psychologists in the future. But he managed to obtain enough ammunition to perpetrate a disaster never seen on such a scale in the UK, and to create heartbreak and havoc in the town of Bonnyholly.

Fred and David learned from Ambulance Control that he burst into the school and started shooting at random in a room full of five and six year olds. The teacher in charge of the children valiantly endeavoured to protect them. As defensive as any animal mother with her young, she tried to shelter them. But McLean was armed to the teeth, and the contest was one-sided. He easily disposed off her and fired again and again from several weapons he carried. In a final act of cowardice, he decided not to face the world to answer for this wanton act of destruction. His objective was to make a name for himself, and in that he succeeded. But it is a name that will be remembered for the outrageous obscenity he perpetrated, and the endless sorrow and misery he brought to a small Scottish town.

Word spread quickly around the close-knit community as neighbours telephoned each other in horror. Susan Montgomery had contacted Danielle to find out if she'd heard anything. Danielle was busy cleaning her house that day with some of her favourite music on the CD player to jolly her through some of her least favourite jobs. She hadn't listened to the radio or television since the early news, before Graham left for work.

In David's room, her eyes automatically focused on some of his childish paintings on the wall. It never ceased to amaze her how tidy he was for a five-year-old. She rarely had to clear up after him as he always put his toys away when he had finished playing with them. He loved reading and being read to, and was doing very well at school. He had a vivid imagination, and could make up stories at the drop of a hat. Danielle sat on his bed. He looked such a little scrap when he was tucked up in it for the night, and it was hard to imagine that one day his small frame would actually grow big enough to fill this bed.

She took his pillow and sitting there for a few minutes, hugged it to her, the precious smell of him still lingering. Back downstairs, for some unexplainable reason, she had to go and gaze at his framed picture taking pride of place on their living room wall. He'd won the bonnie baby competition when he was just one year old, and rightly so, she thought. To every mum, their child is the most beautiful in the world, but to Danielle, David was perfection.

She turned to look at his class photograph. His tiny frame seemed dwarfed by his blazer and shorts. She had deliberately chosen a slightly larger size than he needed, to leave plenty of room for growth. His red hair and piercing blue eyes reminded her of her Irish grandmother. Her identical blue eyes were set in a finely chiselled face, framed by her luscious long red hair – her crowing glory. Danielle always felt the song: *When Irish eyes are smiling* was written especially for her grandmother. Looking at David's photo, she loved the likeness between them – two of her favourite people in the entire world. But David also had freckles, speckled across his nose and cheeks, and she thought they made him look positively cherubic.

Her reflective mood was broken by the harsh ring of the telephone.

'Hello, is that Danielle?'

'Yes. Is that you, Susan?' Susan spoke softly but Danielle heard immediately the urgency in her voice.

'Are you alright? Is something wrong?'

'Haven't you heard the news, Danielle?'

'Heard what news, Sue?'

'You'd better get down here quick.'

'Get down where, to your house, what's up?'

Danielle automatically thought there was something wrong at Susan's and that her friend needed her support. 'I'll be over right away, Sue. Stay calm. Don't do anything rash.'

'Danielle, I'm alright, it's not about me. It's about our kids.'

The mention of the kids made Danielle breathe a sigh of relief.

'Gordon Bennett, they've not been fighting again, have they? You know what kids are like, one minute they're going at it hammer and tongs with each other, the next minute they're friends again. Let's not fall out because of our kids, it can't be anything too terrible. They're just children after all.'

'It's not about them falling out.' Susan sounded tense. She was beginning to get frustrated. Danielle didn't seem to be listening.

Danielle could tell by the change in her friend's tone there was something more than kid's disagreement here.

'What'd you mean, it's about our kids?'

'Danielle, it's not just about your David and my Charlene, it's about the whole Primary 1 class, something terrible has happened.'

'What do you mean?'

'Just get down to the school as quickly as you can. There's been a tragic ...' Susan broke off her sentence as if she could not bear to relate what had happened.

'Tragic, what, Sue, please tell me. Is David involved?'

'I don't know. All I know is there are lots of our children involved. Annabel, Mary, and many of the other P1 parents are rushing to the school right now, which is why I called you. Hurry. I don't want to say any more in case I'm wrong and your son is not involved – I'm going Danielle, must rush, Shawn is waiting for me in the car. I'll see you down there.'

'Sue … Sue … Sue ….'

Susan had put down the phone, not wanting to be sidetracked into a long conversation, and rushed outside to join her husband, waiting with the car engine running to make the journey to Bonnyholly Primary School.

The phone call had left Danielle an emotional wreck. She paced up and down the living room, then instinctively turned on the radio, then the television, and flicked through the channels to see if there was any news. At first, all she could find were the shopping channels and various talk shows. She tuned in to various radio stations in the hope of catching a news bulletin, but there was nothing. Then she thought of the news channels which ran continuously, breaking stories as they happened. Switching to BBC *News 24*, she couldn't believe what was unfolding before her eyes. The newscaster, Sunday Chavez, was talking to reporter, Sandy McDonald, about a possible shooting at a local primary school in Bonnyholly. She turned the volume up.

'Over to our man live at Bonnyholly Primary School,' said Sunday Chavez. 'Sandy, what can you tell us?'

'Well, Sunday, we have here unbelievable scenes. I have reported from Lebanon, Afghanistan, the Sudan and Northern Ireland, but I never thought I would be seeing sights like this here in Scotland. The anguish on the faces of the parents is identical to any I've seen in all the world's trouble spots … hold on, Sandy, here's the first ambulance arriving from Bonnyholly Hospital ….'

Danielle could hear no more, it was as if her ears suddenly stopped functioning. She could see the images, hear the sound in the room, but paradoxically there was utter silence, her brain couldn't make sense of the pictures on the screen. All she could see was Sunday's mouth moving, saying something, but what it was she could not understand. As far as she was concerned, he appeared to be a mute. She went numb, and a feeling of nausea swept over her as her face drained of all its colour and she actually felt bile coming up into her mouth. She urgently needed to run to the bathroom to be sick, and yet another compelling force was holding her transfixed to the screen.

'Over to our man live at Bonnyholly Primary School,' reverberated in her head. She remembered nothing more of the unfolding news. All she could later recall was pacing up and down, finding her car keys, and then putting them down again, mumbling about calling

Graham and starting to dial, then replacing the phone. For the first time in her life, Danielle was almost literally paralysed with fear. Fear of the unknown, fear for her precious son.

'Please God, don't let David be involved,' she muttered to herself. 'Please, please let it be someone else.'

A pang of guilt overcame her for thinking such a thing, and for wishing someone else's child should be a casualty instead of her own. She reasoned that David had already undergone enough suffering in his short life. What had that little boy ever done to deserve something like this? Why did things always happen to him? She and Graham thought they had been through the worst with him, and could look forward to happy times together. Her mind went back to how long it took for him to be conceived, then his difficult birth, and subsequent problems.

At a year old, he had been diagnosed with an intussuception and was referred to Bonnyholly Hospital. The conversation she'd had with the Consultant, Mr Donald Briggs, was still fresh in her mind.

'Mr and Mrs Darling, I'm afraid I've some news for you both regarding David.' Mr Briggs had informed them in his usual professional manner devoid of any emotion.

'I don't want to alarm you as I've spotted the problem in time. I'm sure I'll be able to treat him successfully and he will make a full recovery.' Danielle always felt irritated when she heard consultants speak in the singular.

'What's the matter with him, Mr Briggs?' she asked anxiously.

She and Graham had noticed some worrying symptoms in their one-year-old son. He was experiencing constant abdominal pain, and the baby analgesia did not ease his discomfort. He started vomiting; initially it was his milk, and then it changed colour to green, showing it was bile from his stomach. When Danielle noticed an unusual discoloration in his nappy, she started to worry. The constant colicky pain, the bile, and the alteration of his bowel habits made her panicky. After referral to Bonnyholly Hospital they met Donald Briggs, the Consultant Paediatrician.

'On the basis of what you've told me, I believe your son has an intussusception.'

'Intussusception?' they said in unison. 'What exactly is it, Mr Briggs.' Graham asked.

'You know you have a large and small bowel?' His tone was formal and a touch patronising.

'Yes.'

'We call the small bowel the jejunum, and the large we call the colon. But for some inexplicable reason, we have found in some children like your son here,' he gestured at David, 'the last portion of the small intestine, which we call the ileum, goes into the first portion of the colon named the cecum. This is what we in the medical profession call intussusception. Do you remember the old telescopes?'

'Yes, I remember seeing one in the film *Pirates of the Caribbean*. I think Johnny Depp was in it,' said Danielle

'For goodness sake, Danielle, this is not the time to be funny,' Graham said.

'I wasn't being funny, just showing Mr Briggs I understand what he's talking about,' Danielle said defensively.

Mr Briggs cleared his throat.

'Can I continue please?' he said.

'Oh, sorry, Mr Briggs,' they both said a little shamefacedly.

'As I was saying, it's this which is causing the pain for

your little boy. It can cause stomach blockage, and we have to treat it as an urgent case.'

'How is it treated?' asked the anxious father.

'By x-rays,' replied the consultant.

'Can you please explain?' asked Danielle.

'I was just about to.'

Although a man who appeared to be without any human emotions, Mr Briggs was actually a caring professional. He and his wife had lost a child through illness themselves, making him more understanding and sympathetic. He knew just how parents felt when they worried about their children. He also recognized that he appeared to be rather formal, or even a cantankerous old dinosaur to some, but he cared passionately for his patients. He believed in treating the whole person, and where children were concerned, that included the parents. A negative attitude or emotion expressed by the parents always had an adverse effect on their children who were sensitive enough to pick up all the vibes around them.

'As I was saying, a portion of the small bowel ....'

'The ileum,' interrupted Danielle.

'That's right, Mrs Darling,' he said encouragingly. 'As I was saying, the ileum telescopes or folds into the last portion of the large bowel.'

'The cecum,' said Graham, not wishing to appear ignorant.

'Well done, you've been listening. As you rightly said, Mrs Darling, in Johnny Depp's old pirate telescope, one section goes into another. A similar thing has happened to the bowel in your son's case.'

'You mean one section, instead of continuing straight, has gone into the next?'

'That's precisely correct,' said Mr Briggs in a tone similar to that used by a father praising his children for behaving themselves.

'What's the cure?'

'I was coming to that,' he said patiently. 'As I was saying, by x-rays. Your son will undergo a barium enema examination. If, before the procedure, I establish he is dehydrated, I'll give him something to correct this, usually with a drip of fluids before I proceed. David will also need a nasogastric tube. As the name suggests, this tube is passed up the nose, goes down his oesophagus, or wind pipe as it is commonly called, and then it goes into his stomach. We also use this pipe to drain off the stomach and bowel contents which are causing your son so much discomfort. After that I'll give him a barium enema.'

'Sorry to interrupt, Mr Briggs, but what's that?' asked Danielle with a worried frown.

'Nothing to worry about, Mrs Darling. I, or at times I may use a radiographer, pump air or oxygen into the bowel while x-rays follow the progress. The reason for this procedure is that, by expanding the bowel, the intussusception usually corrects itself. If the enema works well, your son will be able to return home in a day or so. You see the intussusception is actually the site in the bowel where the infection or telescoping has occurred.'

The Darlings nodded, understanding what needed to be done to make their small son better. It sounded uncomfortable for him, but they would do anything to stop him being ill.

'Any further questions?'

'No.'

'That's good. I'll make arrangements for your son's examination immediately.'

'Sorry, just one more thing, Mr Briggs,' said Danielle. 'Do you operate the x-ray machine alone?'

'Of course not, a radiographer does that.'

'And what happens if something goes wrong?'

'I will have a crash team on standby,' said the consultant, sounding a touch pompous.

'If there's a team on standby,' said Danielle, 'then why do you always speak in a singular tense, as if it was you on your own?'

Mr Briggs was rather embarrassed and attempted to save face.

'It's just that … err …um .... What I mean is …. Let's just say it's easier to understand ....'

Danielle nodded, and asked no more questions.

David was transferred to the children's ward and under the guidance of the radiographer Linda Soggins, underwent a successful barium enema that day. Afterwards, Danielle said she had never known radiographers were involved in this kind of operation. Graham agreed. He'd assumed all they did was take pictures of broken bones.

'I hope we don't have to bring David here in the future, because of broken bones,' she said.

'Danielle,' said Graham affectionately, 'he's a boy, and I'll eat my hat if during his childhood we never see the inside of a hospital because of broken or dislocated bones.' Little did Graham know the next time his son visited Bonnyholly Hospital it would be under very different circumstances.

After that flashback to their early dealings with the hospital, the television news brought Danielle back down to earth. On the screen were pictures of parents outside Bonnyholly Primary School gates. The reporter was still describing the scene.

'It can't be true, please, oh please, it can't be true,' she mumbled over and over again, as she stood rooted to the spot by what was going on. The constant live reports and updates by the reporter and the rolling newsflashes along the bottom of the screen were like watching a horror film. Danielle continued to stare blankly at the screen unable to function, frozen and frightened. Then with eyes still transfixed on the TV, she began to mumble 'must phone Graham, must phone Graham. But what can I say?'

Almost hypnotically she started to dial Graham's number at work. As her fingers slowly pressed on each digit she suddenly thought 'Oh no, I can't tell him yet, what if I'm mistaken, is there any point upsetting both of us? No, I know what I'll do, I'll phone my mum.'

So instead of calling Graham, she phoned her mum.

'Mum, can you come over right away, I need a lift,' she said, barely able to hold back her tears. Sharon Moffatt could tell something was wrong. Perhaps Danielle's car had gone on the blink, but it was quite new. She almost suggested her daughter should call the AA breakdown service, but something in Danielle's voice made her pause. This was something more than a car breakdown. With typical motherly concern she spoke reassuringly.

'I'll be right over, dear, just give me a minute to make sure I've switched everything off.'

In the car, Sharon did what she always did, and turned on the CD player, which meant her car was a news blackout zone. Blissfully unaware of what was happening or what news awaited her, she drove calmly to her daughter's house.

Meanwhile, Danielle waited anxiously for her mother, the dreadful television pictures from Bonnyholly Primary School repeatedly echoing in her head. Her heart was pounding; she was in danger of hyperventilating. She staggered to the kitchen, ran the tap till the water was cold and filled a tumbler. Her hand was shaking so much she splashed it as she tried to drink. Still in a stupor, she reeled to the settee and sat down hard, wishing her heart would stop pulsating so loudly.

Now the TV crews were beaming live footage of the parents gathered at the gates of the school. Some looked visibly shaken, others were crying. There appeared to be some kind of hysteria as police cordons were trying to keep them back. The whole scenario was unbelievable.

'This can't be true,' Danielle kept repeating. This was not some G8 protest meeting with activists trying to get their points across. These were law-abiding parents, watching helplessly as one ambulance after another screamed out of the school. It was too much for some, and she saw some parents collapsing onto the ground.

'Mum, where are you, can't you hurry up,' she kept whispering.' Her body started to go into shock. A clammy feeling enveloped her and beads of perspiration glimmered on her forehead.

She couldn't stand it any more, and stood and turned off the television. With the silence came a measure of relief. She sat down again and began to sip her water. Slowly, her temperature began to subside, although she still felt clammy. Occasionally she would shiver and her body would shake. 'Mum, where are you?' just like the call of child when in trouble. It's as if mum can fix anything. She remembered when she fell off a tree as a child, she had run to her mother in tears. A cuddle, a bandage and a kiss made it better. How she wished she was a little girl now. How few worries she'd had then. 'Mum, where are you?' she repeated, desperately.

As if on cue, Sharon arrived. She rang the bell and immediately the door was flung open by her sobbing, incoherent daughter.

Mother and daughter were complete opposites. Danielle was serious, a worrier, liberal in outlook, and an agnostic – or was it an atheist? She was never quite sure. Sharon, while she could be serious, was jovial and open. She took religion seriously and was a fatalist, believing people were powerless to change anything that was meant to happen. Danielle, on the other hand, believed certain circumstances could be avoided by the use of prudence. At times she joked that her mother had been given the wrong baby at birth, but the close bond between them was obvious.

Sharon Moffatt had brought up her daughter alone. They had shared many ups and downs and now she put her arms around Danielle.

'My dear, whatever's the matter?' she asked.

'Oh, Mum, you'll never believe what's happened?'

'Come on, I've always told you there's nothing so bad that it can't be fixed. What is it?'

For the answer, Danielle switched the television on again. The story was still being told, retold and updated.

'What's happening - is that Germany or something?' said Sharon naively.

'Mum, it's not Germany, listen to the reporter,' Sharon glanced at her daughter and then back to the television. There were texts running at the base of the image. Wearing bifocal spectacles, Sharon had failed to spot them at first. She read 'Breaking news live at Bonnyholly Primary School'. Then the voice of the reporter Sandy McDonald.

'Another ambulance has just left Bonnyholly Primary School. I understand from my sources there are children on board. I can't confirm who they are, or what injuries they may have sustained. All I can say is their condition appears to be critical. Sunday, the scene here is unbelievable. I've never in my whole life seen such carnage and pandemonium ….'

'Are all these people at the school?' asked Sharon.

'Yes, Mum,' said Danielle, trying hard to hold back tears.

'Is there a fire or something?'

'Something worse.'

'What can be worse than a fire at a school?' It suddenly dawned on her this could be no ordinary school fire. There was no smoke, for one thing. Living near a chemical plant, she automatically thought of a chemical incident. But she quickly dismissed that notion, as none of the personnel she was watching were wearing any protective clothing. Even the reporter was smartly dressed in a suit and tie, with no breathing apparatus. Perhaps it could be a terrorist attack. She dismissed this idea as too preposterous. That sort of thing didn't happen in Bonnyholly. Danielle broke into Sharon's thoughts.

'Mum, Susan's just been on the phone, there's been a shooting and those people are parents.' Now she was sobbing again.

'Oh, Mum, it's so terrible; I don't know what to do. I don't know if David's all right. I'm shaking too much to drive there myself. Please take me now.'

Sharon looked at her daughter more closely than she had when she arrived. Her usually bright blue eyes were clouded with tears, and mascara had run down her cheeks, smudging under her eyes. Her hair was unbrushed and lank and her finger nails, always so well manicured and polished, were rough and bitten.

Sharon knew she had to keep a cool head for Danielle's sake, for her precious little grandson's sake, too. As she switched off the television and the picture faded, the rear of the first ambulance with flashing blue lights could be seen manoeuvring through the school gates on its way to the hospital. Her heart aching, she took control. If both of them panicked, nothing would be achieved.

'Danielle, I've brought you up through thick and thin. We're not going to let a nutter beat us. Come on, dear, stop worrying. It may not be as bad as you think. When Jerry dropped all those bombs on us at Clydebank, even after three days the Home Guard still managed to get people out of the rubble. So stay positive. Do you hear me? That's my girl now, that's the fighting spirit.'

Her words comforted Danielle. She reached for a tissue and wiped her eyes. Her mother gently took the tissue and dabbed at the smudged make-up. Her loving care made Danielle realize she wasn't alone; she could depend on her mother, who'd always made things better. The words of the James Taylor song *You Have a Friend* flashed briefly across her mind. Her mum was most definitely her friend.

Sharon had had a hard life but it hadn't made her bitter. She'd lived by the rule 'what's for you won't go by you.' Danielle didn't go along with that but she respected her mother's point of view. She felt that at times things can happen just because you are in the wrong place at the wrong time. And she reflected that if she and Graham had taken a holiday this week, then David would have been safe. But the idea was shelved because the Government had brought out new procedures which penalized parents if they removed their children from school during the term without valid reasons.

'Come on, Dani, get your coat now,' said Sharon. The use of her nickname brought a bleak smile to Danielle's cheeks. Whenever her mum was consoling her, she always called her Dani, but it was Danielle when discipline was needed. She switched everything off, grabbed her box of tissues, coat, and house-keys and together they headed for the front door.

'How about Graham, should I phone him?'

'No, no need to worry him yet. Have you brought your mobile phone?'

'Yes, Ma,' said Danielle affectionately.

Sharon grabbed Daniel's hand, gave it an affectionate squeeze and then, moving her head slightly to one side, gave her daughter a wink followed by a smile. The result was not a feeling of dreaded foreboding, but one of quiet resignation. It was as if she could now cope with anything she was about to experience. At times, Danielle had wondered what her life would be like if Graham was no longer in the picture, would she be able to cope? Her mum would – she could cope with anything. Sharon possessed a strength Danielle secretly envied.

Sharon's grit was now in danger of failing her. Although she gave the impression of being optimistic, she was fearful. But she knew that, irrespective of what was about to unfold, showing fear would not help the situation. There was a sickening feeling at the base of her stomach, but she mustn't show any weakness to Danielle, who, even though she was thirty-five years old, was still her little girl, the one she had made tremendous sacrifices for.

The scene that awaited both women was far worse than they had imagined.

Chapter 8

Fred and David eventually got their ambulance through the cordon, and the screaming hysterical crowd of anxious parents.

'Poor blighters, I know how they feel,' said Fred.

'Err ... do you have kids, Fred?' said David

'No. Why?'

'Then how could ye possibly ken how these parents are feeling. Believe me, if ye've no been a faither or mither and nursed a child, you'll never know what I mean. But in all honesty, Fred, ye have nae a scoobie do you? Efter all you have nae been a shining light with the lassies have ye?'

'Och,' said Fred. 'Is that in reference to a certain relationship?'

'Well if the cap fits, wear it, but until ye've been a faither, and then taken your responsibilities seriously, let me say this loud and clear, in case ye did nae hear me the first time, you dinnae have an inkling what these parents are going through,' said David.

He suddenly realized that was a bit below the belt and the pressure was getting to him. Before Fred could reply David said:

'I'm sorry, Fred, I didn't mean what I jist said, please forgive me. It's just the strain we are both under the day. I've just taken number one to the morgue and that face is still fresh in my memory. Ah jist cannae make sense o' aw this.'

'That's all right, buddy. I understand.'

'Tell you whit, Fred, before the end of the day we'll both probably say and do things we'll no be proud of; let's be determined that whatever happens we'll tak things that are said wi a pinch o' salt and not go off in a huff. I'm sure we'll never in our lifetime experience another situation like yon. OK pal?'

'You're right, Dave.'

'Aren't I always?' said David repeating his usual catchphrase.

They reported to control and were given further instructions. David, being the more experienced, spoke to Ambulance Controller Shaun O'Connell.

'Shaun, I dinnae mean tae be rude, but we are nae taking more than one serious child at a time again. We've had a traumatic experience with the last one. I was nae able to give one-to-one attention and I feel it could hae contributed to me losing him. We'll tak another passenger but it has to be someone with a minor injury. We're no taking twa critically ill patients in this ambulance. You can place me on report if ye like, but I'll nae do it, Shaun, I tell ye I'll nae do it. And neither will Fred.'

Shaun had known David for many years and had the utmost respect for him. He was fully aware of the situation, and for David to make such a stand meant business. At such a critical time he needed all his team pulling together, and the last thing he wanted was mutiny.

'All right, David,' said Shaun in his broad Irish brogue which at times required a translator.

'And to be fair to the rest o' the other crews, may I tactfully suggest ye apply the same rules tae them too?' continued David, knowing he had achieved a valuable concession.

'Tactfully be ...' said Shawn. Before he could complete his sentence, David added, 'and dinnae be including any profanities now Shaun.' As if in tacit acknowledgement of David's concerns, Shaun changed tack.

'My word, David, since when have you been tactful when making a point you feel strongly about, you're like a bull in a china shop you, yea, a bull in a china shop.' Shaun had a habit of repeating himself whenever he wanted to emphasize a point.

'I've been in touch with our neighbouring crews in Glasgow and Perth. They're sending all available crews to us,' he added.

David thanked him and went over to the Incident Controller, Richard Baincroft, to find out who was next to be evacuated.

When Richard got the first call, he was stunned. Immediately he assembled his mobile crew. A helicopter had been scrambled from the nearest airport and was waiting for them in the hospital front yard. A special grassy patch had been reserved for emergencies. Living near the hills and glens, there were regular flows of patients from the hills. Walkers suffering from frostbite, occasionally broken limbs and even fatalities.

The crew climbed aboard the helicopter, and in what seemed a fraction of a second, they were at the school and landed safely on the playing fields. In scenes reminiscent of a 'drop down' in a war zone, they jumped down from the helicopter, crouching low to avoid the downdraft, then they all rushed to the school, looking as if they were under fire from an unseen enemy. There had just been a downpour and their boots were squelching as they crossed the grass. At that very moment, a rainbow appeared above them, seeming to end right where they were. In a ghastly paradox, the school was to be the site of the most horrendous scenes ever to confront the Scottish public in peacetime, and yet a rainbow, a symbol of peace, glimmered brightly overhead. The domestic animals in the surrounding fields were also munching away at the fresh grass, peacefully unaware of the heinous crime that had taken place on their turf.

The medics from the helicopter worked methodically, assessing who was breathing and who was not. Then they graded the casualties in order of severity, and assigned them number tags. Names could come later; the important thing was to get the children to hospital for treatment as quickly as possible. Richard wasn't new to this kind of situation. He had been an A&E doctor in Northern Ireland and had vivid memories of knee-cappings, gunshot wounds and bomb injuries.

Looking at the children brought back memories he thought he had put on the back burner. There were some terrible memories, but even the terrorists in Ireland did not go out deliberately to shoot children. There had been a number of deaths amongst kids, and they were distressing enough, but the gunmen and bombers, on both sides of the divide, always said it was unintended; collateral damage was the euphemism. What he did not see in Ireland was slaughter of innocence on such a scale.

He remembered how x-rays had been used to find embedded bullets and pellets. He'd seen them destroy the patella - the bone in front of the knee. Two x-rays would be taken, one always at right angles to the other, to enable the surgeon to gauge the depth and location of the fragments. Usually, the patient was left crippled for life. A similar fate perhaps awaited these damaged children.

He pulled himself back from his thoughts and moved towards another of the injured, a little boy. He assigned him tag number one. His breathing was shallow, and his pulse was weak. Richard shouted to someone to bring some adrenalin. He tried to find a vein but the child's temperature was falling, and the veins collapsing to preserve heat in the small body. He finally succeeded in finding a vein, administered the adrenalin, and shouted to a colleague.

Jenny Sanderson came rushing over.

'I think this is our first patient. We need to get him to A&E immediately. Where are the ambulance crews?'

'Outside, waiting for instructions,' replied Jenny.

'Tell Control I've number one ready for evacuation. We've stabilized him for now.'

Jenny went on the radio and relayed the information to ambulance control, who in turn informed Fred and David. They put a cervical collar on the boy, transferred him to a trolley and wheeled him to the ambulance. An attachment was placed on his index finger so his vital body functions would be constantly monitored. The same procedures would be followed in meticulous order as Richard and his team moved systematically to examine all the children.

Meanwhile, Sharon and Danielle were making their way to the school. Sharon tried to take Danielle's mind off the situation while they drove.

'Do you remember the time I went to Bonnyholly Hospital?'

'Mum, you've been there so many times. I don't know which time you're talking about. Was it when you took me?'

'No. Remember I'd been there to have a mammogram.'

'What's this got to do with what's happening now?' said Danielle, whose mind was racing ahead of her, picturing the scene they would find when they arrived at the school and trying to hope it wouldn't be as bad as she dreaded.

Sharon continued. 'Well, when I went there, I feared the worst. I'd just had my usual three year x-ray and had had a recall, and they only recall you if there's something wrong.

'Oh I remember that now,' said Danielle. 'But I still don't understand how that has anything to do with what's happening now.'

'Well,' said Sharon, 'I expected the worst. I thought I'd got the dreaded big C and that would be me for the knackers' yard.'

'Oh, Ma, you can be so silly at times,' said Danielle.

'No honestly, Dani, I thought I was a gonner. Anyway I went to Bonnyholly Hospital and sat at the x-ray department, what a bonnie place. All those nice pictures on the walls ...'

'Mum, get on with the story, please.'

Sharon was always getting side-tracked and Danielle had to bring her back to the point. She put that down to old age. But for once Danielle regretted interrupting her. She appreciated the tactic was to distract her from what could lie ahead.

'Sorry, Mum, go on,' she said, 'what happened?'

'Well I met a radiographer called Isobel Anderson. What a lovely woman. You know, she looked a younger version of me. Anyway, I asked her what the machine was called, and she told me it was an x-ray machine. But it didn't look like one; the others I'd seen were much bigger. Isobel told me it was a special machine for examining breast tissue, and I asked her why it was special.'

'So why was it special, Mum?' said Danielle.

'She told me that the construction of the breast was

very different from the rest of the body, and was mostly soft tissue, so it didn't need as many x-rays as you would for bones. And she said she needed fine detail so she used a low kVp and a high mAs – all very baffling to me. She explained that kVp is the power of x-rays, and the more kVp, the greater the power of them. However, give it too much power and it passes right through the body and does no earthly good. So the trick is to give the right amount.'

Danielle didn't interrupt her mother, although her attempts at distraction were hardly working. Sharon continued.

'I asked her what mAs meant, too, and she said they are the amount of x-rays, and the radiographer has to balance the kVp, or the punch with the mAs - the amount. There is a subtle relationship between the two, she told me. Give it too much and the film appears too dark, too little and not enough x-rays will get through. But there's another thing the radiographer has to take into consideration, she said, and that's the dose of radiation. If the settings are too low, the x-rays just move about in the body and all they cause is potential radiation risks in the future. In mammography, the radiographer uses a low kVp but a high mAs; that way, she gets to see all the small details that are in breast tissue and can detect any subtle changes. Isn't it clever?'

Danielle nodded to show she was listening, although it was half-heartedly. Her mother went on.

'Isobel also told me that nearly every woman will come into contact with a radiographer sometime in her life – even if she's never had a day's illness. And even if she's never been inside a hospital.'

That caught Danielle's attention.

'How come?' she asked.

'Well, nearly all women go for a mammography at a certain age, but there are mobile Breast Screening Units inside vehicles that take the x-rays to people who can't make it to a hospital; they take the units to people's workplaces, and to car parks and things like that. You know, I never realized what an important role radiographers play in the community. Mind you, the mammogram's not comfortable with that paddle thing that squeezes your breast. But Isobel told me there are ultrasound machines for the breast now, so maybe when your turn comes, you will be able to have that instead.'

'I had an ultrasound scan when I was pregnant,' said Danielle.

'So you did,' said Sharon.

The conversation had had the desired effect. For a brief moment, Danielle closed her eyes as her mother's rather monotonous voice went on. She drifted off slightly, because of the heat and tiredness. She had been pumped up with adrenalin on the journey but as her mum talked, her body started to relax slightly. Feeling hot, she opened the car window and breathed in the fresh June air.

She relaxed in her seat and tried to focus her mind on what her mother was saying. Her mind automatically went back to her childhood. As a young girl, her mother always read her bedtime stories and she remembered the comfort - the inexpressible comfort - of feeling safe and secure. She turned to Sharon.

'Ma, I'm so glad you're here. I never told you this, but I really appreciate all you've done for me all these years, and if there's anybody I would've wanted to be here with me now, it would be you. Don't get me wrong, I love Graham, but I feel with all we've been through together, waiting so long for a baby, then David's illness when he was little, I think he would've found the situation too difficult to cope with. At least, whatever happens once we get to the school, I know you'll help me to be prepared for the better or for the worst. Let's be honest, Ma, we don't have any idea what awaits us at Bonnyholly. It's just too frightening to think of.'

'I went through the blitz, Dani, and if I coped with bombs and bullets I can cope with anything. Hitler never got me down, and I'm not going to let any nutter destroy my family. Let's just keep a positive attitude eh? But we have to be realistic – we don't know what we are about to find.'

'Come on, Ma, let's go and get David,' said Danielle. Softly she began to sing Celine Dion's famous song *Because you loved me.*

'You and your singing; you haven't changed, have you? You used to do that in the bath when you were a child. Then when you grew up, it was the hair brush as microphone. I tell you, Dani, I'm awfully proud of you. Mind you, I can't say that about your singing.'

And with that, mother and daughter headed to the school hoping to bring David home safe and sound, and yet preparing to accept that perhaps he could be a casualty.

Chapter 9

'X-ray, Mark here, how can I help you?'

'Trauma series please,' shouted Mrs McLeish on the internal phone in resus.

Mark turned to Margaret.

'Resus bay two, trauma series please.'

In the x-ray department, Mark and his team knew this was it now.

'I'll come with you, Margaret,' volunteered Fatima immediately.

'No!' said Mark, in a firm voice that took everyone in the department by surprise. Margaret shot him a questioning look.

All in the department were surprised at his assertive tone. Realising how it had sounded, he continued.

'I need Fatima here to process the images. I want to use this situation to enhance her experience which will help her.'

They all knew this was far from the truth, and so did Mark. In that instant, he had tried to protect Fatima from what he knew was going to be a gruesome sight. He had a sudden flashback of a scene from Lockerbie. He thought he'd dealt with this, but the memories were returning to haunt him. A cold shiver ran down his spine.

Margaret, knowing speed was of the essence, ignored Mark's comments, grabbed a number of cassettes and a grid, and headed for resus. Realising that she needed help, he added,

'Oh and take Jenni with you.'

'OK.'

As soon as Margaret headed out to resus, another call came. The casualties were arriving so quickly now.

'Trauma series please.' This time it was Anne, Rose McLeish's protégée.

Mark turned to Drummond.

'Trauma series, Drummond.'

'OK, on my way. Who do you want me to take?'

'Take Nick with you. And use the first mobile.'

On leaving the department, Drummond couldn't help but notice that Fatima was not pleased at being ignored.

In anticipation of what was going to be needed, Mark had brought all the mobile x-ray machines from the hospital to A&E. The quality of the pictures was not as good as those of the static machines, but they produced diagnostic images.

Mrs McLeish and Mark had decided on a strategy for patient care. All serious cases would be dealt with in resus. Once the resus bays were full, then patients would be diverted to the general rooms. She would work from the wrist-band attached to each patient by the Incident Controller and would handle each difficult case personally; Anne would deal with the less severe ones, and the minor injuries would be given to more junior doctors in the General rooms situated some distance from A&E.

In resus bay one, Margaret arrived to a chaotic scene. David and John the porter were wheeling number one out of the bay. She caught some kind of commotion between them, but she was too busy to notice what it was about. For a moment, a sickening feeling engulfed her, not because she hadn't dealt with children before; she had, but not on this scale.

She recalled a similar incident in resus when the ambulance crew brought in a Road Traffic Accident victim. A female patient was in bay one and her five-year-old daughter in bay two. Mrs McLeish had pronounced the mother dead and switched off the machine. The slow steady staccato blip had announced this to Margaret, as the bays were only separated by curtains. Her duty then was to attend to the little girl. As she was x-raying her, the girl was whimpering:

'Where's ma mammie. I want ma mammie.'

Margaret remembered the dilemma Mrs McLeish had faced at the time. The next of kin, the little girl's father, had to be informed of his wife's death, and what was happening to his small daughter. The trick was to tell him in such a manner he would not be a casualty himself in his haste to reach the hospital.

Margaret gathered her thoughts. A trauma series involves the examination of the cervical spine, chest and pelvis. David and Fred had transferred number two onto the resus trolley by the use of a pat slide. Immediately, Rose McLeish and her team had swung into action. They had practised this drill countless times. No words were exchanged, everyone knew what to do. Carol Shanks, the A&E nurse, clamped a monitor attachment to number two's index finger. The monitors came to life and announced they were working by the use of their particular computer language, lights and bleeps.

The trolleys had been designed to carry adults, but the small build of child number two on the white sheets was particularly poignant. His feet reached only a third of the length of the trolley. One bullet wound could be seen on his chest, another to his skull and small trickles of blood were oozing out of the wounds. Rose McLeish found a vein and venflon to give ready access to any fluids the little patient might need. Carol read off the stats.

'Come on, Carol, lets give the wee fellow our best,' said Rose. She was concerned about his breathing, and placed her stethoscope on his chest.

'The left appears clear but I can hear some crackles on the right. I think he's got a right sided haemothorax.'

This is the condition where the air in the lung cavity escapes and mixes with blood in the rest of the body. This is a serious condition, which must be treated. The lung has two membranes, the visceral and parietal. It can be likened to a bicycle tyre and an inner tube working in harmony. The tube and the tyre usually encounter each other, but not so the lung's membranes which are separated by a space. This cavity in turn is filled by pleural fluid. The two are held together by surface tension, just like the way a drop of water prevents two sheets of glass sticking to each other. If the chest wall is punctured then either air or blood, or a combination of both, can enter the space and this interferes with breathing. If this malfunction is not corrected, the lung will collapse with dire ramifications for the patient. The projectile had caused this condition.

Rose was glad it was on the right. The heart is on the left side and had a bullet penetrated there, it would have posed considerable problems. She was waiting for the chest x-ray results to confirm or refute her suspicions.

Margaret set up her cassettes. She placed a 24 x 30 cm cassette lengthwise to the boy's head and manoeuvred the overhead x-ray machine ninety degrees. Placing a lead apron on to protect herself, she shouted out 'x-ray', the cue for anyone not wearing a protective apron to either leave the room or retire to the protective lead screen separating the bays. Rose and her team remained in the room; knowing that many x-rays that would be required, they had all put on lead aprons under their green ones.

Margaret began exposing the cassettes, then passed them to Jenni who took them to the computer in x-ray. There, the details of her patient were confirmed before the cassettes were read. In resus, Margaret moved to the next examination and then, having completed her trauma series, and with Jenni acting as a runner, she returned to the main department.

As soon as the cassettes were entered into the Kodak reader, the images could be seen. Margaret had heard the consultant's concerns about a possible right-sided haemothorax, and was looking earnestly at the chest image gradually appearing. The speed of the image reminded her of a sunset on an African savannah. She had always marvelled at the sheer beauty and the speed of this celestial phenomenon. Once the full picture appeared, she carefully examined it and there were the tell-tale signs of a haemothorax.

'Jenni, can you please tell Mrs McLeish her chest and cervical spine x-ray images are on the PACS system. Thanks,' said Margaret.

The PACS system was a computer archiving system which held all the x-ray images. Any hospital in the UK linked to this system could access any x-ray. Mrs McLeish clicked on the images. She looked at the cervical spine to rule out any fractures so the collar could be removed, and thus enable further examinations to take place without this restraining device. She started to count the cervical vertebrae.

'1, 2, 3, 4, 5, 6, 7, ah T1, 2.'

She was not surprised she had managed to see the top two thoracic spines. In heavily built men and women, this was very unlikely and to assess these important junctions, another supplementary view had to be used, known as the *swimmers view*.

In number two's case, this wasn't necessary. Mrs McLeish traced all the cervical lines methodically to rule out any deviations from the norm. Any abnormality would suggest a fracture. She started with her first line and after examining the spine she moved to the chest x-ray.

'I thought so. We'll need to insert a chest drain.' Carol blurted out. 'His readings are down; we'll need to act quickly.' Rose McLeish turned to her.

'Can you see if the skull x-ray has come thorough yet?'

A trauma series usually involved a lateral C spine to check for the alignment of the cervical spine. But because of a possible object in the boy's head, she wanted to establish exactly where it was. For that she'd requested a full skull x-ray.

'The skull x-rays are through, ma'am,' said Carol.

Rose McLeish moved to examine the images. She knew number two was having difficulties, but she had to establish where they were coming from. The skull x-ray showed a bullet embedded in his head. The problem was establishing its location to enable the surgeons to assess its danger.

Ordinary x-ray images were limited in that they were two dimensional; what was needed was a more accurate method of assessment, a CT scan. The image of the body attained this way enables a more accurate diagnosis of a patient's pathology in some cases. CT acquires images by literally slicing through the body.

Rose knew she had to get number two to CT and then off to the operating theatre on the first floor of the hospital as quickly as possible, but she had to stabilize him first.

Carol raised her voice slightly.

'He's deteriorating.'

As if confirming her concerns, the machine raised its electronic voice by increasing the tone of its bleeps.

'Is CT ready?' Rose asked.

'I'm sure they are, but I'll find out,' said Carol who then called Mark to confirm everyone was ready in CT.

'Right, how about theatre?' Rose knew this was a rhetorical question. She had already been through these checks and appeared to be repeating herself. She was curious as to why she was behaving in this manner. A lack of trust in her own judgement was beginning to affect her.

It was then she remembered Stuart Mctavish's words. 'Do not, I repeat, do not feel any affection for them. I know it may sound callous but if you do, you will never be able to treat them. You will freeze. You may treat one, but after your third or fourth you will be overcome with emotion. Blank out their faces, Rose, it is the only way that you will manage to care for them.' Recalling those pearls of wisdom had the desired effect; it was as if a bucket of cold water had been thrown into her face. Her response was immediate.

'Right, Carol, get the sterile trolley ready.'

'Yes, ma'am.'

Rose McLeish prepared to insert a chest drain into number two to ease his distressed condition. Carol knew exactly what to do. They had worked together on countless patients. Stabbings were a regular feature of their work and they could almost literally perform this procedure with their eyes shut. What made it more difficult this time was the size of the patient. Number two looked like one of the dummies they had practiced on while at university when learning injection techniques. He looked so serene and peaceful, but the crimson stained sheets told another story.

Carol pushed the sterile trolley towards number two's right side. On it were the needles and drips needed. Rose went to the sink and washed her hands thoroughly, then put on sterile gloves and began the delicate procedure.

'Hydrex Pink Scrub,' she ordered.

Carol had already poured some of this sterilising fluid into a container. Using tongs, she washed away a section of his right thorax and Rose began to trace his ribs. She knew the fluid was more likely to be at the base of the lungs as fluid tends to pool downwards. Had it been a pneumothorax, which is when air fills the pleural cavity, it could have been in any of the divisions of the lung: the upper, middle or lower lobes.

Although she knew the probability of the haemothorax location, once again she seemed to be faltering. The delicate bone structure she was tracing to establish an entry point for the Seldinger needle was concerning her. She mentally began to note where the haemothorax was located from the chest x-ray. The machine's bleeps increased, giving the procedure an added urgency. Her concentration returned and she began to silently count the ribs. The noise of the machine increased again, 'bleep, bleep, bleep' in increasing intensity.

'Can you turn the volume down a bit please, Carol?' Rose appeared irritated by the louder tone of the machine. Carol complied.

Mrs McLeish made a neat incision to the skin, stretched it, and then satisfied she was in the right location, she inserted the needle. Immediately, a hissing noise could be heard, the noise of the machine abated and the bar coded readings decreased. She replaced the needle with a large draining tube and a collecting bag which fixed onto to the trolley, and to make quite sure the procedure was effective, she checked for the tell-tale signs of the retrieved fluid oscillating in the draining bottle.

'Is CT ready for number two?' she enquired again.

'Yes, I phoned Mark earlier and he said they're all ready,' Carol replied.

'Can you double check please, Carol,' Rose said. This was unusual but to humour her, Carol did as she was asked and phoned Mark a second time. He called Melanie Griffins at CT.

'Mel, are you ready for my first patient?'

'Has the request card been signed?'

'Yes,' said Mark

'Send him along then.'

Mark then called resus and told Rose McLeish that Melanie was ready for the young patient. She thanked him for his speedy response.

'Och, it wasn't just me. It's all team effort, Rose.'

'I know but it's good to show appreciation. Before I send him to CT, could I have a check x-ray please?'

'Sure,' came the response. 'I was a bit puzzled why you didn't ask for one. I'll tell the porters to hang fire for five minutes.'

It was customary, but not always necessary, to ask for a check x-ray after the insertion of any drainage to ensure the implement was in situ. Normally, this followed admission to the ward or when the doctor in charge was not happy with the initial results.

With that, Rose proceeded to resus bay three, where a small girl was awaiting attention after number one had been removed to the mortuary. As she walked hurriedly towards her patient, she reflected on what Mark had said.

He was right; it was working well for number two because of a TEAM effort. Things were still in the balance, but at least he now had a fighting chance. This would not have been possible without the radiographers. It was x-rays that had pinpointed the exact location of the haemothorax. It would be x-rays again in CT that would enable surgeons to gauge the position of the bullets and once in theatre, x-rays would guide the surgeons to the exact spot. Without radiographers, number two's life would surely have ebbed away.

Rose realized how undervalued these members of the medical team were. The funny thing is, she thought, if number two survived, no one would give the radiographers a mention. The communications team would in all probability wheel out Mr Briggs who would wax eloquently about the complexities of the case. No doubt they would also ask her about it. No one would mention the role of the radiographers, or report that, without their diagnostic skills, the A&E consultant and the surgeons would all be groping in the dark. There was no doubt in her mind that from that day onward, she would see radiographers in a different perspective. If she was included in any press briefings, she would ensure the radiographers were given recognition as a vital part of the team.

Back in the x-ray department, Mark decided to give his team a confidence-boosting talk. He praised them for their quick reaction and commended Margaret for her fine imaging.

'You're all aware the casualties are kids. None of you have ever experienced - and I sincerely hope never will again - what we're about to do today. I was in Lockerbie and it can be very hard on the psyche. But in Lockerbie, the majority were adults. Here, we're dealing with children, who through no fault of their own have become victims. I want to say to anyone who feels they can't go on to feel free to come to me privately and voice any worries. I'll not consider them weak, nor should they feel they're letting the team down. We all have different thresholds of pain and emotional turmoil. It's a sign of strength to acknowledge you're out of your depth. So I repeat, you do not have to carry this load if you just feel you cannot go on. We have dealt with our first patient and there are going to be many more.'

'How many?' interrupted Fatima.

'To be honest, I don't know. All I can say it's in double figures. So whatever we've done now it's just a start. We're going to experience this scenario throughout the day.'

There was an initial silence, broken by Drummond, who injected a lighter note into the bleak atmosphere.

'Hey, Mark, how about our overtime payments if we don't know when we will finish?'

'Just put it on your expense account,' said Mark sarcastically.

Everyone smiled as they knew it was a dig at the current furore going on about MPs claiming all and sundry in their expense accounts. Had the MPs known, their behaviour would provide a little light relief to some distant radiographers who were about to experience what was euphemistically called 'hell on earth', they may have taken a different view of the pillorying they were currently receiving in the press and media.

The mood of the team lifted slightly as the first case had taken its toll. Mark knew from experience it was better to forewarn them of what to expect rather than leave them to plod along. He was also glad of Drummond's wit. Although a sombre time was ahead, the low key humorous comment had, albeit in a small way, relaxed them all for the moment. The brief respite was interrupted by the incessant ringing of the phone. Mark was right; there would be no breathing space for any of his team that day, not even for a tea-break.

Chapter 10

Sharon and Danielle were in a slightly more philosophical mood as they made their way towards the school. A mile from the gates, they were confronted by a line of traffic.

'What's the hold up? It's like the lights are stuck on red or something. We'll never get there,' said Danielle.

'Now, now, Danielle, what did I say - positive thinking now,' said Sharon.

The traffic began to inch forward, very slowly, like a turtle on a beach heading for the ocean in search of food. Eventually, about 800 yards from the school, they were confronted by a policewoman, PC Sangria Hughes who waved them to stop. They complied, wound down the window and waited. She bent and peered into the car at the passenger side.

'I'm sorry, madam, we're diverting all traffic from the road leading to the school today.'

'Why's that, officer?' said Sharon respectfully.

'For emergency services vehicles. There's been an incident at the local Primary School.'

'Is it serious?' asked Sharon trying to subtly weed out information from the officer, who, being an old hand at the game, knew exactly what the purpose of the question was. After all, she was in the habit of regularly interrogating suspects more canny than these two women.

'Can I please ask you to go by the alternative route

signposted?' she said.

'But it's important we get to the school,' insisted Danielle.

'And may I ask what business you have there?'

Tension was building in Danielle's voice.

'My son's at that school and I need to make sure he's fine, all right?'

'Madam, I don't mean to be rude, but there are all sorts of people trying all kinds of excuses to get to the school today. It is imperative I keep the road clear.'

As they were talking an ambulance with blue flashing lights could be seen approaching in the distance.

'Now do you see what I mean?' said PC Hughes, 'I'm not trying to be awkward.'

At the sound of the ambulance siren, Danielle, who had been calmed a little by her mother's positive outlook, felt hysteria rising.

'Please, Officer, I've to get to the school,' she cried with urgency.

Experience told PC Hughes this woman could be genuine, but she'd had her orders.

'I'll let you through if you can provide a means of identification. Do you have a picture of your child?'

'Of course I do,' said Danielle naturally. She wanted to tell this police officer why her son was so special, and that not carrying a photo of him would have been tantamount to a betrayal of her love for him. She reached into her bag, retrieved her purse, and showed a beaming picture of her proud son in his pristine school uniform. As the officer examined the picture, Danielle thought back to the circumstances that had led to that photo.

They had looked forward to his first day at school, and going shopping for his school uniform was a highlight she would never forget. They headed for the department store in town. The family's finances were beginning to recover after her expensive IVF treatments, but there wasn't enough to enable them to afford made-to-measure clothing, and anyway, children grew up so quickly. They went into the shop and headed for the childrenswear department. There was a whole section specifically dedicated to school uniforms.

'Now, David, you're going to be the most handsome boy in the entire world when you go to school in two weeks' time. Here, try this on.' She took a blazer off one of the racks and tried it on him and then laughed 'Oh no, this is far too big for my precious.' The sleeves hung way over the end of his arms and the blazer nearly reached his knees.

'You know if I bought this, I'd not need to buy you short trousers!'

'I'm not going to school looking like this, no, no, no, no, never!' His bottom lip quivered.

'Now, now, no tantrums, or I'll make you wear it.' This had the desired effect as David was well aware that his mother meant what she said. Danielle looked at the label.

'Size what? No wonder you looked silly in it, you need three sizes smaller than that one.'

He tried on another blazer, this time it was the opposite effect.

'You look like a stiff little robot in that blazer.' The poor mite's outstretched arms made him resemble one, not the modern humanoid kind but like one of the early prototypes seen in movies. He couldn't even raise his arms if he tried, it was so tight.

'Mum ….'

'Yes I know … I'm not going to school in this either, no, no, no ….' she repeated her son's often favourite words of *no*, *no*, *no*. They both laughed. Their third attempt was successful and the blazer was duly bought. Danielle then picked up trousers and ordered a cap with the school's motto.

On that first day at school, her son was her pride and joy. He was indescribable as far as Danielle was concerned, as she got him ready before leaving the house, and with a tear in her eye, she knelt to straighten his tie.

'What's wrong, Mum?' he said in his soft voice with a slight Scottish lilt. For a child of five, Danielle was amazed at his powers of perception.

'I'm so happy. I never ever thought I'd see this day. My, you're more handsome than your daddy, my wee darling.'

'I should think so, too,' he said happily.

That statement was an understatement. With his blazer, white shirt and tie, he looked so grown up. He was no longer her baby, and she had a lump in her throat as she finally put his cap on the glowing red hair.

'My, you're handsome, my wee prince,' she said. To her, he was not just her knight in shining armour; he was a prince equal to any of the ones in the stories she had read to him before tucking him into bed.

'I know, Mum,' he said, 'you've told me that before.'

'Just a minute,' said Danielle.

'What for?' came the impatient reply.

Danielle was amazed how he could watch one of his DVDs for over ninety minutes without even a toilet break, and yet give him something of a more mundane nature, and she could not keep him amused for a few seconds.

'Kids, eh,' she thought, 'they say women are strange, but has anyone done studies of children? If women are from Venus and men are from goodness knows what planet, who can explain where in the universe kids come from?'

She rushed to the living room cabinet, opened one of its drawers then rummaged around in it.

'Come on, Mum, what are you doing now?' asked David.

Danielle was still looking for something, wondering why it was that you could never find what you were looking for when you wanted it. But eventually she found it at the bottom of the drawer. She picked up her digital camera and turned back to her son.

'Taraa! Found it.'

'Found what?'

'My camera.'

As soon as he saw the camera, he grimaced. He hated his photograph being taken.

'Come on my little prince, smile for Mummy please.'

A half hearted smile crossed his lips. In a pleading and warm tone, Danielle looked at her son's piercing blue eyes and pleaded again with him, this time more softly.

'Please smile for Mummy – pretty please!'

His furrowed forehead began to un-crease, and as if brow and lips were working in unity, a wide beaming smile covered his whole face. Danielle looked at the preview for a split second, almost speechless. Here, standing in front of her, was the results of years of worry, sacrifices and tears. She felt a lump come into her throat, and tears welled up in her eyes. She sniffled, slightly trying to hold them back; this was a happy day. Stevie Wonder's song *Isn't she Lovely* came into her head – the words would do just as well for a boy, she thought.

'Mum, come on, please,' begged David impatiently but respectfully, a testimony to his nurturing. Danielle loved this about her son. She had seen first hand the disrespectful attitude of some of her son's school mates to their parents. Whenever he appeared precocious or was developing a bad attitude, she would sit down with him and in a loving manner try to re-adjust him. Seeing his responses to loving instruction had all added to the sterling bond existing between them. Danielle's mother always blamed the TV and the media for some of the bad behaviour that seemed prevalent these days. Once again, Danielle disagreed with her as she felt good parental upbringing in a loving environment could offset any negatives happening in her child's life.

'Smile please, my wee darling,' she repeated.

'Mum, I am smiling, come on I want to go to school and meet my pals, please can you hurry up?' Then he added, 'and when I grow up, I don't want to be a prince, I want to be a doctor so I can help people.'

There was a flash, then the camera clicked, followed by a whirling sound as it reloaded the next frame, and the beaming picture of her handsome son with his straight smiling white teeth standing in his smart attire was captured for all eternity.

'That's a lovely photo. You did very well keeping still for me, David. Thank you. No, thanks a lot.' Danielle had lived by the maxim correction does much but encouragement does more. Even if she had to discipline her beloved son, she always ensured it was never in anger and it was always followed by encouragement. This had been a successful formula she and Graham had followed meticulously and here, standing in the frame, was the proof that it was working.

Danielle's thoughts were broken by PC Hughes, passing the photograph back through the window.

'That's fine, madam. Thank you.' The photo gleamed in the sun and emphasized the boy's cherubic features. 'That's a bonnie wee laddie you have there, you must be awfully proud of him,' she said.

'I am, believe me, I am,' said Danielle.

'Tell you what; I'll give you a wee ticket. The sergeant has developed this system to weed out anyone who shouldn't be allowed near the school. Anytime you meet another officer just show them this ticket and they'll let you through the cordon.'

As Danielle started to close the window, PC Hughes reached into the car and touched her gently on the shoulder.

'I hope you find him safe and well.' She spoke softly and sincerely.

'Thank you.' Sharon started the car again and they drove towards the school gates.

'What a nice officer, she'll make someone a good wife one day,' said Sharon warmly.

'Mum, will you mind your own business. Stop always trying to pair people off. After all she may already have a partner you know P ... A … R …T ... N … E … R - after all not all women have husbands these days you know.'

Nearing the school, they were stopped by several police officers, but eventually they found a parking space about a hundred yards from the gate. The surrounding streets were lined with cars, which wasn't all that unusual, as parents normally picked up their children, but the numbers there at this time of day made Danielle start to panic again. Many of them looked as if they'd been abandoned, not parked. Half walking, half running towards the school, her legs felt wobbly and as they approached, they heard an announcement from a megaphone:

'Please do not obstruct the road. Please keep the road clear for emergency vehicles. It is important you remain on the pavement.'

This message was relayed six times during their unsteady progress towards the gates. Fifty yards from the entrance was a barrier of police tape, and behind the tape a large group of parents had gathered, some silent, some distraught. The police had formed a human chain on both sides of the pavement and were keeping them hemmed in. The loudspeaker message was repeated.

'Please do not obstruct the road. Please keep the road clear for emergency vehicles. It is important you remain on the pavement.'

None of the parents knew what was happening; all they could see were the police officers fighting to keep the road clear to let the stream of ambulances through.

Sharon and Danielle joined the crowd. Next to them was another mother. In an attempt to find out what was happening, Danielle spoke to her.

'My name is Danielle Darling. My son is in Primary One. Do you have a child there too?'

'No, my daughter Ruth is in P7, and she's contacted me on her mobile phone to let me know she's fine.'

'That's a relief for you then.'

'Relief, that's an understatement. I heard about it from neighbours. How about you?'

'I haven't heard anything yet. My friend Susan phoned me and said she was heading for here. I was hoping I'd bump into her. Apart from that, all I know is what I've seen on the news.'

'They say there's been a shooting or something, but the police aren't giving anything away,' continued the unnamed parent in a fearful tone.

'Oh, pardon me for being so rude, I never asked your name.'

'Och, I can understand, your mind is all fuddled up, well don't worry, so's mine. My name is Helena. Helena

Sugden.

'Pleased to meet you, Mrs Sugden.'

'Goodness, this is no time for formalities, just call me Helena. She put out her hand to Danielle to shake hands, then in a heartfelt gesture of solidarity, hugged her.

'It's the way I brought her up. She can't help it,' chipped in Sharon proudly.

For once, Danielle agreed with her mother. She couldn't fault her in that aspect of things. When she was young she thought her mum was too strict, wanting to know about boyfriends, who she was visiting, etc but in hindsight, now that she had a child of her own, she understood better. It would have been a dereliction of her duties, a betrayal of loving concern, had her mother not been concerned about her friends, interests and activities. Indeed, there had been the arguments, the rows, but in the end she had always acceded to her mother's wishes, and in hindsight realized now this had been the right thing to do.

'Pleased to meet you too, Danielle,' said Helena.

'And me too,' said Sharon, not wanting to be left out of the conversation.

As they were speaking, another ambulance was heading towards Bonnyholly Hospital.

'You know, I've been here for forty-five minutes and that's the fifth ambulance I've counted. My friend, who lives down the road, said she saw a helicopter land in the playing field with some medical people. I don't wish to be alarmist, but I don't like what's going on. I've got a bad gut feeling,' said Helena.

So had Danielle now, after talking to Helena.

'Can you still get in touch with your daughter Ruth?'

'Why?' asked Helena.

'I just want her to find out if those in Primary One are

fine,' she said in a worried tone.

'Well I'm afraid I can't do that, Danielle, because in her last text, she told me the teachers were confiscating all the mobile phones. Look, here comes another ambulance.'

Six ambulances now, thought Danielle, trying to quell the panic she felt.

'And here's another coming back,' her mum called out.

'And another … that makes ...'

'Quite a lot,' said another parent standing next to them.

Rumours were spreading around the crowd. With no formal information, the gathered families began to speculate. Some said the ambulances contained five bodies each, others said ten. Then there were those who theorized that very few children had survived, others the opposite, that all had and had suffered only minor injuries. With so little to go on, the parents became extremely agitated and angry.

'Who do they think they are, not telling us what's happening to our own children?'

'Aye, they're treating us like weans.'

'You'd think we were ane o' the bairns in the class.'

'I've had enough; I'm no gaunae staund for this any mair.'

'I've had it up tae here. They may think we're eejits, but we're no.'

'Or maybe bampots.'

'Yea, you're right,' another took up the chorus, then another.

Spontaneously, the crowd started to surge forwards. The police officers tried to contain them. The cordon now behaved like a sidewinder snake moving in an S-line across the desert sand. It was only a matter of time before the thin plastic tape barriers gave way. Senior Police Superintendent Andrew Dimble was in charge of the officers who were trying to control the crowds milling around the school gates, all anxious for news. He went on his hand-held radio and spoke to Chief Constable Fiona Mctaggart, who had been flown by helicopter from Glasgow to handle the situation.

She was an experienced woman, having risen through the male-dominated police force. She had graduated from South Bank University in London with an honours degree in Social Work. Dealing with the rehabilitation of criminals, she was constantly annoyed at the revolving door which took them back into the Criminal Justice System again and again. Seeing at first hand the abuse of children, and the difficulties of the system she worked under, were constant frustrations. The old adage 'damned if you do, damned if you don't' haunted her profession. The last straw occurred when her department was blamed for failure to act in a child abuse case, which became widely reported in the media.

After resigning from the social services, she joined the police, and as a probationer, impressed her superiors and was fast-tracked through the system because of her aptitude. Many of her male colleagues were piqued, insinuating she'd got her promotion by subterfuge, while others maintained that it was merely a case of window dressing by the Glasgow Police Force. Despite all the negative comments, which she treated with contempt, she made rapid progress.

Her shinning hour came in the high profile case of the serial killer dubbed 'Dodgy Dave' by the media. Using all her skills gained in the Metropolitan Police and Social Services, she was able to bring a successful conclusion to a crime wave which had terrorized the whole of Scotland.

The perpetrator had tried to confuse the police by spreading his tentacles all over the country. Leading a mostly male team of fifty officers finally brought her the recognition she rightly deserved.

'Ma'am, we seem to have a problem here. Over.'

'What is it? Over.'

'Ma'am, we can't control the crowds and they're starting to be really agitated. I don't know what we can do to hold them back from venting their frustrations in an unlawful manner. Over.'

'Why? Over.'

'They're angry about the lack of information about their children Ma'am. Over.'

Suddenly, as if to emphasize their grievances, the crowd started to chant repeatedly, 'We want answers.'

On cue, Danielle started to sing, 'Why are we waiting.'

'Listen to this Ma'am. Over.' The officer held the radio towards the chanting crowd.

'Can you hear them, Ma'am? With all due respect, you'd better come up with a solution soon or we'll be dealing with a full scale riot here,' said Superintendent Dimble, then for good measure he added, 'and I can't say I blame them. Most of my officers have children too, and if we don't start informing these parents of what's happening, they'll surge into the school. And, Ma'am …' he continued with conviction, 'I'm sure you know what'll happen then. Over.'

The officer was referring to the carnage awaiting any parent who dared to enter the Assembly Hall. At the mention of a crowd of anxious parents bursting into the school, the police officer's voice took on a note of urgency. It didn't take Chief Constable Fiona Mctaggart long to agree with him.

'You're absolutely right. We have to start informing

them of what's happened. I'll be in touch in a few minutes; tell the families an announcement will be made soon.'

The superintendent went towards the crowd of parents, grandparents, aunts and uncles. He took the megaphone from the officer who had been informing the crowd about keeping the road clear for emergency vehicles.

'Can I have your attention please?' he said.

'Why are we waiting? Why are we waiting?' came the chanting, drowning him out. He tried again.

'I have an important announcement, but I can only make it if I have your full attention.'

'What did he say?' one father asked.

'Something about an important announcement,' came a reply.

'About what?' queried another voice. And as if in reply to their queries, the megaphone boomed.

'About the children ....' the officer paused. The crowd began to nudge each other into silence.

'Let's hear him out,' said a pleading voice in the crowd.

'Aye, shush everybody. Give the man a chance to explain,' said another.

Superintendent Dimble stood for a minute as the crowd slowly fell silent. He knew he had to get things right. He must woo the crowd.

'I have to find common ground,' he thought. Raising his megaphone he began.

'I know what a difficult time it's been for you all and for me and my officers as well.'

'Aye, that'll be right, ye dinnae hae bairns in there,' a heckler shouted.

'That's not correct; some of my officers also have kids who attend this school. They are just as worried as you are. They're human beings who love their children just as much as you do.' Those remarks silenced any further heckling.

'It's been difficulty, as I said for *ALL* of us. None of us has experienced such an occurrence in our lives. You may think we're hardened coppers, or screws as some of you prefer to call us. But we're humans like you, with feelings just like yours. We're horrified about what has happened. But you must understand that the priority was to get the children to hospital immediately. It would have been time consuming to try and establish who was who and talk to you first. It's a fact of life that children sometimes play 'swapsies' with toys, sweets and books, and unfortunately for us, they do this with school uniforms too. So one kid may have put on another kid's clothes. You can see the dilemma this poses for us trying to confirm their identity.

'We could not afford to tell any parent the condition of their child until we knew for a certainty what had happened to them. All the children are being allocated to hospitals in Bonnyholly. We have tried to keep them as close to you as possible but it's been a logistical nightmare. Some children have been taken to Glasgow. Now we can't tell which child has gone where until we establish their identity. Please be patient with us and give us room to work. Chief Constable Mctaggart has suggested the following.' He paused. The crowd was hushed, waiting for him to carry on.

'It would appear the majority of the children's parents are here. The classes are being dismissed right now. Please take your children home as soon as they arrive at the school gates. Don't loiter about or try to make conversation. The rest of you parents, please don't try to solicit information about your child. It may be inaccurate and cause unnecessary upset. I repeat, once you have your child, please go home. Those of you whose sons and daughters do not leave the school now, will be spoken to after all the remaining children have left the building. Thank you for your co-operation.'

And for good measure he added, 'we stand shoulder to shoulder with you in this, your darkest hour; remember, some of us have kids here too. Thank you again for being so understanding.'

'Well that's fair enough,' came a response.

'At least we know what to do,' said another in support.

To ease the tension, Danielle and the crowd broke into applause in appreciation for the Superintendent's speech. Once again, the effect on the crowd was amazing; the mood lifted momentarily. It was more an outlet for their frustration than a show of gratitude.

Danielle felt she had to do something with her hands. She could not wring them or shout with clenched fists at the officers, who were after all only doing their duty.

For a moment, there was a milling about as the restless crowd calmed down.

'Here's another ambulance coming away,' said an anxious parent whose voice broke into the quiet that followed the superintendent's words.

'And another returning,' Danielle said, craning her neck to see properly.

'How do you know it's the same one returning?' said Helena, standing next to her.

'Because I'd know those two in it anywhere. That's David and Fred, they took me to Bonnyholly Hospital when my wee boy was born,' replied Danielle.

The crowd now tacitly assisted the emergency services. Anytime an ambulance appeared they retreated from the edge of the pavement.

Soon, the children started to be led, class by class from the school. Their head teacher, Bruce Carlisle, had specifically told all of them not to mention any details of any child in the school, or to talk to anyone except their own families. 'Now imagine that's your wee brother or sister, would you want your mum or dad to worry unnecessarily until they knew the full facts?'

All the kids had agreed to keep silent about the day's events until the headmaster or another teacher had contacted the parents.

Primary Seven left first, followed by Primaries Six, Five, Four, Three, and Two and finally the last child appeared. As each year left the school, mixed emotions were experienced by the parents. There was jubilation for the parents who received their children, holding them close in relief, and ever more sickening feelings filled the remaining parents. By the time Primary Two's last child had left, Danielle was thinking the worst.

'Perhaps I'm being punished for saying that I wished someone else's child had died instead of mine. Please, God,' she continued, addressing a deity she didn't believe in, 'I wasn't thinking straight. I was just upset; don't take my outburst out on my wee boy, take it out on me.'

Before she could destroy herself with further feelings of guilt, a police officer arrived.

'Will all those whose children are in Primary One please follow me,' he said in a firm but compassionate tone.

Just as the crowds anxiously followed the officer out of the corner, at the corner of her eye, Danielle witnessed a heart-warming scene. The last Primary Two child was being hugged tightly by her mother. Then she administered an affectionate and gentle slap on the head.

'That's for giving me the fright o' ma life.'

formative years. She believed this sacrifice would pay rich dividends in the future. Occasionally, she would undertake some cleaning work to supplement the family's income. They lived in the local council estate - their house a tad cluttered, but clean and generally tidy. Certainly, there were no luxuries like a thirty inch plasma TV, or the latest surround sound system. They were perfectly content with their old television and audio equipment. Her brothers and sisters ranged in age from six to sixteen.

Being the youngest, she was sometimes spoilt by her older siblings. There was the occasional fight with the brother, only older by one year, who always enjoyed teasing her. Mealtimes were always a pleasant affair. There were no microwave instant dinners for them. Because she chose to stay at home, her mum always made sure the family had a cooked breakfast and dinner. School dinners were unaffordable and although they were entitled to free school meals, her mother, from similar circumstances herself, knew the stigma attached to them. She remembered all the kids in her school getting their tickets and the teacher tactlessly mentioning those having free meals. She vowed never to let any child of hers have similar experiences and kept her word. All her children went to school with nutritious packed lunches which included the delicious home baking she was famed for. Her brood were the best fed in the school and their lunchboxes were much admired by other mothers. At one parents' meeting, teacher Stephanie Learmouth had asked her where she got all her recipes.

'What's that got tae dae with ma wee lassie?'

'It's just that your daughter is the envy of the class, and I've heard other kids complaining to their parents that they wished they had a mum like you. I must admit, even I've been jealous of your home cooking.'

'Och, that's very kind o' ye but I enjoy daein things for ma kids.'

'We've noticed that, and that's what I wanted to say to you. The headmaster and I want to congratulate you and your husband for the fine work you've put into helping your youngest girl. Her reading is excellent.'

'That's guid. He may no hae a university degree but ma man enjoys reading. Once the bairns hae all come hame and had a wee rest, he makes sure that they dae their hamework. Ane day he'll read tae them. The next day the kids aw choose a book they like and they read portions tae us.'

'I can see that's paid rich dividends. Your daughter is the best reader in the class and at times she asks so many questions, I can hardly keep up! It's always "why, why, why" and I have to tell her to be patient and let the others have a chance. Perhaps that's the only criticism I have of her and it's not a negative criticism, just a point to bear in mind. You see, it can put off other kids who are too shy to answer.'

'I'll consider that, Mrs Learmouth, the nixt time we are haein our daily chin wags. Oh, and by the way, I'll bake a wee scone fir ye to show ye me and ma man are pleased wi all you do for our kids.'

'Thank you very much, Mrs Faichnie. This is one offer I will definitely not refuse. It will not influence your daughter's marks mind you!'

'If it did ye'll get nae mair scones.' They both laughed.

Stephanie Learmouth was pleased with Tricia Faichnie's reactions. From time to time, some parents mistook positive criticism for an attack on their parenting skills and immediately became defensive of their child even if the comments were warranted. In her opinion, some parents were stunting the development of their children by being too indulgent, but that wasn't true of Tricia Faichnie. Stephanie thought back to university when she studied psychology and distinctly remembered her professor, Walter Mischel, and his *Marshmallow Theory* test. In a trial to test children's self-control and to see if it had wider ramifications for their future well-being, the professor had selected a group of four year olds. They were put in a room with a marshmallow on the table. The acid test was whether they would eat the marshmallow immediately, or wait twenty minutes to receive two marshmallows. On the face of it, this may seem a ridiculous study, any child given a sweet and told to eat it would not need a second prompting, but the option of an extra sweet tested the self control of the child. The professor found that the children who could delay gratification, or who showed self-control, went on to do better in school and in adolescence than those who could not. It proved that whatever background people came from, they were really masters of their own destiny, and the environment they were reared in played a significant role in countering many negative influences in their lives.

In the Faichnie household, this theory, although they didn't know it, had been applied. The whole family sat together round the table and conversations were lively, friendly and loving. They were taught patience and to wait their turn for food to be passed round. Any problems that came to light were discussed one-to-one with their parents.

At times, more perplexing questions would be put to the rest of the family and all suggestions for a solution listened to seriously. Number ten had grown up in this environment. Living in a rural area, the children had been allowed more freedom than those living in cities. With so many youngsters, they'd had a number of contacts with radiographers and had lost count of the number of visits to Bonnyholly Hospital and the x-ray department. There'd been the usual greenstick fractures, and occasional broken arms or legs as they grew into active teenagers. One or other of them was invariably in plaster. Colin and Tricia Faichnie sometimes worried that the hospital would be suspicious of their frequent visits, but their fears proved groundless.

Young Colin Faichnie, when his full set of adult teeth emerged at the age of thirteen, needed to be seen by an orthodontist and without treatment, he probably would have grown up with teeth to compete with a walrus. But even this skilled professional would be working blind, were it not for the skill of radiographers.

Before any treatment could begin, all of young Colin's teeth had to be x-rayed and assessed. A panoramic image followed by what is called a *lateral ceph* provided the orthodontist with all the information he needed to correct the problem. After a brace was fitted, subsequent x-rays ensured its correct positioning and when it was finally removed a few years later, young Colin had gleaming straight teeth he could be proud of.

There was no more name calling at school and instead of mumbling in a vain effort to conceal his uneven teeth, he now not only spoke coherently but made every effort to flash a beaming smile. His nickname of 'Bugs Bunny' became irrelevant. The old adage 'sticks and stones will break my bones but names will never hurt me' was a false one for young Colin. The taunting words had hurt him very much, and he withdrew more and more into his shell.

Once his brace was removed, his parents noticed a

marked improvement in his behaviour, and that had a knock-on effect on his school work. Instead of slinking about hoping no-one would notice him, he began to speak out in class, offering answers and thoughtful opinions.

The positive changes were remarkable and the Faichnies were astonished that a cosmetic brace could have had such far-reaching consequences.

Once again, the radiographer had proved valuable. Dental radiography is a specialty in its own right and is a skill seldom mentioned or appreciated by the public.

Mick Watson's thoughts about number ten and her home life were interrupted by Rose McLeish.

'What have here, Mick?'

'Oh this is number 10. Her obs are ....' and he relayed his findings.

'Well done, Mick.'

'Thanks, Mrs McLeish.'

Mick always made it a habit to give the consultants their due respect. He felt it was being presumptuous to call them by their first names.

'We'd better get some x-rays and see what we're dealing with. Taking the readings, and what I can hear in her chest, I don't think there's any likelihood of either a pneumo or haemotharax, but we'd better do the right thing and rule them out completely, don't you think?'

Rose looked at number ten. The blonde hair and pale skin suggested a Scandinavian origin. The child's eyes were closed. So Rose reached towards the trolley and gently prized her eyelids open, shone a torch into her pupils to test her reaction and closed them again very tenderly. They were very blue, the colour of the sky on a summer morning. Rose thought perhaps she was called after one of those Norse goddesses such as Freya or Ursela. The tiny figure gave no indication of the kind of adult she would grow into. Perhaps she'd do medicine, or become a nurse or a radiographer, or perhaps something quite different like a teacher, a dancer, an artist or even an astronaut. Mrs McLeish didn't know about the conversation number ten had had with her mother only a few days ago.

It was bedtime. She had been bathed and was in her pyjamas. Her mum picked up a bedtime book to read but number ten interrupted her.

'Ma, dae ye mind if we jist blether tonight?'

'Of course not, ma dearie, what dae ye want to blether aboot?'

'Well, at school today, Mrs Learmouth was talking aboot what we all would like tae be when we grow up. Johnny said "Spiderman"; Daniel said he'd be better than that, he wanted tae be "Superman". Then Jennifer said she wanted tae be "Storm" o' the *Fantastic Four* who would be better than baith o' them put the githcr. Mary told her that she wanted tae be a "prime minister" like Margaret Thatcher, but I dinnae ken who she is.'

'Oh that's braw,' said her mum, trying to suppress a giggle, and trying not to stifle any discussion by being negative, 'and what dae ye want tae be?'

'Guess,' she said excitedly as she bounced up and down on her bed, with legs crossed like a Buddha, in Barbie pyjamas.

'Noo let me see,' said her mum trying to string her along, 'ye want to be a pilot?'

'Wrang ....'

'A bus driver then?'

'Wrang agane ....'

'Well then, a model?'

'Och nae, Ma, yir so, so wrang ye'll nivver guess it, jist gie up.'

'Richt, I gie up. What dae ye want tae be then?'

'A want tae be a radiographer.'

'A radiographer? What in heavens name is that? Do they operate radios?'

'No, Ma, dinnae be daft. They tak x-ray pictures.'

'Of course. I kent that aw the time, I was only testing ye.' Her mother blushed at the white lie.

'By jings, how on earth did ye come tae that decision?'

'Do ye mind whan ye took us to Bonnyholly Hospital aboot yer foot?'

'Aye, I mind, I'd an awfie lot o' trouble wi it.'

'Well ye asked one o' the radiographers to leuk after me.'

'Aye I mind noo, yer faither was at work and could nae get the time aff and I could nae get a babysitter so I took ye wi me.'

'Well,' continued number ten, 'I asked her loads and loads o' questions and she showed me some x-ray pictures. She was a wee bit lik ye, Maw.'

'Oh, how?'

'Well, she said she could see richt through us.'

'That's richt.'

They both laughed. Tricia Faichnie then started to tickle her daughter resulting in both of them rolling about on top of the bed, the little one shouting and giggling.

'Oh stap it, Maw, I cannae stap laughing,' said her daughter.

Tricia stopped, tucked her daughter in bed, kissed her goodnight, and went downstairs to join her husband.

'Colin,' she said, 'do ye ken what our dochter has just telt me, do ye ken what she wants tae be?'

'A cook, nurse, doctor, brain surgeon, astronaut or mebbe a rocket scientist?' Colin answered without looking up from his newspaper.

'Aw dinnae be daft, Colin,' said Tricia, 'I'm serious.'

'Tricia, kids change their minds aw the time. When I was young I wanted tae be in the merchant navy and be a ship's captain and jist leuk at me the noo,'

'Well ye may no hae become captain o' a ship, but you gey near reached yer goal.'

'Are ye trying to tak the Mickey? I'm an operative at the terminal, a faur cry frae a ship's captain, dae ye nae think?'

'Aye, and whaur's the terminal?'

'Nixt to the sea.'

'So ye got hauf what ye was efter.'

They both started to laugh.

'But you ken,' said Colin, 'tae be a radiographer is no a baud thing. Leuk at the number o' times we've been up and doon the hospital wi oor lot. Jings, I think we've shares in the place.'

'If it was nae fir them I may no hae been diagnosed,' said Tricia.

'What dae ye mean?' said Colin.

'Well ye mind I'd been ranting on fir months aboot my fit.'

'Aboot fower months, tae be precise,' chipped in Colin, 'an I bore the brunt o' it, dinnae forget,' he added.

'Ye're sae rude butting in whan I'm speking. Can I gae on…?' said Tricia in frustration.

'Och, sairie,' said Colin, 'gab awa.'

'Thanks. As I was saying, afore somebody nicked in twa or three words, I was in pain in ma richt fit fir months. I tried aw kind o' things if ye mind. Immobilisation, rests, they creams and potions, ye name it, I had tried them aw. Then whan our wee lassie an I went to Bonnyholly Hospital fir an x-ray, I did nae ken that place was to change her and ma life foriver. Well, the bonnie radiographer, Fatima, I think she was called, and she was a new graduate, well she x-rayed me while a Margaret leuked efter our bairn. They telt me the results in a week and they said I had a stress fracture o' the navicular. What a fancy name fir a bit o' bone eh? I kent aboot the metatarsals cause o' David Beckham bit I'd niver heard o' the navicular. Onieway, they weren't shuir so I haud tae gae fir a bone scan and I met anither radiographer.'

'A bone scan? Jings, hoo auld are ye? Ye dinnae need a bone scan, isn't it jist fir auld women wi that fancy disease osteothingummy ....'

'Och yer jist so daft at times, Colin. Ye mean Osteoporosis. A bone scan is no jist fir old women. Blokes git it too ....'

'Aye that'll be right,' he said.

'Can I go on? Stap yer butting in, it's so rude.'

'Sairy dear,' he apologised again.

'As I was saying, I met anither radiographer?'

'Anither radiographer? Hoo monie radiographers are ye going to meet in ane day?'

'Why dae ye keep wearying me?'

'It's jist that I thocht radiographers jist teuk x-rays pictures. I never kent they teuk bone scans an aw.'

'Well noo ye ken see! I was like you. I asked the same question of the bloke that did it. I think he was called Drummond, and he said aye, they did bone scans an aw. He explained tae me that he qualified as a radiographer and studied some mair tae become a nuclear medicine specialist. Anyway he did a bone scance.'

'What's a bone scance?'

'Ah here's the clever bit. Do ye ken when ye go fir an x-ray, whaur the x-ray comes frae?'

'Frae that whacking great big machine they

radiographers lumber aboot in the x-ray room.'

'Aye that's right. But in a bone scance they put the radiation in yer body, and then they tak a picture.'

'So do ye become like yon man the Hulk?'

'Dinnae be daft, Colin, yer taking the Mickey oot o' me .... Be serious.'

'Sairy darling, I was only joking. Onieway, what happened?'

'The radiation thingummy travels to yer bluid and gathers in bits that are nae normal. They ca' this either het or cald spots. Onieway this bone scan went tae ma fit. Drummond telt me there was an increased uptake in the navicular and he also telt me mebbe I had a stress injury.'

'So what did they do fir ye then?'

'They decided to leuk mair intae it, and sent me fir an MRI.'

'Oh, thae muckle machines like a doughnut.'

'Aye, they're full o' magnets and ye ken how claustrophobic I am.'

'Aye. I mind ye spending some o' my hard earned cash on thae relaxation tapes. Did they work at aw?'

'Aye they did. And dinnae forget it was nae jist your cash. I did that wee cleaning job mind ye, so get aff yer high horse.'

'Oops … sairy.'

'Onieway, nixt stop MRI and I met anither radiographer Brian Richardson. He was ever so nice. He teuk time tae explain why a cannae go in if a have onie metallic objects.'

'I always wondered why. What did he say?'

'It's do wi the way the machine works. Dae ye ken what MRI stands for?'

'Nae. But yer going tae tell me onieway.'

'He telt me it's short for Magnetic Resonance Imaging.

If ye put a body in a powerful magnet, the body does nae stay the same, and the clever clogs, the scientists, fund ways o' making pictures frae the changes o' the body in a magnet.'

'So that's aw then?' said Colin.

'No I went fir mair tests. They sent me to someone called Linda in ultrasound and then to Mel in CT.'

'Ye went through a hail lot o' radiographers eh? I did nae ken there were so many. What was the outcome then?'

'They faund ma problem, and when the orthopaedic surgeon spak tae me he said I had an accessory navicular ossicle.'

'Whit causes it?' he asked.

'Twa or three things, like shoes that dinnae fit, a heap o' exercises, or trauma.'

'A telt you yon jogging was nae doing you onie guid.'

'But I needed to jog to de-stress after looking efter aw they kids. I would nae need tae de-stress if I had help frae a certain buddie spread aboot on the seetee. Onieway I'm alright the noo. The operation at Bonnyholly finally cured me. I'm a new wumman now.'

'Ye ken,' said Colin, thoughtfully, 'a radiographer would be a great job for our wee lassie. Leuk at your case. There was a radiographer who did yer x-ray, anither did yer ultrasound, anither yer MRI and then anither yer CT and finally this nuclear thingy, it was a radiographer that scanned you an aw. That makes five different kinds o' radiographers that leuked efter ye. If ye had gan tae theatre ye would've needed a radiographer agane. My, we do underestimate what they dae in a hospital eh?'

'Aye you're richt, we dae,' Tricia agreed.

'And by the way we've forgotten something else radiographers dae,' he said.

'What?' said Tricia.

'Mind when young Colin turned thirteen and he had to hae a brace fitted?'

'Aye I mind that too. His teeth were a richt mess.'

'Well who mended them?'

'Mr McLeod the orthodontist,' she replied, but the penny was beginning to drop.

'Aye, but before he got his teeth sorted, he had tae have them aw x-rayed by a ….'

'A radiographer of course,' said Tricia finally.

The crime perpetrated on that day had robbed some children of their futures. Number one, now lying in the mortuary, had wanted to be a doctor to save lives. He was gone. Number ten wanted to be a radiographer, and her life now hung in the balance. As she was being taken to CT after another series of trauma x-rays, her future was now dependent on the skill of the surgeon, Mr Roger Whitmore and his team.

Included in that team would be a radiographer who would skilfully manipulate his image intensifying x-ray machine to enable the surgeon to locate and remove the bullets embedded in her small body.

The very profession number ten had said she wanted to join, radiography, would now play an essential part in saving her life.

The sadistic assault on defenceless little children had resulted in the loss of an unknown number of potential scientists, artists, doctors, carpenters, plumbers, comedians, radiographers. The cost was immeasurable. It was possible that this crime had deprived the world of a future discoverer of a potentially fatal or life-threatening disease. The parents still left at the school were to find out if their future prodigies were alive or dead.

Chapter 12

The procession of singing parents finally reached the front doors of the school, still not knowing what had happened to their children. Fate was to deal them a terrible blow and those jealous and vengeful Greek goddesses, the Moirae, were playing tricks to torment them further. The parents assembled in the entrance hall of the school. Headmaster Bruce Carlisle had deliberately kept them from the scene of the crime, knowing it would be too appalling for their eyes. He was correct. No loving parent would have been able to comprehend such an inhumane and merciless ending to the life of their beloved offspring. Bruce Carlisle and Chief Constable Mctaggart came slowly down the stairs. Each step, painfully deliberate, reminded them of each casualty. One, two, three, four ....

They knew the families were looking for answers, and those answers had to be given in a direct and dignified manner. After all, they were parents too. Both wondered how they would feel if they were among the crowd assembled below. They reached the last step, number forty. This raised them slightly above the height of the waiting crowd of anxious relatives, as if they were standing on a platform. They paused for a moment, surveying the parents who had been singing in harmony only a few minutes before. For Fiona Mctaggart in particular, the sight of these desperate people wrung her heart. It made the message she was about to deliver so very hard.

In a touching display of support, the parents still held each others' hands, several taking this show of solidarity further by wrapping their arms around each other. The common denominator of fear in these unimagined circumstances had spontaneously generated a kind of parent-to-parent bonding. At other, better times, this group of people might not have had anything in common, or they might have been pushy parents, almost competing against the others; perhaps complaining if their child was not given the lead role in either the Christmas or Easter Play, when their little star was obviously the best. Parents, indignant about who was to play Joseph or Mary, or who would be humble shepherds or even sheep, had caused many a headache for the headmaster.

Now the carping paled into insignificance. For once, they all realized their petty squabbles had been infantile. It had been the sort of behaviour they might have expected from their children. They held each other, not only for support, but to tacitly acknowledged how stupid and foolish the *dog-eat-dog* attitude had been. Some parents had taken umbrage to such an extent that friendships had been broken. Long after the children had sorted out any misunderstandings among themselves, the parents had continued their puerile behaviour. Now they were friends united in grief. Now they needed each other.

Bruce Carlisle recognized some of the faces instantly. He caught sight of one mother whose child he believed to be a child prodigy, with reading abilities years beyond his age. Now and then in his or her career a teacher would have the satisfaction of saying 'I played a part, albeit a small one, in this boy's development.' It was one of the joys of his profession.

Side-by-side, the two officials stood at the foot of the stairs. Both were used to dealing with crowds. One, with unruly adults, the other, boisterous children. Bruce Carlisle was glad he had the Chief Constable beside him.

Before descending the stairs, they had rehearsed in cold blood what to say. They had their own reasons for not wanting the parents to see the scene of the crime. The headmaster had actually been a witness of the carnage, and didn't want any parent to see the devastation for themselves; the Chief Constable didn't want any further contamination of the crime scene to hinder police investigations.

With different objectives, they were united in needing to protect these mothers and fathers from the nightmare image of where their beloved children had suffered. It would be indelibly imprinted on their minds, and many wouldn't be able to live with it. In a nutshell, both felt they owed all these people a duty of care, until support systems were in place to look after them and enable them to cope. The Chief Constable could never understand why some people wanted to see the actual spot where their loved one had suffered a calamity.

It was now four o'clock. An earlier thunderstorm had passed and now the sun was shining and a rainbow glimmered in the sky. Shafts of sunlight shone through the windows, rather like x-rays finding their way through bones, illuminating each person in turn, almost as if singling them out for analysis. The faces of those bathed in sunlight looked radiant for a brief moment; those in the shade looked drawn and dark. 'Was this a portent of what was to come' thought the headmaster. Some, he knew, were about to be utterly devastated by the news they would hear, their lives never to be the same again; for others, there would be a measure of relief through the pain. Or perhaps he was just reading too much into a natural phenomenon.

Their brief pause lasted less than a minute, but to the parents it seemed like hours. Bruce Carlisle spoke first.

'I,' he began, but on catching a sideways look from the Chief Constable he started again.

'We know you've all had a difficult day, and like us, you'll be wishing you could wake up and find this had never happened.' He paused, giving Fiona Mctaggart an opportunity to speak.

'I agree with Mr Carlisle. You're all aware I'm a Police Officer, and never in my thirty-five years in the force have I had to deal with an incident like this. I can honestly say I thought I'd seen it all, but I never ever imagined I would witness a day like this, or a crime of this magnitude.'

'We're not being alarmist; we're trying to prepare you for what we have to tell you.' Bruce Carlisle cut in.

'Where are our children?' came a voice from the crowd.

Bruce looked at the Chief Constable who dipped her head as if to say 'go ahead, answer that question.'

'I have to tell you they're either in Bonnyholly or other satellite hospitals,' he told them.

'What dae ye mean ither hospitals? Hoo monie are casualties or maybe even deid? Fir goodness sake tell us,' someone called out. The headmaster responded nervously.

'Well, at the moment we've counted ....' He could not bring himself to speak the number out aloud. A wave of distress swept over him, making it impossible for him to continue. It was hot with so many people crowded into a confined space, and the news he had to give was unspeakable.

Fiona McTaggart, more accustomed to dealing with the public, stepped in with authority.

'As Mr Carlisle was about to tell you, at the moment the casualty figure stands at forty-five.'

There was an audible gasp from the hundred or so gathered in the small space at the foot of the stairs. Unseen by the two officials were the hands linked together, tightening as if trying to hold onto something – anything; others at the back buried their heads into the shoulders of their partners.

'Dae ye ken onie names?' came another voice.

'We're still trying to establish the identity of some of the casualties,' the headmaster told them.

'Surely you know who's who in your school?' an astonished voice asked.

'Yes, of course, but there are complications,' Bruce spoke defensively.

'What dae ye mean by complications?' said someone else.

Bruce and Fiona could see the lack of information was starting to cause anger and animosity towards them. Understandably the parents wanted answers, but they were not yet in a position to give a full and accurate account of what had happened here within the school, where children should be safe.

'You see, our investigations are still ongoing. We've established the identities of some, but a number are proving difficult.' Bruce was nervous.

'For goodness sake,' came an angry response from the crowd, 'we send our kids to school. We entrust them into your care, and now you stand there and have the bare faced cheek to tell us you don't know who's at school or not? Do you expect us to believe that?'

'Aye, she's richt. Do youse tak us for fools or

uneducated cretins?'

The Chief Constable spoke quietly. 'Listen, please. Superintendent Dimble informed you earlier of the difficulties we're experiencing. We don't want to go into details, but as he told you, some kids had swapped uniforms, and blazers, and others we couldn't identify immediately.'

A barrage of questions came from the now near hysterical parents clamouring for answers.

'Do you mean they were so disfigured you didn't even know who they were?'

'Why don't you know who the casualties are? You have a school register don't you? What would've happened if there'd been a fire - you wouldn't be able to tell the fire brigade who was still in the building?'

'I start tae smell a rat,' said another.

'Aye, nae jist a rat, there's something fishy going on.'

'We have to know about our children – now.'

Fiona Mctaggart wished she had chosen her words more carefully. Her initial words were to return to haunt her. She had inadvertently sown the seeds for a range of conspiracy theories. One would centre on whether the police were covering up their incompetence by issuing a gun licence to an individual, they well knew from past experience was unsuitable to be granted one. She tried to reclaim the initiative.

'What we meant was that because they were all playing and had on face paint it was difficult to identify them.'

That was not true, but she felt it was not the right time or place to tell these distraught people the full details of what had happened in the school's Assembly Hall. This had to be done on a one-to-one basis, not in front of everyone else. To make matters worse, the class teacher, the only one who could formally identify all the children, had herself been one of the casualties.

In a valiant attempt, like a hen defending her brood of defenceless chicks, the teacher had confronted someone she deemed to be a maniac. Before the Chief Constable spoke again, she pictured a scene of unimaginable bravery as a lone woman whose only weapon was words, probably tried to reason with a madman. It has been said 'the pen is mightier than a sword' and perhaps speech is mightier than the pen. But no words could have diverted that lunatic from his set course of action.

There was no contest; bullets against words; there could be only one winner. Winston Churchill, the British Prime Minister during WW2 had waxed lyrical about the bravery of the fighter pilots during the Battle of Britain, dubbed 'Britain's Finest Hour.' Those men, it is argued, probably turned the tide of the war.

Churchill's epithet 'Never in the field of human conflict was so much owed by so many to so few' is well known. The actions of those few, it is suggested, saved many and human history is dotted with selfless and courageous acts like theirs. Total strangers at times put their own lives at risk, or surrender them, in order to save others. And much of their bravery goes unreported.

The valiant actions of the P1 teacher that day would not result in a memorial in perpetuity, or cause politicians or poets to celebrate her courage; no blue plaque would adorn the wall of the house where she'd been born; books would not be written specifically about her; certainly no special day would be set aside to commemorate her bravery and no Hollywood film mogul would be buying the film rights about her or well known actresses queuing to portray her.

How many would remember the bravery of twenty-six

year old Shona Henderson in the future? Her slight build and small stature would belie her strength of character. When she stood in for an absent Primary Seven teacher, it was sometimes quite difficult to distinguish between pupil and teacher, as some of the pupils were the same height as she was.

She was dazzlingly pretty with long curly blond hair, which some of her girls, said was just like Rapunzel from the fairy story she'd read to them. A perfect bone structure with high cheekbones, clear milky skin and piercing green eyes made people turn round to look again as she passed. Plump rosy lips opened to reveal perfect white teeth, when she smiled or laughed. Framing her eyes were long curling lashes which her pupils jokingly said reminded them of the giraffes they had seen at the Safari park she taken them to on a school outing.

Delicate hands which somehow didn't seem suited to the bass guitar she spent long hours playing, and shapely legs, completed a vision of beauty. Had nature been more generous in giving her another few inches, she would not have been out of place on a catwalk.

Nevertheless, with a beauty to rival any film star, and which could have made her vain and conceited, her greatest asset was her compassion. She sacrificed a possible acting career to pursue the teaching profession because 'she loved children'. This love went beyond the call of duty, causing her to devote her own special time in helping those whom she felt could do with a little extra encouragement. Her warm personality and her caring nature endeared her to so many, adults and children alike.

The media would make much of her stunning looks, but would say little about the beauty of her character. In time her memory would fade, but to the parents of the children who were in her care, once the full facts of her bravery were revealed, she would be their heroine and they would never forget her.

Like so many who knew her, they wondered what made her become super-human that day. Was it just a protective reaction, or perhaps a rush of adrenalin causing all reason to fly out of the window; or maybe it was love, an unselfish love for those children in her charge, which motivated her to lay down her own life while trying to save theirs. Such love is found on planet Earth in all races, genders and social classes, it's an intrinsic part of the human psyche. She took the answers for her actions to the grave, but for a brief moment, her bravery caused a diversion.

The intruder, in directing his attention and weapons towards her, expended precious energies that enabled many more children to be saved. Some ran into the Victorian-built cupboard, and with speed and dexterity, even while in excruciating pain with her life and strength ebbing, Shona Henderson shut them in and with a final super-human effort, threw the key out of the opened window. The last image the gunman saw of her was as she smiled mockingly at him as if she was saying she'd cheated him from achieving all he had set out to do by saving some of the children from his sadistic and cruel intentions.

One of the children Shona saved was Donald Anderson, a Primary Five pupil. He was the school tennis champion and had been sent with a note by the PE teacher to inform her class of the next tennis practice session. Shona had often watched him play and could see great potential in his raw talent. He'd already won many junior championships. Donald was handing the note to Shona when the shooting began. He was one of the few Shona's last desperate action saved.

In the following years, very few would remember the name of a teacher called Shona Henderson, who went beyond the call of duty to help little children in her care. Her heroic actions that terrible day would live in the hearts of not only the grateful parents, but also in the lives of the survivors she died for. The words of the Native American Indians could have no greater meaning than in her case. 'They are not dead who live in the hearts they leave behind.'

The children she gave her life for would grow into adolescence and then become adults. They would then go on to have children of their own, so her actions would have saved the lives of thousands through the ensuing generations. They would owe their very existence to the bravery of a small-town school teacher whose bravery equalled that of the fighter pilots, whose daring saved a nation.

And how would she have advised the survivors of that brutal attack? To remember her and the children who lay dead and dying – or to remember her for her kindness and to pass it on, echoing the words of the poet Henry Burton.

The best way for the surviving children to tell all and sundry they truly appreciated the sacrifice of their beloved teacher would be by the way they lived their lives.

For any of them to become the sort of individual that mowed down their chums and their teacher in cold blood would sully her memory and her sacrifice and she would have died in vain. Nor would she have wanted their lives to be consumed with hatred to rob them of peace of mind. If they plagued themselves with feelings of revenge, it would serve no useful purpose but only perpetuate their own suffering.

To those who knew Shona, her final act of bravery

was completely in character. The gunman had proved he was too cowardly to face the consequences of his crime and the judicial system. By taking his own life, he had denied the families justice.

In the Assembly Hall, the Chief Constable's words appeared to have calmed the parents for the moment.

'We're going to call you individually to tell you what the current situation is in regard to the casualties.' The Chief Constable tried to sound less official in her attempt to connect with the parents, but over thirty years of bureaucracy and police jargon could not be forgotten overnight, and she sounded a little stiff and formal.

'The headmaster … err … I mean, Bruce and I have divided you all between us. You'll all be told which hospital your children have been taken to. Please don't ask us what condition they are in as we're not medically qualified to make such assessments. You'll receive full notification of their condition on arrival at hospital. Police officers will provide an escort for you after we've spoken to you. Tickets will also be provided by me to be presented to the car park attendants, who will help you to park close to the hospital. Counsellors will also be made available to help you and for those not wishing to return home, provisions have been made at the local hotel for accommodation. Please don't worry about the cost. The police will bear the brunt of this from its contingency funds. Thank you for your attention.'

One family at a time, the parents were taken aside and told where their children had been taken, then provided with an escort to the appropriate hospital.

For some, the nightmare would end when they found their children alive and only slightly injured. For others it would be a waiting game; tragically for the rest, their ordeal would just be beginning.

Chief Constable Fiona Mctaggart and the headmaster were fully aware of the casualty figures. It was a white lie that this information was unknown. But they believed letting skilled professional counsellors talk to the parents in their distraught frame of mind would not only be the correct, but the merciful thing to do.

The Scottish Government had an up-to-date register of skilled bereavement counsellors on their database. These professionals were immediately contacted and asked to come and help. They were all used to dealing with high profile and harrowing cases, a number of which had been highlighted in the media. None of them had dealt with the numbers involved on this occasion, and to be confronted with the fallout from a crime perpetrated on so many children would be a challenge even to these veterans.

All the counsellors were dispatched to the various hospitals and each assigned to a family. The sheer numbers of victims proved to be a logistical nightmare. Counsellors had not only to be provided for those directly involved – the families of the casualties - but also for those indirectly caught up the in the disaster who could experience psychological reactions later on in their lives.

After a lengthy and agonising wait, the headmaster had finally spoken to Danielle and Sharon. They went back to Sharon's car, and with their police escort, headed for Bonnyholly Hospital, not knowing which category they would find themselves in or what had happened to David.

Sharon prepared herself for the worst. Her mind in turmoil, she knew a positive attitude was crucial. Danielle was quiet and brooded silently as they made their way towards the hospital. She hardly dared let herself think of what might await her there.

'Mum, I think I'll have to phone Graham now to let him know what's happening.'

'Yes, you should, he's bound to have heard something by now.'

'I'll tell him to meet us at the hospital.'

Danielle had debated in her mind whether to call Graham or not and wondered why he had not called her. Now she knew. Retrieving her mobile phone from her bag, she realized she had turned it off. 'Imagine doing that today of all days, why did I do that?' she asked herself. When she turned it on, the phone displayed six missed calls, and some text messages. Accessing them, she found they were all from Graham, who had heard the news at work. She called him.

'Are you alright, Danielle? I've been trying to get hold of you. The whole office is stunned about what's happened. It's on all the TV channels and on the web. I was just about to leave here. Is David – is our son …? Danielle cut him off.

'I'm all right. Mum's with me.'

'Oh.'

'And what'd you mean by that?' Danielle was tense and her voice brittle.

'What I meant is it's good to hear that. I'm sure she'll be a tower of strength at this moment.'

'You're such a bad liar, Graham.'

Danielle knew Graham wasn't pleased she hadn't told him immediately about the involvement of their son in this terrible incident. He felt his mother-in-law at times had too close a relationship with her daughter. He was even reluctant to tell her things, because invariably it would be relayed to Sharon. This had been a bone of contention all their married life. Nevertheless, although he was slightly aggrieved about not been kept in the loop, he knew that at this precise moment Sharon was the best person to provide the emotional and psychological support his wife clearly needed. Sharon knew she was the subject of the conversation.

'And what's my son-in-law saying about me? I can hear you, Graham Darling,' she said loudly.

'Oh, Mum, he's only saying he's glad you are with me.'

'Oh sorry,' she said apologetically.

'Anyway,' continued Danielle to her husband, 'we're on our way to Bonnyholly Hospital. Can you meet us there?'

'Sure. I'm on my way. How's David, is he alright?'

Danielle did not answer his question directly but merely repeated, 'meet us at the hospital, Graham, I'm losing the signal. I can hardly hear you ... bye ... are you still there?'

That was not exactly true. She could hear him clearly, but didn't feel she could carry on a conversation about the condition of their son over a mobile phone. She switched it off and put it back in her bag.

'You've done the right thing turning that contraption off, dear. We wouldn't want to worry him unnecessarily, would we – and we have so few details yet anyway.'

'Yes, you're right, Mum,' said Danielle.

The journey took them through the town centre which was unusually quiet. It seemed everyone was sitting glued to the television for the latest bulletin. With their police escort and blue flashing lights, they attracted immediate attention. People they passed all stood and stared in silence, some pointing fingers, others simply waving as if in silent recognition of their ordeal. Danielle acknowledged their support with a half-hearted wave. An elderly man in his nineties, bent over with age and shuffling along, on hearing the police siren, had stopped and turned round. Recognising the meaning behind the police escort, he attempted to stand straight and raise his hand in a gesture of sympathy.

'I bet he was in the blitz and knows what we're going through,' said Sharon and in the same breath added, 'you know, I always wanted to know how the Queen felt when she was being ferried around places with all those people greeting her – now I know.'

Danielle remained silent, engrossed in her own thoughts of what awaited them, but fully aware her mum was making small talk just to keep her mind occupied.

Suddenly, something caught Danielle's attention. A mother was walking with her young son, but she was holding firmly on to his hand as if to prevent him darting off. The boy was the same size and age as David. She wondered if she would be afforded that kind of luxury ever again. Silently she vowed, 'If I ever I get him back safe, I swear I'll never let him out of my sight again.'

Her mother, having seen the young child with his mother, and, knowing her daughter, knew intuitively what she was thinking. Taking one hand off the steering wheel she patted her daughter's knee. Startled, Danielle shouted at her.

'Mother, for goodness sake will you keep your hands on the steering wheel. What you just did is every bit as bad as using a mobile phone while you're driving. Do you want us to end up like ....' her voice trailed off and she burst into tears.

'Mum, I'm so scared. What are we going to find at the hospital - what are we going to find?' She was absolutely distraught. For once in her life Sharon was speechless. She had no answers and trying to find words to describe what might be waiting for them was futile. She trotted out her usual repartee.

'Listen, dear, I coped when I threw out that no-good

cheating Dad ... err … husband of mine. I survived the blitz and I'm sure as heck not going to let a maniac get my daughter down. Don't assume something has happened when it hasn't. OK?'

Sharon could think of nothing else. She turned the radio on and continued the drive. It was ironic the song playing was *Someday we'll Be Together* by Diana Ross and the Supremes.

Chapter 13

Having being assessed, number ten was wheeled to CT by the porter John Campbell. He wasn't usually a fast worker and his slowness had long been a bone of contention among his colleagues as they felt he was not pulling his weight. The porters had a heavy work load and without their tireless efforts, very few patients would be transferred between departments in the busy hospital.

Their duties included running samples between wards and laboratories, taking lunches to the wards, ferrying patients to various departments for x-rays, scans and tests, and countless other things too numerous to mention. It would be no exaggeration to say they were the backbone of the hospital. This was brought sharply into focus during a particularly acrimonious dispute with management when the porters downed tools. The speed at which their grievances were resolved proved how essential they were to the smooth running of the hospital. Any slackness in their work flow affected patient care.

Number ten, a precious small patient, had been entrusted to John, and for the first time in his life he rose to the occasion, caught up in the emergency like all his colleagues. The speed at which he transported her to CT amazed them all, and as he deftly avoided any obstacles on the way, he proved he was capable of working quickly if he wished.

Mel, the CT operator, was standing at the opened door

waiting for him. He wheeled the desperately-ill little girl into the room. Mel and her colleague Robyn Maxwell, with the assistance of two nurses, 'pat slided' number ten onto the CT couch. The weight of the little girl made the use of the pat-slide unnecessary; she could very well have been lifted single-handedly. Nevertheless, even in such dire circumstances it was important that correct protocols were followed. With so many people turning to litigation for the smallest of infringements by health professionals, it was the norm to always follow the right procedures.

This had long been a bone of contention with Mark, the Superintendent Radiographer. He had found that more and more often, doctors were ignoring their own clinical judgements and sending patients for x-ray, irrespective of whether they needed it or not. The prevailing attitude was 'better to be safe than risk being taken to court and being struck off'.

The litigation culture had affected everyone in the health service from management to the cleaners; no one was exempt. Everyone could see how much it was costing the NHS, and knew how much more could be done with the money for patients.

Once number ten was on the couch, Mel shouted:

'Is the anaesthetist here?'

'Why?' asked one of the nurses.

'Because if I'm going to give her contrast, he needs to be here in case there is an adverse reaction,' she said.

'He's waiting for her in theatre,' Robyn told her.

'Well if he can't come, will you make sure someone from A&E is here please? Ta.' Robyn rang Rose McLeish who despatched Anne to CT. Once all the staff had vacated the examination room, Mel went into the CT control room. There, through the radiation-proof glass, she surveyed her fragile little patient. She looked so small and peaceful in that giant doughnut of a machine.

'I wonder if she would have been so quiet if she'd been awake,' Mel wondered.

Most people asked her why radiographers always withdraw either behind a screen or into a separate control room before exposing the patient and she always told them the simple answer was to avoid radiation contamination. The ordinary man in the street would encounter x-rays only spasmodically, seldom on a daily basis like radiographers, she would inform them.

Radiation is not lethal in small doses, but it does have a cumulative effect. Exposure to radiation on a daily basis increases this cumulative effect, and gives those working with it a higher risk of radiation induced cancers. There are strict limits as to the amount they can tolerate and to ensure these are adhered to, all radiation workers are issued with badges to monitor their exposure, which are sent to a central unit for checking every three months. Radiation Protection Advisers are employed by each department to ensure this procedure is always carried out.

Mel began her examination. First she took a 'scout view' to enable her to plan her procedure, and then started to scan the small body. The diagnosis was poor. The bullet had penetrated a vital organ. The usual protocol of chest, abdomen and pelvis were followed, but Rose McLeish had also asked for a contrast enhanced study to enable her to examine the major vessels. The way to do that was to find out from the patient if they'd had an adverse reaction, which posed no problems if the patient was conscious. If not, it was much more difficult and although the study could still be instigated, it was hospital policy to have an anaesthetist on hand, or a doctor who could administer drugs to reverse any adverse effects immediately, and that's why Rose had sent Anne to CT.

'Anne, take a look at this,' said Mel after the scan. It had begun at the head and finished at the lower pelvic region. They both peered at the screen as Mel scrolled down the images. She knew CT was an excellent tool for diagnosing head injuries. It surpassed ordinary x-rays in that it sliced through the body in seconds. The various ventricles of the brain and the brain itself, both white and grey matters, were easily discernable. Any abnormalities could be seen immediately.

CT training, in fact all radiography, hinges on a fundamental principle - that of knowing what is normal. The human body, like most things in the animate and at times inanimate world, hinges on symmetry. Therefore, usually what is found on the right side must also be on the left. A trained eye soon spots what is normal and picks up any slight variation from this. For example, the adult body has 206 bones with children having approximately 231. The radiographer has to be able to name all these bones and know which ones interact or connect. So, instead of studying every possible abnormality, the radiographer and the radiologist study normality, and any deviation from normality that needs investigation.

The CT had confirmed in greater detail what the earlier x-ray had pin-pointed. To Mel, it was very obvious that this small patient had to go to theatre as quickly as possible and she said so.

'I know,' said Anne, 'but the five operating theatres are working to capacity already.'

'For goodness sake, Anne, can't you see what we've got here? If we don't act quickly she's going to die.'

For Mel, the urgency was due in part to the fact she

had once lost an elderly patient in her CT suite. She had agonized over that, even though he was quite old, and she dreaded it happening again, especially to this little girl.

She often wondered if people knew what a CT radiographer actually did. Most victims of road traffic accidents would pass through general x-ray, and might possibly be referred to CT. She told anyone who asked, that for example, angiograms or heart repairs could seldom be carried out without a radiographer operating an x-ray machine and that anyone who has had a heart bypass is more than likely to have needed a radiographer. Without the skills of a radiographer, the surgeon would be working blind, which could have dangerous implications for the patient. Sometimes, if people were interested, she told them about another largely unknown branch of her profession, where radiographers administer radiation therapy.

An alarm coming from the examination room abruptly interrupted her train of thought. Automatically, she looked at her control console; there were no warning lights. Then Robyn shouted:

'It's the wee girl's monitor. It's coming from in there Mel!' pointing to the examination room. Mel and Anne bolted from their seats and in their rush, nearly became wedged in the doorway.

'What's the matter?' Mel asked Anne.

'I think her heart's beginning to fail. The poor little mite has been through a lot.'

'Can't you do anything for her?' For once, it was Mel who appeared worried, not Anne. Mel couldn't fathom it why Anne was being so matter-of-fact about it. Her mind went back to the CT. She had seen the images from the scanner. Even if the wee girl survived, her quality of life would be severely impaired. She wondered if this was why Anne didn't seem to be treating it with urgency, but she wasn't willing to give up so easily. She hit the panic button that summoned the crash team and shouted at Anne.

'For goodness sake, are you just going to stand there?' Mel was almost in tears.

'The crash team will be here shortly,' Anne replied.

'You're an A&E person, surely there's something you can do in the meantime?' said Mel, her voice rising with tension. She was getting frustrated and it seemed as if Anne was thwarting all her suggestions.

'Well I'm not going to stand here and do nothing,' she said.

She remembered very clearly how she'd felt after losing her elderly patient. He'd had a good innings, and nobody could live for ever, but as far as Mel was concerned, if anyone arrested on her watch, she was going to do her utmost to help them, irrespective of their age. Her hospital first aid course had ensured she knew what to do to keep this child's heart functioning until the crash team arrived.

'ABC,' she said out loud. 'ABC,' she repeated, and as if she'd been struck by a pang of guilt, Anne suddenly sprang into action.

'Is her airway clear?'

'Well you're the expert, you tell me,' said Mel cynically, immediately regretting her disparaging tone. Anne ignored her, and with the expertise characteristic of someone who had done this procedure countless times, Anne used all her skill to try to keep number ten's heart beating until the crash team got there.

'Where are they for goodness sake, where are they?' Mel repeated. In desperation, she re-activated the crash team alarm just as the door burst open and the team appeared. Immediately they began to work on the child.

Mel withdrew into her control room and from her vantage point, watched the drama unfolding before her eyes. The room was soundproofed, and communication was only possible by a two-way radio system. She turned on the speaker and listened to the conversation between the members of the crash team. The team leader had attached the usual monitors to her chest and was trying to use the defibrillator on her. Another was pumping air through the Hudson mask into her lungs, followed by chest compressions. Mel could see the anguish in their faces. When the team leader shouted 'Clear!' everything stopped, while the defibrillator was activated, and the tiny body would arch suddenly, as if she was having an out-of-body experience. It was torturous to witness the unconscious contortions of the little girl, but she felt no pain.

The same couldn't be said for Mel, who almost seemed to feel pain on the child's behalf. She was disturbed and, refocusing on her control panel, she began to go through the images once again. The door opened and Anne came in. Mel already knew what was coming, as the microphone had been left on, and, unbeknown to Anne, she and Robyn had witnessed the hopeless fight for life in the next room.

'I'm afraid we've lost the wee girl. We did all we could to save her - you both know that, but her injuries were far too extensive. I know it may sound callous but, had she survived, I don't know what quality of life she would've had. She'd suffered serious brain injuries, so maybe it's a blessing she ....' Anne didn't finish her sentence, and Mel had already tuned out of the conversation.

She felt like calling Anne all the names under the sun,

but refrained because she knew, in her heart of hearts, the doctor had made a valid point. She realized that in any case, being angry with Anne would have been totally pointless; she hadn't fired those bullets, and Mel's anger would be better directed to the perpetrator of that outrageous and devastating crime.

The phone rang and she answered.

'Mel, is that you? Mark here, are you ready for another patient?' Silence greeted his enquiry.

'Mel, are you OK? Can you hear me?' Mark's voice became anxious.

Mel was distracted; she was contemplating what had just happened, and wondering how many similar scenes she would be party to today. The memories of the elderly man dying on her shift, and now the little girl, kept echoing through her mind like a computer caught in a loop before reverting to the blank blue screen.

Her head was buzzing; she knew she was being unrealistic; not everyone would survive this monstrous act, but she did not expect to see a child on her watch die. Now she had to face the possibility of seeing not just one, but perhaps several children's lives ebbing away. If the small patients were referred for a CT scan, she knew this was because the doctors had very serious concerns about them. Bullets have a very destructive effect on any human frame, and these victims were just little children.

Mel thought about Mark's talk to the whole department before the mayhem began. He'd said then that if anyone felt they could not continue, then he would not think less of them if they were honest and said so.

She finally answered.

'Mark, I've just ….' she found the words difficult and her inability to complete her sentence made an uneasy Mark more perturbed.

'Mel, what is it?' Mark asked. 'You can tell me, we've all had to deal with all sorts of circumstances we certainly weren't trained for, and yes, we've dealt with children too, but never on such a scale as this. We're all in uncharted territory here. When I was at Lockerbie, I saw some terrible things. I'd to x-ray bits of limbs to help the forensic scientists and the pathologists and I thought I'd seen the worst humans can do to each other. But this is something else ...'

Mel interrupted him. Her face was drawn, and her eyes dark and bleak.

'Mark,' she said, not giving him a chance to complete his sentence, 'I feel I can't go on, I can't cope with this, and you said earlier ....' It was now Mark's turn to cut across her.

'Mel, before you decide to throw in the towel - and believe me I will respect any decision you make - please consider this ...'

'No! My mind is made up,' she said with determination, interrupting again.

'I know, Mel, but consider this ....' Mark tried again to get her to listen.

'All right, what?'

'Well, you're the most experienced in CT and have trained Robyn and others. At least you have seen someone die on the CT table before, but these young ones are inexperienced. If you leave now, Mel, how are they going to cope? Think how easy it is to let something that frightens you become a phobia. The automatic human reaction is to avoid any situation that makes you frightened, but let me give you an illustration. Have you ever been bitten by a dog?'

'What kind of question is that at this moment in time?' Mel was exasperated.

'Yes, I know it's a stupid question, but humour me, Mel. Have you ever been bitten by a dog?'

'As a matter of fact yes, but what's that got to do with anything,' she said, not seeing where this was going.

'Well, what was your reaction to the dog bite?'

'I suppose I was a bit scared,' she replied in a long-suffering tone of voice as if to say 'well, what did you expect?' But Mark didn't let her sardonic attitude get under his skin. He needed to get through to her, to make her listen and think about what she was doing. He didn't want her to take a rash decision she might later regret.

'That's right. You either avoided dogs, or the next time you were about to pat a dog you were probably a wee bit cautious?'

'I see what you're getting at,' Mel replied, more thoughtfully.

'And the point is …?' he asked her.

'Well I suppose you're trying to say that if I don't confront my fears, I'll avoid any situation that'll remind me of the dog bite, and also, because I've dealt with it once, the next time I come across a similar situation I will be more cautious.'

'That's right. I've been involved in something terrible like this before. As soon as we heard there was a major incident, I knew what to expect. The initial experience was incredibly awful, but it's been a good teacher. If you still feel, after our conversation, that you can't go on, that's fine, Mel, I'll understand. We all have different thresholds of pain, tolerance, or, come to think of it, anything in life. But it's your call; I won't press you one way or the other.'

Mel paused, deep in thought. 'You know, Mark, I feel I've got to say cheerio to that wee girl, just to have closure. If more of these kids are going to come to me, I have to face my worst nightmare.'

'That's the spirit, Mel. I always knew I could count on you,' said Mark encouragingly as he put the phone down.

The conversation had the desired effect. Mel was re-focussed on the task in hand. She felt able to cope again. She sat down at her computer screen and was about to review the images, but catching sight of her own reflection in the screen made her reflect on her decision to become a radiographer.

She was in her early thirties when she had graduated from Glasgow Caledonian University, and after a few years training in general radiography, she had decided to specialize in CT. When she started, CT machines were in their infancy and scans took ten to twenty minutes. Because those older machines took longer to do the examinations, it resulted in higher radiation doses than with the modern ones. These can do similar examinations in seconds rather than minutes, so the dose is reduced and therefore safer.

When CT scanners were first available commercially, they were referred to as CAT, short for Computed Axial Tomography, but this was later shortened to just CT, the axial being omitted. Now they are used so routinely, people take them for granted.

CT can detect skull fractures better than ordinary x-rays; scans are invaluable in the analysis of aneurysms, which are ruptured or leaking vessels in the head. CT has proved its worth in the evaluation of strokes, brain tumours, hydrocephalus, and sinus problems, to name just a few areas where it has become an invaluable diagnostic tool.

Mel knew you could stop anyone in the street and ask if they had heard about CT and it would have to be someone living on another planet who hadn't; but she knew, too, that if you asked them who operated and worked with the CT machines, the answers would be less certain. Some would say doctors or nurses, others might think hospital technicians, but only a small number would think of radiographers. Yet, without their professional skills, expertise and experience, very few people would benefit from this technology.

Mel could tell anyone who asked how specialized this area of training had become. She'd done a post-graduate course to get as far as she had, and would explain to her younger colleagues that specialisation was now essential to get the very best from the diagnostic machines.

Coming back to the present, Mel and Robyn sat down and began reviewing the images she'd taken so far this dreadful day, before sending them to the PACS national system.

This was a national database for all radiographic images. Any medical personnel with the right access code could now view the pictures on the PACS system. Mel was constantly amazed at the progress in reporting diagnostic images, and how widely these were used around the world.

The United States, although there was a shortage of reporting radiologists there, was able to make the best use of the system by sending images overnight to India where they were plentiful, and because the time difference of between nine and twelve hours worked in their favour, a report could be ready and waiting the following day.

Glancing at Robyn, Mel thought about the change in attitude of some of the graduates. They had to be confident of course, but she had found some of the new ones verging on the precocious, thinking they knew better than senior staff, and believing they could give them advice or instructions.

In her previous hospital, it had always annoyed her to see this, but she was so pleased to find this didn't happen in Bonnyholly. All the 'new starts', as the more mature radiographers referred to them, had fitted in well and were learning by the example and encouragement of the more experienced members of staff.

As she and Robyn worked together, Mel felt she had to offer the young woman a few words of warning about the situation they found themselves in.

'I want to be honest with you. You won't see just one death today, but perhaps several. It will be a baptism of fire for you and hard to deal with. None of us has faced a disaster like this before, but we can't just run away when the going gets tough. You saw my reaction.'

Robyn nodded silently and Mel continued, 'I nearly did just that, nearly ran away – and although I've witnessed many traumatic events in my career, nothing prepared me for something like this. If it has this effect on a mature person like me with loads of experience, then I expect it will be even worse for you young ones. I just want to say, Robyn, if you feel you can't go on, tell me now. I won't think any the less of you, and I'll ask Mark to send me a replacement. What do you think – can you cope with all this?

Chapter 14

In A&E, it was complete pandemonium. The shuttle service with the casualties was constant. Ambulances came and went, delivering their damaged and dying small patients; porters wheeled trolleys as quickly as possible between the different departments; in resus, doctors and nurses tested for vital signs and examined wounds that could never have been imagined on five year old children.

In the x-ray department, many dozens of x-rays and CT scans were carried out with the results being urgently relayed to the medical teams.

Mark's staff was now seriously overstretched.

'Trauma series,' Rose McLeish called out again and again.

'I'll go with Margaret,' yelled Fatima.

'Fatima, I need you to do something else please,' said Mark. 'The parents will all be arriving shortly, and I'd really like you to make sure the corridors are kept clear of people so our work flow is not hindered.'

'What's the matter with you, Mark? Every time I want to go to resus you do all you can to keep me away? Why are you treating me like a new start? I've been here ages now.'

'She's right,' Margaret agreed. Mark knew his authority was on the line. Fatima continued.

'What is it you're scared of, Mark? Do you think I'll

behave like a baby and run away screaming,' she said, almost sneering.

Mark was stunned at her tone of voice. Respect for those senior to her was one of Fatima's strongest points, and he'd never heard her speak like that before. He didn't quite know how to handle the situation, and felt slightly aggrieved because he thought he'd had her best interests at heart.

He resisted retaliating in the same vein, forcing himself to see the situation from her point of view. She was professionally trained, after all, and he could see that she wanted to put that training into practice. Maybe she was right; certainly Margaret thought she was, and this was not the right time to go into the reasons why he was trying to shield her from the carnage in resus, and the deeply distressing sights she was likely to witness there. He had to acquiesce.

'OK, Fatima, go with Margaret. I'll get someone else to keep the corridors clear.' He hoped that comment would instil a feeling of guilt in her for not doing this important task when he had asked her to. His attempt to make her change her mind failed. Fatima said nothing more to him, but turned to her colleague.

'I'll bring the cassettes along, Margaret.'

Together they went into resus. All the bays were full and the sight that met them was beyond belief. To Fatima, it seemed there were crowds of people everywhere you looked. Every bay had doctors, nurses and anaesthetists hurrying everywhere. The noise was overwhelming. Every doctor was shouting instructions and how each nurse managed to decipher which instruction was meant for them was remarkable. It was a bit like a gathering of bats, each emitting its own unique signal which was picked up by the others so they could fly in the darkness without any collisions.

The curtains round each resus bay were all closed so Fatima couldn't actually see much of what was going on inside, but she could hear the orders being bellowed by various members of staff in their desperation to try to save the children.

Some voices held a note of urgency, others confirmed a situation had been stabilized; now and then the demands were punctuated by requests for x-rays when additional views were required, or trauma series when a new patient arrived.

'Get me theatre.'

'Has haematology been contacted?'

'X-ray please.'

'Onto it.'

'Crash team please.'

'Adrenalin.'

'Can you put a chest drain in?'

'X-ray please.'

'Mark has been contacted.'

'Are the films on the PACS system yet?'

'Just checking.'

'We appear to be losing this one.'

'Crash team here, who bleeped us?'

'Over here, quick!'

'Has CT been contacted?'

'Trauma series.'

'Can the porter take this one to CT please?'

'Where's the porter?'

'Jist coming.'

'Resus Bay is free.'

'Nixt patient has jist arrived. Need help tae pat slide him onto the trolley.'

'Trauma series please.'

'Need x-rays here as well, can someone get a radiographer please.'

The orders and instructions were endless. What Fatima noticed most was the silence of those who were being treated. There were no cries of anguish from frightened little patients; no childish tears or crying out for their mothers. In all the mayhem, they remained completely and heart-breakingly quiet. Fatima suddenly froze and Margaret noticed immediately that her young colleague seemed unable to move.

'Fatima,' she shouted, in an effort to jolt her back into action, 'Look after resus bay two, I am going to three.' With that, she disappeared and for the first time in her life, Fatima felt vulnerable and completely unprepared. She began to wish she had listened to Mark.

Ever since she'd arrived in the department, Fatima had held Mark in high regard. He had always treated her with courtesy and kindness and, although completely disinterested in any religion himself, respected her right to follow hers as long as it didn't interfere with her work. He made it perfectly clear he was not one of the PC brigade and his philosophy was to treat everyone exactly the same. Fatima's respect for him was based on the fact that he did just that.

'I'm not into positive discrimination,' he told his staff. 'You either qualify or you don't, pure and simple.' He was a great believer in team work and was fond of using the vertebrae by way of illustration in his team building talks.

'I want you all to realize the value of teamwork and the contribution each of you can make, not just in patient care, but helping one another to get the job done. Think of the human vertebrae. Each piece is capable of only a small movement by itself, and yet together the vertebrae engender astonishing movements, like those of a gymnast, for example. So, as each separate piece of bone or cartilage is important, so are all members of a team. Working together we can all contribute to the whole and achieve more.'

Mark had travelled extensively during his chequered youth, and had found good and bad in every nation he'd visited. He'd told Fatima of the hospitality he'd received in some of the poorest countries; how families with very little would rather starve than see a stranger go without. His travels had been an education in all sorts of ways and had enabled him to develop an empathy with most of the people he came across in his day-to-day life. Having visited so many places where health care was expensive and often well beyond the pocket of ordinary people, it really irritated him when people berated the NHS. He would tell them they didn't know how lucky they were to have it, and add that it was the envy of many other countries around the world.

It was Mark's fairness, and the way he treated everyone equally, that was his most endearing quality. He was admired and looked up to by his staff, and patients loved him because he dealt with each one as if he or she really mattered most. His jokes and banter made them laugh and put them at ease, so when they talked about him, they described him as 'that lovely man in x-ray'.

Perhaps they meant his looks when they used this term. Mark was tall, standing six feet, four inches without his shoes. He was lean and lanky. His face, swarthy and rugged, bordered on that of a rugby player, although he was not. He had a large Roman nose and his crisp dark hair always looked a touch greasy. His long arms hung loosely by his sides and ended in the largest hands Fatima had ever seen, while his huge feet, everyone in the staffroom agreed, gave him a 'good grip of Scotland'.

He was a giant of man and would have rivalled Gulliver in his travels in Lilliput, but he didn't swagger as he strolled through the hospital corridors with his powerful dark eyes that hid his past pains. What made Mark really attractive, though, was his character; everyone knew he would go out of his way to offer help to anyone. Often, he would juggle the rotas and give up his own holidays to accommodate the wishes of his staff.

The whole department also knew of Mark's burning desire to have children. How he'd met his wife was a source of mystery, leading to all kinds of theories and assumptions. Some said he'd met her on the internet; others that she was a pen-pal bride.

He'd confided in Margaret, telling her of his inability to have children and how he and his wife Sonia had finally decided to adopt a child and were right now going through the final checks and security clearances. According to Margaret, he was ecstatic.

Fatima had aroused his paternal interest. He'd seen her potential from the very beginning, and everyone in the department knew he saw her almost as a daughter.

Going through her own moment of crisis in resus, she thought back to Mark's encouraging words when he told her he was not into positive discrimination; in his department, achievements were on merit alone, and that applied to everyone. She knew her inclusion in the team was not because the hospital had a quota to fill.

She was still frozen to the spot, unable to do as Margaret had asked her. She heard her phoning Mark before going into bay three.

'Can you send another assistant to help Fatima?'

'For goodness sake,' bellowed Mark, 'have you left her on her own?'

'Listen, Mark,' Margaret replied defensively, 'it's chaos in here. You're sitting in your ivory tower issuing the orders while we're doing all the donkey work. Get down here and see for yourself; the whole place is chaos and everyone's got to pull their weight if we're going to get anything done. I've had to put her on the mobile-ray machine as I'm using the overhead tube, but I think she's struggling.'

At that moment, Mick, one of the A&E nurses, popped his head round the curtain.

'Trauma series please, Margaret.'

'Can you send another radiographer down, Mark,' she said into the phone. 'Mick's just shouted for another trauma series in bay one.'

Margaret was irritated by Mark's attempts to shield Fatima. 'Why doesn't he cut the apron strings?' she muttered to herself

'OK. I'll send Nick to help Fatima, and Lynne and Lindsey with the last mobile to the other bay.'

At last, Fatima seemed to come out of the trance-like state that had kept her rooted to the floor. In resus bay two, she looked down at the little boy on the trolley. He appeared so still that only a slight movement on his torso gave any inkling he was still alive. He looked just like her little brother Ravi, only lighter-skinned.

Her mother had told them of the time they'd had to leave Uganda; the time when the president had decided that all the Asians in his country should be 'repatriated', mostly to Britain. Her family had arrived in Scotland with nothing but the clothes they stood up in. Through sheer hard work and determination, her father, a doctor, had regained a position in a local hospital. He'd had to cope with some hostility at first, and a few complaints that foreigners were coming in and taking local people's jobs, but most people in the community had been welcoming and kind.

Fatima's parents had always encouraged her to take a positive view of life and not let the negative views of others influence her outlook. She found it quite funny that they also used to say the same things as Mark did about there being good and bad people wherever you went, and how it was.

The behaviour of the Ugandan president and the treatment of his people had been widely reported in the press and broadcast media around the world, but Fatima's parents had experienced the hospitality of many African people when they were stripped of all their assets. And now, here in Scotland, she was standing looking at the proof of what they and Mark had said. There certainly were good and bad people everywhere.

She set up her portable machine, but placing the cassettes turned into a nightmare. Dealing with Road Traffic Accidents had become a matter of routine, but she had never dealt with a child in this condition and in these circumstances before. Her emotions threatened to overwhelm her and her hands began to shake as she tried to place the cassette for a lateral C spine. It dropped noisily to the floor. Anne, who was looking after the patient, shot her a sideways look.

'Any chance of going a wee bit faster, Fatima?' she asked, aware of the girl's hesitation.

With Anne watching her, and the tenuous hold on life of her small patient, Fatima was even more nervous. She bent down, retrieved the cassette and tried once more to place it, only to drop it again. In desperation, she began to swear in Arabic and although Anne didn't understand what she was saying, she got the gist, and this time she looked angry and impatient.

'For goodness sake, if this is too much for you, why don't you just go back to Mark and tell him to send someone else,' she said sharply.

The whole atmosphere was beginning to be highly charged. The all-important ethos of teamwork was starting to break down, and any lack of co-operation meant patient care would suffer. Fatima's initial reaction to Anne's brusque reprimand was to ask her who she thought she was, talking to her like that. Couldn't Anne see she was nervous? But she checked herself and managed to put the cassette in place. This time she was successful and putting on her lead coat she shouted the usual warning.

'X-ray.' People scurried behind lead screens separating the bays. She exposed the film and shouted again.

'All clear.' Everyone came back, but just as she finished, Margaret bellowed.

'X-rays.' Again there was a scuttle for protection.

'X-rays.' This time it was Nick. In the space of a few seconds there were three exposures but this was only the beginning. Each victim had to have chest and pelvis x-rays as well. The A&E staff, who were normally patient, began to be exasperated with the radiographers. Some were heard muttering under their breath.

It seemed as if an insidious cloud of gloom and negativity was slowly leaking into the resus room, and it got worse with the arrival of each little patient who was unconsciously contributing to the deepening atmosphere.

The frustrations, the age of the casualties and the heat of bodies in A&E, aprons and lead coats were all beginning to take their toll. Inevitably, it was only a matter of time before someone exploded. The murmurings of exasperated and worried staff were becoming more vociferous. One spoke out and voiced the dissatisfaction of most of the others.

'If they got things right in the first place instead of dropping cassettes and goodness knows what else they can't hold onto, we wouldn't need to stop doing things every few minutes.'

The discontent was infectious. Each complainant tried to outdo the others.

'What's all that racket?'

'We can't do our work with all this commotion.'

'And they call themselves professionals.'

'No wonder no-one knows what they do in a hospital.'

'Very little, it appears, if this is what they do when under pressure.'

'I say it shows you can't send a boy to do a man's job.'

The whole episode of sarcastic biting exchanges between the various staff culminated in vitriol.

'You mean a girl to do a woman's job.'

Fatima knew this referred to her but she ignored the comments. Rose McLeish, the A&E Consultant, also knew who the comments referred to, and could not let it go without remark. From her perspective, the pressure of the staff working under stressful conditions was finding an outlet in blaming someone – anyone – for the frustrations and pent-up emotions. She knew quick thinking was needed to tackle the situation before it got any worse.

'For goodness sake, everybody,' she shouted above the din. Her authoritative tone brought an immediate hush. 'Can we please, please stop all this nonsensical and ridiculous behaviour NOW. You'd think you were all in a playground complaining about one of these kids stealing your sweets. How can we help them if we're all bickering amongst ourselves?'

Her outburst had the desired result, and the silence that

had suddenly descended, was broken by Rose again, before she resumed her painstaking work on another child.

'Hannibal' she quoted, 'said the behaviour of each one will determine the outcome of each other. It might be as well to remember that. Now I suggest we all get back to work. There's still so much to be done.'

With her partner acting as a runner for the exposed cassettes, Fatima finished her examinations and reported back to Mark in the x-ray department. As soon as she entered the room, Mark knew all was not well. He resisted saying 'I told you so', merely asking:

'How did you get on?'

'Fine. Can't wait to go back.' Margaret, who'd heard all the commotion, knew this was far from the case and glanced at her in indignation. Fatima knew what the silent stare meant but she was determined to prove them wrong if they thought she couldn't hack it. She wasn't going to let them see her crumble, and had every intention of keeping going.

'Mark,' she said with a confidence she didn't feel, 'can I go the next time Mrs McLeish calls for x-ray?'

Mark hesitated.

'Actually it's Drummond's ….' He didn't get time to finish his sentence.

'He's been five times already and I've only been once. Why are you trying to stop me going down there?' Fatima thought she had now worked out why Mark was trying to keep her away. She was determined not be treated differently from the others, but she was ignorant of his real reasons for protecting her.

She couldn't see the effect the sights in the resus room were having on her. As insidious as any x-ray, her constant exposure to the horrific scenes she was witnessing was proving harmful, and her false enthusiasm for the task was merely hiding the fact. Mark saw through this easily. While in Lockerbie, he'd seen the same sort of adverse effect on a colleague. He had to protect Fatima, and in any case, her behaviour was disturbing the other members of staff in both his department and in A&E. It wasn't good for anybody.

'You know, I dropped the cassette when I saw that poor wee boy ... I was just about to tell Anne to go and get …' she stopped, seeing an expression on Mark's face she'd never seen before.

'You were about to tell her what?' he asked.

She didn't answer, but changed the subject.

'How's my positioning, Mark? I bet you can't find fault with me now, you perfectionist.'

'I think you need a tea-break,' he told her.

'Tea break, my ....'

'Fatima!' Mark was growing annoyed.

'Oh here we go again. Fatima can't go here, Fatima can't go there, Poor wee Asian Fatima, or is it poor wee Scottish Asian Fatima?'

This was the last straw. Everyone knew Mark was completely impartial and he made no differentiation between race, gender, colour or creed. Was Fatima just being annoying or was she playing the race card? The whole department was stunned into silence. They had never experienced such a scene, and all wondered how Mark would deal with this outburst. Would he excuse it as the rantings of an overworked young girl, or would he take firm action? The department waited, almost not daring to breathe. The silence was only broken by the telephone ringing, yet again, in the background.

Chapter 15

The police escort terminated one hundred yards from the hospital. The officers waved Sharon and Danielle on, made a U turn and returned to the school to repeat their journey with another set of desperate parents. They finally arrived at Bonnyholly Hospital at 7.00pm and pulled in into the car park. Spaces had been especially reserved for the parents of the young victims. To make sure this happened, only those with a slip of paper signed by Chief Constable Fiona Mctaggart could park in the area next to the hospital entrance. The car park attendants had been briefed about the need to be dignified and respectful to all these people.

Sharon approached the attendant slowly, stopped, and lowered the window. Carefully positioned on the dashboard was the official parking ticket which she handed to him. He nodded, passing it back, and voiced his support.

'A howp things turn oot fine. Youse hae my deepest sympathy. Jings, I hae bairns an aw. I ken how youse are baith feeling.' He didn't mention that he had a child in Primary Seven who had arrived safely home; his sympathy was heartfelt and genuine.

'What a nice young man,' said Sharon finally breaking the silence. Apart from her one outburst, Danielle had not spoken since they'd left the school. Sharon followed the attendant's instructions and tried to park the car only narrowly missing another.

'Mother, be careful,' said Danielle automatically.

'It's those blasted architects; look at the space they give you. I'd need a Robin Reliant to get into that space. I'm glad I'm not driving one of those monstrosities,' she added, pointing to a large car in the distance.

'Mum, if they can afford it then it's up to them. Maybe you're just jealous.'

'All right, but what happens when they knock down some poor wee ....'

She stopped, horrified by what she had been about to say. Here they were about to find out the outcome of all this horror on the one thing they always agreed about, their beloved boy, and they were arguing about the size of parking spaces.

Silently, as if in a huff with each other, they walked towards the entrance of the hospital.

Danielle suddenly realized the numbness she had been feeling had developed into a pounding headache. She compared this visit to the hospital with earlier ones, especially when her son was born. She remembered every detail as if it was yesterday and instinctively she looked over to the mountains half expecting a miraculous rainbow to appear.

Looking back to her childhood, she recalled her mother telling her the Bible story of Noah and the appearance of the rainbow. Sharon had explained that a rainbow always appeared after a storm, and it was a symbol of peace. How much she needed a peaceful outcome today. The encircling mountains offered her a small measure of comfort as they seemed to wrap themselves protectively around the hospital and its environment. She wished they would wrap themselves around her too, and protect her from what was to come. She wanted to run, to get inside the hospital and find her son, but her feet refused to obey her. It was as if her brain knew what was in store and was putting off the evil moment.

The arguments between Sharon and Danielle never lasted long. Although they agreed on very little, Sharon was still the understanding mum, and was glad she was there to help and support her daughter.

'Come on, dear, let's go and find out what's happened to our lovely boy.'

As they went inside, they found Graham waiting for them. He had left work immediately after receiving the call from Danielle. As soon as she saw him her heart melted. He was visibly shaken and his face was white. His usual wonderful smile, which she found so endearing, had gone. His lips were tightly closed and his brow was furrowed with anguish. Looking at him, Danielle was reminded of the day they'd bought David's school blazer and how he'd frowned in exactly the same way when he'd tried one on that was several sizes too big. The resemblance was uncanny. His red hair and sparkling deep blue eyes, which she'd always compared to her Irish grandmother's, were actually a copy of his father's. They even shared the appealing freckles which sprinkled their noses and cheeks.

Where David was small and slight – Sharon called him 'a wee slip of a lad' – Graham was always described as 'a fine figure of a man.' To de-stress from his office-bound job, he had joined the local gym and worked out religiously. Danielle had joked that he worshipped at the temple of gymnasium, and certainly it had produced startling results. When they'd married ten years ago, although tall, at six feet, three inches, he'd been a bit skinny, and definitely not fit. Now his meticulous routine had produced bulging biceps, a six pack and muscular calves that wouldn't have looked out of place among the mythological Greek gods. Danielle used to laugh at the 'height of nonsense' as she used to affectionately call him. Now she called him *Adonis*.

He was self-conscious about his height and before his fitness regime, had walked with a slight stoop. He'd been in danger of developing Kyphosis or curvature of the spine, but as his muscles became tuned and he started to appreciate it, his back straightened and the stoop began to disappear. To further train his back, he had invested in a spine brace and now he was a man proud of his height and physique.

As he came forward to meet them just inside the hospital entrance, for a moment it occurred to Danielle that he looked slightly stooped again, but she thought it was understandable if he appeared bowed under the weight of the present situation. The bitter anxiety of not knowing what condition their son was in had obviously affected him deeply.

'Oh, Graham, I'm so glad you're here,' she said, tears filling her eyes.

'Have you seen him?'

'Not yet,' said Danielle.

'Let's go and see what's happening,' he said, and then, as if suddenly realising that their son wasn't alone in this horror, asked about David's friends. 'Do you know exactly what's happened at the school? Are there other children involved? How about wee Jamie, and bonnie Susan, and Rhonda - are they OK?'

His questions were coming out rapidly, and although Danielle was petrified about what they might discover, Graham's concerns for others emphasized why she loved this man. Here was someone who might not be taking his only son home again; he didn't know if David was paralysed, or in a coma, or worse, and yet he was also concerned about the wellbeing of the other children. Graham had enjoyed getting to know the kids in their son's class who had come round to play, and had had fun joining in their games. He cared about them as if they were his own flesh and blood.

His very real concern for the fate of the others was even more poignant because he had only one precious son, and there was practically no chance of another child for him and Danielle. None of the other children he knew were only children, and if any of them had died, although they themselves were completely irreplaceable, their parents would have some small measure of comfort in their siblings.

Danielle was holding Graham's hand very tightly, and they both seemed to hesitate, as if unsure what to do next.

Sharon took the lead.

'Can I suggest we check with reception and find out where our wee lad is?'

'That's an excellent idea, mother-in-law.' Graham always called her that when he was trying to be polite and nice to her. Danielle said it was patronising but Sharon didn't see it that way. They approached the reception desk and Graham opened his mouth to speak.

'Can you please tell me where we can find ....' said Sharon, taking over as usual.

The receptionist interrupted.

'Are you here about the incident at the primary school?'

'Yes,' said Sharon.

'Can you wait a minute please?'

'Yes, but I hope it won't take long,' said David's granny.

The receptionist waved her hand and an official

looking man approached them. He was dressed in an immaculate black pin stripe Saville Row suit with a crisp white cotton shirt, red silk tie and gold tiepin. The shirt sleeves, with double cuffs fastened with gold cufflinks protruded from the jacket. Graham knew straight away this was no ordinary hospital official. This was serious.

'Are you here about a relative, sir?'

Speaking what could be described as upper-class English, he addressed his question to Graham but looked at Danielle and Sharon at the same time. His direct gaze seemed as if it was trying to penetrate their very souls for any hint of the torment inside.

'Yes, we are,' replied Graham.

'Do you have any means of identification? For data protection reasons we have to ensure we are not speaking to the press.'

'What if we were the press?' said Danielle.

'Firstly, your demeanour is a giveaway. Secondly, if you are, then I can refer you to our press liaison officer.' With a limp flick of his wrist he pointed to a man with a clipboard.

'Can I see any form of identification please?' he repeated.

Danielle reached into her purse, opened it and showed him the picture of their son in his school uniform.

'That's one handsome young man. You must be very proud of him.'

'He is, and we are,' said Danielle, while Sharon and Graham both nodded. As they spoke, the official continued to scrutinize them, and finally satisfied these were genuine relatives, he told them to follow him, and then he paused.

'Oh, I'm so sorry,' he said, 'how rude of me not to introduce myself. I'm John Pottinger, Family Liaison

Officer.' He didn't even attempt to shake their hands. 'And you are?' Mr Pottinger looked in a detached way at the three of them standing nervously in front of him, almost willing him to give them good news.

'Sorry.' said Danielle, 'we should have said. We're Graham and Danielle Darling, and this is my mother, Sharon Moffatt.'

The three of them followed the rather stiff official down the corridor. As they left, they could hear someone greeting another set of parents, and wondered what news awaited them.

The long corridor was familiar. Danielle looked at the yellow x-ray line on the floor and for a moment her mind went back to the time she and Graham had followed that line to the x-ray department, then to ultrasound department where Linda the sonographer confirmed the news they had hardly dared to hope for, that indeed a baby was growing inside her womb. 'Six years ago we were oh so happy,' she said to herself and smiled at the memory. She squeezed Graham's hand, and he squeezed hers back, sharing the memories and offering support to each other.

She also recalled the same journey when their son developed intussusception. Again it was to the x-ray department they went, and this time it was Linda Soggins, the Barium specialist, whose skills intervened and corrected the problem.

She noticed there were no visitors in the hospital corridors this time; they only passed members of staff and everyone seemed to be in a sombre mood. Even the cleaners were going about their jobs quietly and without their usual chit-chat. Eventually they reached a door labelled 'PRIVATE DO NOT DISTURB' and Danielle became more frightened.

'Why aren't we going to A&E or a ward?' she asked, 'Why here?'

'I'll answer any questions you have inside this room,' answered the rather starchy official. He opened the door, held it ajar for them and waited for them to go in. Danielle was insistent. Her voice was tense and rising with fear.

'Why aren't we going to A&E? Is something wrong? There is, isn't there? Please tell us what have you done with my son .... Please don't tell me he's ....' she started to cry and became hysterical.

'Now, Danielle, love, don't let's jump to conclusions. Let's hear what this gentleman has to say, eh?' Sharon put her arms around her daughter. Graham still held on to her hand. She calmed down a little and reluctantly entered the room; the door was closed behind them. Inside was a square mahogany table capable of seating six people, and lying on it were several files with numbers on them, a computer screen, a telephone and a notepad. Mr Pottinger pulled out three chairs and placed them in a row side by side. Danielle sat in the middle flanked on either side by her husband and her mother, each holding tightly to one of her hands. He pulled out another chair and faced them.

'May I see the photo of your son again please?' he asked a little less formally. With shaking hands Danielle tried to get it out of her handbag, but could not do it.

'Here,' said Sharon, give it to me,' and she quickly pulled out the small laminated picture and handed it to Mr Pottinger who accepted it without comment. Looking at it, he began to manoeuvre the mouse, comparing it with pictures that appeared on the computer screen. Then he stopped, glanced briefly at the parents, then back to the photo and the screen. Picking up the phone he dialled a number and spoke without any hint of emotion.

'If the hospital wanted to keep parents in suspense,' thought Sharon, 'they've chosen the right person. This man has no emotions whatever. You just cannot read anything from his body language.'

He spoke into the phone.

'Mike; John here, can you join me in the special room please, I have the parents of number one here.'

At the mention of 'number one', a piercing pain went through all three. How dare these people refer to their darling as number one; whatever had happened, at least they should give him his dignity and call him by his name.

The same thought went through all their minds. Danielle and Sharon had both learned at the school why numbers had been used, the headmaster had explained, how important it was to get the children away and treated quickly. Graham didn't know that.

Saying nothing further, but deep in contemplation, the Family Liaison Officer continued to leaf through the rest of the files. Sharon counted at least thirty. He put the remainder aside and kept one in their full view. It was clearly labelled 'Number One'.

'Why are your files titled with numbers?' asked Graham, genuinely perplexed.

Mr Pottinger proceeded to relate in meticulous detail why this had been done, all the time emphasizing this was in no way intended to dehumanize or treat their offspring with disrespect. Graham nodded.

There was a knock on the door

'Come in,' said John Pottinger.

Mike Reid, the social worker-cum-bereavement counsellor came into the room. He pulled out a seat next to Mr Pottinger who opened the file, showed him the picture from Danielle's wallet and then pointed to the screen. Neither spoke, their actions reminding Sharon of mime artists.

Then came the questions, the endless, agonising questions. Mike Reid had been specially chosen for this role because of his kindness and his gentle and caring manner, and the articulate way he could explain difficult situations. His voice, it was said, could send a baby to sleep.

'Mr and Mrs Darling, and …?' He looked at Sharon.

'Sharon Moffatt, Mrs Sharon Moffatt, I'm Mrs Darling's mother,' she added.

'Do you mind if I call you by your first names? It sounds so impersonal when we start calling each other by titles instead of names.'

It would have been hard to refuse him and they all agreed quickly, and told him their first names.

'Danielle, Graham, could you all look at this picture?' He reached into the file labelled number one and retrieved a large colour photo which had been blown up to A4 size.

'Please look at the child circled.'

Graham looked at it first. It was the school photograph, the same one that stood on the shelf at home; the one where David looked so grown up in his school uniform. He passed it to Danielle who looked down at her precious little boy. She gave it to her mother, who looked silently and nodded. Sharon handed it back to Mike.

'Did you recognize anyone in the picture?'

'Yes, of course. The boy circled is our son David,' said Danielle getting agitated. 'Is he all right? Please tell us,' she was beginning to get hysterical again.

Mike Reid gently took control of the situation.

'Are you sure?'

'Of course we're sure, man,' said Graham backing up his wife. 'Look at his hair for goodness sake, there's no one else in the class with hair like that.'

'Are you blind?' Sharon interjected, 'look at the photo, look at Graham; they're like two peas in a pod.'

Without displaying any emotion, both men continued to look at the three agonized people in front of them. Mike Reid cleared his throat.

'There is no easy way of saying this, and of course we have to verify it, but ....'

'Is he alive? Is he injured?' Danielle was pleading now.'

Mike had been a counsellor for a long time, but he found this more difficult than anything he'd ever had to do before. Relaying the death of a child was always the most unpleasant aspect of his work. There was never a right way of giving this kind of news or explaining the circumstances surrounding it. He could never quite decide whether he should come out with it bluntly and say the child is dead, or if he should just try to skirt around the issue, using all kinds of euphemisms to try to soften his message. He believed in being truthful but always with tact. He remembered in his early training his instructor giving him the definition of tact as 'not giving unnecessary offence.' But how could you avoid offending someone who has lost a cherished child, he thought, it was practically impossible. He had to come straight to the point and the longer he delayed the more distraught they were becoming.

'Mr and Mrs Darling - sorry - Graham, Danielle and Sharon, I've searched in my heart for the right words to say. But I can't find any. On the basis of what you've told us, I have to tell you we believe your son is the child we call number one.'

'Where is he, for goodness sake, tell us.' Danielle begged, feeling a chill settling over her, and her eyes filling with tears again.

'Danielle,' he specifically addressed her, aware of the tight bond that existed between a mother and her child. 'Danielle,' he repeated, 'I'm afraid we think your son was the first casualty brought into Bonnyholly Hospital. The ambulance crew did all they could to save him, but his injuries were too extensive. They were unsuccessful. He has been taken to the morgue and we have to ask you to accompany us there so you can formally identify him.'

Watching their stricken faces, Mike thought how much he hated his job at times. He paused and waited for the family's reactions. Graham was silent; his face completely blank; the only other sign that he had taken in the news about his son was the constant drumming of his fingers on the table. Sharon appeared emotionless, putting her hand out to touch her daughter's shoulder. Whimpering like a wounded animal, Danielle buried her head in Graham's neck. After a few moments when all that could be heard was the sound of Danielle's distress, she lifted her head from his shoulder and, with all the strength she could muster, she clenched her fists and began to pound Graham's chest, sobbing uncontrollably. Graham did nothing to stop her, he shared her intense pain and he just sat there, letting her continue to pummel him as hard as she could, until it ran its course. Gradually the pounding stopped and Danielle's sobs abated.

Mike repeated what he'd said before.

'I'm afraid I have to ask you all to follow me to the mortuary for formal identification.'

'Did he suffer? What were his last words?' asked Graham.

'As far as I'm aware, he passed away quickly. His

injuries were too serious for him to survive the journey to the hospital. He was unconscious and I can assure you he did not suffer. I only hope that brings some relief to you.'

'And the other children in his class? Are they all dead too? Are they the ones on your table?' asked Graham as he pointed to the second pile of files.

'I'm not at liberty to divulge that kind of information, Graham. Once all the parents have been informed of the condition of their child, they can talk about it if they wish, but now ….'

'Yes, I know about data protection and all that, I work in an office you know.' Graham's emotion was beginning to show.

'I just hope some of the other children are all right. I'd hate any of their parents to go through what we're going through just now.'

In a last ditch attempt to keep them positive, Mike said:

'Let's wait till we get to the mortuary and establish definitely that number one is your son. Could you tell me, for the record, what was his name?'

'His name was David,' said his father, the lump in his throat threatening to choke him.

'That's a lovely name,' acknowledged Mike.

'Yes, we named him after the ambulance driver who took Danielle to Bonnyholly Hospital when her waters broke,' said Graham.

'Did you say David, the ambulance driver, a paramedic?'

'Yes.'

'Well, if it's him, then he brought young David to the hospital today.'

'You mean to say he was near at his birth and he was there when he died?'

‘Yes, and it appears he also took him to the mortuary’

‘What a strange coincidence,’ said Graham.

With that, they all headed towards the morgue for official confirmation of number one’s identity.

Chapter 16

In A&E, Fatima's behaviour was giving cause for concern. Margaret approached Mark whilst she was in the resus room. She had finally persuaded him to observe the pandemonium for himself.

'Mark, are you seeing what I'm seeing?' she asked.

'What do you mean?' he said, trying to appear diplomatic.

'Are you blind?'

'Blind to what?' he replied innocently.

'You know exactly what I mean.' She wasn't fooled, but Mark was trying hard to avoid the obvious as it stared him in the face. Fatima's behaviour was out of kilter, odd, disturbing. He was rescued from the conversation by the demanding ring, ring of the telephone.

'Excuse me, have to dash,' he rushed to get the phone.

'It's all right,' said Nick, 'I'll get it.'

'No, it's probably theatre, I'll have to organize someone to go,' said Mark.

'But you already have,' said Margaret, adding, 'you arranged that George and Fiona are to go as soon as the theatre co-coordinator phones when the patient's in the anaesthetics room.'

'Oh, you're right, so I did,' then as if he was contradicting himself, he continued on a completely different tack.

'I'll have to organize two to go as we only have two

Image Intensifiers.'

Image Intensifiers are x-ray machines which produce live or real time images of an operation. The images are then fed onto a computer screen. Before this invention, radiographers had had to take static x-rays and process them in a special darkroom next to the operating theatre.

There was very little room for error. There had been cases in the past where frustrated surgeons had hurled things at radiographers who had failed to provide diagnostic images. The Image Intensifier had proved invaluable in all kinds of surgery and diagnostic procedures. Young David had benefited from a similar machine, when radiographer Linda Soggins, together with paediatric consultant Donald Briggs had corrected his intussusceptions.

Suddenly, Fatima appeared in the x-ray department:

'Oh my goodness, it's so gruesome in there. There's so much blood. My cassettes are covered in it, and I'll need to clean them … no, I'll just put them in the reader first then clean them later. Oh drat! I can't do that, can I? Mrs McLeish is waiting for results, but I need to think of infection control. Now, should I put them in first and clean them later. Or do it the other way round? No, now. No, later. What shall I do?' As if caught in a loop she kept repeating incoherently, 'In now or clean first, in now or clean first.'

Then, as if a safety valve was being released, she screamed at everyone in the room.

'Can't somebody help me? You're all standing there like complete idiots gawking at me. What's the matter with you lot? Am I the only one working today? And you, Mark,' she stopped and pointed a finger in his direction, 'you couldn't organize a ....'

She paused as if trying to find something dreadful to

accuse Mark of, then dropped the cassettes on the floor and standing alone in the middle of the department, began to weep. For a second, no one knew what to say or do. The blood stained cassettes remained on the floor waiting to be rescued and their vital information retrieved.

Margaret bent down and picked them up.

'Give me the request card. Whose is it?'

'Number thirty,' Fatima managed to splutter through her tears. She was on the verge of hysteria.

Hearing that number, Mark was jolted into reality. He suddenly realized they had examined thirty little children in horrendous circumstances. Because of her irrational exuberance, Fatima had borne the brunt of these examinations. Each child had had a minimum of four x-rays, which amounted to more than 120 in all. Mark was taken aback. He moved over to the RIS system and looked at the number of examinations at the base of the screen. It stood at a staggering 210. In addition, he was fully aware Fatima had taken some flak from the staff in resus. He chided himself for not looking after her better.

He was, of course, mistaken. He had tried everything in his power to shield her from the resus room, but all his efforts had failed as Fatima interpreted this as him being overly protective and stopping her doing a job she loved. The truth of the matter was that the nature and pressure of the work involved was clouding everyone's judgement, leading to the wrong conclusions. More bitter tears cascaded down Fatima's brown cheeks.

She looked so vulnerable standing by herself in the middle of the department. Her confidence, along with her warm smile, had gone. The crying had made her mascara run, giving the impression she was wearing war paint ready to do battle. Perhaps that wasn't too far from the truth. Fatima was now engaged in a battle of her own; a fight to save her sanity. Dressed in theatre blues which showed off her slim figure, her depressed demeanour was a far cry from her elegant arrival at the start of the shift. Her tunic was stained with blood, and smudged with make-up.

She'd failed to follow the rigid hospital protocol of inserting cassettes into disposable plastic covers whenever there was likelihood of contact with contaminating bodily fluids. Her arrival back in the department clutching blood-stained cassettes under her arms indicated her deteriorating mental state.

Mark didn't know what to do. His normal ability to deal with any situation completely deserted him. He just stared at Fatima, dumbfounded. Margaret took matters into her own hands. Gently she passed the request card she'd taken from Fatima and handed it to Nick. Without a word he began to enter the details into the computer system.

'I think someone needs a break, Mark,' Margaret said quietly. Mark, still speechless, just nodded.

Taking the weeping Fatima by the hand, Margaret spoke softly.

'Fatima, you've done a lot today. None of us has had a tea break. Why don't you and I take five, eh?'

Sniffing and shaking uncontrollably, Fatima nodded without looking up. It was a sad and pitiful sight; the usually vibrant young woman, the epitome of tall, dark and beautiful, now reduced to this babbling unkempt creature. As Margaret led her out of the department, many wondered if she would ever return.

For Mark, it was a bitter pill. It was a case of déjà vu as he'd envisioned just such a situation and had tried hard to prevent it happening. All he could do now for Fatima

no backup, except for a phone link, she had to be technician, as well as radiographer.

His reverie was interrupted by a commotion in the corridor. Outside, there appeared to be a distraught parent venting her anger on Rose McLeish because the A&E Consultant had refused to let her go into resus.

'Why can't I go in? Why won't you let me see my son?' the distressed mother was demanding. Rose was trying to inform her there were procedures in place to assist parents. She should have checked into reception, and been assigned a counsellor to accompany her in the hospital, but somehow she had managed to bypass the system and was now at the doors of resus.

How Fatima's gentle services were needed now, Mark thought. If only she had listened to him at the start of all this. She had a way of pacifying distraught people and she would have been the ideal person to deal with this. It was the main reason he had not sent her home. He sighed; the young were so impetuous, so impatient, always thinking they knew best and what was good for them. Observing the scene in the corridor, he knew his intentions had been honourable and the role he'd had in mind for Fatima would have shielded her from what she had actually experienced. Rose McLeish was having very little success with the parent.

'I'm going in and you can't stop me,' said the mother, raising her voice even more.

'I know you're upset, and I fully sympathize with you, but have you considered that perhaps your child isn't in here?' Rose was trying to reason with the parent. She failed.

'I don't care. At least then I'll know something. Nobody has told us anything,' she replied.

'That's not correct,' said Rose, exasperated that this

encounter was taking her away from the life and death task in hand. 'Procedures are in place to help you. May I suggest you go back to reception and check with them, they'll be in a better position to ascertain the condition and the whereabouts of your child. After all, they may not be here and then you will be faced with further anxiety as you try to track them down.' The last remark was an attempt to win the parent's trust.

Mark knew Rose was right. Relatives in resus were a bone of contention among medical staff. Some believed relatives should be present when attempts were being made to resuscitate a patient, others fiercely disagreed. Some experts had postulated the theory that there are distinct advantages in that the relative can be a witness to the efforts of the medical team. They suggested a final embrace, last words, or actually being an eye witness to a last ditch effort, could act as a closure mechanism, enabling relatives to accept the demise of their loved ones more quickly. Others took an opposite view, seeing family members more as a hindrance than a help. In their view, terms used by the medical profession could easily be considered offensive.

Mark was of the latter opinion. Trying to x-ray patients with relatives in the vicinity could have its downside. But ever the pragmatist, he always tried to accommodate relatives' wishes as long as it did not interfere with his staff and their work. He moved forward to give Rose some support.

'Hello, I'm Mark. I'm just in the x-ray room over there. Can I help?'

The furious mother turned to Mark for support, repeating her intention to go into resus. Intentionally lowering his tone an octave so as not to appear harsh, he spoke gently.

'It's terrible what's happened, eh?'

'Terrible - that's an understatement,' she retorted. 'It's absolutely shocking, and do you know, I don't even know where my son is,' she confided desperately to Mark.

'Were you at the school?' Mark asked.

'Yes,' she replied.

'Did you attend the meeting with the headmaster and the Chief Constable?'

'Oh, I was there in the back row but once he mentioned a figure of casualties in the thirties or forties, I didn't hear any thing else,' she confessed.

Mark realized this poor woman was in shock and needed to be helped. He called another of his radiographers.

'Karen, can you look after the phones for me while I take this lady to reception. I think she's lost.'

'That's OK, Mark,' said Karen. He turned to the mother.

'Will you come with me please?'

'Can't I go in to that room? I want to go in. Please let me go in. Let me just have a look, at least I'll know he's not there.' She was insistent.

'Madam, it'll do you no good until we establish where your child is. Would you like to see a scene that has no relevance to your son and might be very upsetting to you?' said Mark.

'Well, no, but at least I'll know the kind of treatment he will be getting,' she persisted.

'Suppose he doesn't fall into that category and doesn't need the treatment you'd see in resus, isn't that giving you unnecessary worries?'

Mark was right. There was a distinct possibility the child might not need any treatment at all, but it wasn't his place to act as counsellor. The tactic worked; the mother hesitated and Mark took advantage of the lull in her pleadings.

'Please ....' Mark said, 'Please come with me to reception.' The sympathetic tone had the desired result at last. The unhappy parent stopped her protestations with Rose and started to accompany Mark.

'Thanks, Mark,' the consultant called out as they walked away.

'No problem,' he said with a backward glance.

They walked slowly towards the reception, Mark trying some small talk and the mother's only concern being to establish the whereabouts of her child. Nearing the end of the long corridor, they passed Graham, Danielle, Sharon and their counsellor heading towards the mortuary. For no apparent reason Mark stopped to look at them. The parent he was taking to reception became slightly agitated again.

'What are you waiting for?' she said, annoyed at the delay, 'I haven't got all day you know.' Her loud voice caught Danielle's attention. She looked up to see what the commotion was all about. Her eyes met Mark's and a deep pang of sorrow was felt by them both. Mark couldn't explain it, but something told him this woman was about to suffer an agony he could not begin to imagine. Her body language told him she was going through indescribable pain. Her downcast eyes, dulled and brimming with tears, and her faltering, unwilling footsteps, told him she had lost someone dear to her that day. She appeared only half alive. Little did Mark know there was a song going through Danielle's head. There was always a song for her, saying the things she couldn't put into words herself. This time it was *Don't Forget to Remember* by the Bee Gees.

Chapter 17

'Theatre co-ordinator here, can we have a radiographer for Theatre One please?'

'Will send one up,' said Karen, who had temporally replaced Mark.

'Nick, will you go to Theatre One please.'

'What's it for, ORIF or …?'

'They didn't say, probably, they'll let you know when you get there,' she told him.

'By the way, who's the patient?'

'I think it's number thirty-four, because she's been through CT and Mel said her chest was fine.'

'That's great news, Karen; the bullet missed her vital organs. Actually I x-rayed her in resus. I think she's got a shattered tibia; so that's probably what they're trying to fix. Did you get the name of the surgeon?'

Yes, it's Mr Bendrix.'

'I'm all right then,' and Nick headed out of the department.

John Bendrix was a consultant orthopaedic surgeon or 'Orthopod', as the radiographers called them. He'd had his fair share of tragedy and recently had had to deal with his mother's death after she had been a victim of a hit-and-run. This had affected him profoundly. It was not public knowledge among the staff but Nick had x-rayed his mother and he wondered how the surgeon would react to the current situation.

Nick was another example of the changing face of radiography. Previously, the average age of radiographers was eighteen, but he was fifty when he qualified. He was one of the mature students who made up a staggering seventy per cent of all new recruits. In addition to studying, nearly all the older applicants had to hold down part-time jobs to support their families. Gone were the days when students were offered means-tested grants. In Mark's day, no student would have had any debt when they qualified, which was a very different picture to the present one. Nick's success also proved the old adage 'you're never too old to learn.'

He'd been educated in Glasgow before heading for London and a degree in Business Studies. His plan was to become a company secretary eventually, but for some reason he couldn't even explain to himself, he changed direction and returned to education after a twenty year gap. He was the oldest student in his class.

He was the first to admit his career path had been a chequered one, working at office cleaning and even running his own business which employed twenty people. After being caught out in a severe recession, during which he lost everything he'd worked for, he tried all sort of things just to keep the wolf from the door.

The turning point came when gall bladder problems took him to hospital, where he was diagnosed by a radiographer who chatted about the work his job entailed. That was it. Nick was fascinated and decided there and then to retrain to embrace this profession.

During his training and afterwards as he started working in a hospital, Nick found his maturity, rather than being a hindrance, was actually an asset. His mentors were constantly commending him about his patient care, and where the younger trainees were sometimes reticent when dealing with older patients, Nick was the opposite, talkative and friendly.

The downside of his training was juggling family responsibilities with university schedules. But looking at his first year's salary, he was glad he and his family - especially his wife - had made the sacrifices. Now, three years after he'd qualified, he felt able to meet most diagnostic challenges, but like his colleagues, for him this day was the greatest challenge of all.

University certainly hadn't prepared him for slaughter on such a scale as he was now witnessing. His thoughts suddenly turned to Fatima, silently willing her to cope; she had looked so brittle and so vulnerable.

Nick collected his white theatre shoes from his locker and headed upstairs to the operating theatre. There, he slipped off his work clothes and replaced them with theatre blues. He liked the colour, the blue was serene and calming, and the lightness of the clothing was a welcome change from his normal uniform.

In the theatre area, he picked up his II or C arm and proceeded to Theatre One, where he set up the machine and awaited the arrival of the young patient, who was presently being anaesthetized.

While he was waiting, Nick reflected on the work of another largely unsung group of medical professionals – anaesthetists. He believed very few people knew exactly what they did, and yet no operation could proceed without their consent. He had often watched them as they constantly monitored patients undergoing operations, checking that everything was OK all the time, and ensuring that the surgeon was warned immediately if any of the observation parameters were breached.

The little girl was transferred onto the operating table; her small feet barely came half way down the table. The anaesthetist had taped her eyelids to maintain vital moisture on her delicate eyeballs and to prevent them drying out during the operation, causing damage.

The theatre suddenly became a hive of activity as each member of the operating team took up their own particular role. They had one purpose: to ensure this small injured girl would walk again. Once scrubbed, the surgeon in his blue sterile theatre gown, splash proof mask and sterile gloves, resembled an astronaut. Underneath his sterile clothing was a lead coat to protect him from the x-rays issuing from the C arm.

Before the operation could commence, the child was covered in blue sterile drapes. Only those who were part of the operation team and clad in sterile blue theatre gowns were allowed to touch her now. Any inadvertent contact would render the person and the area contaminated, and the whole process would have to start again from scratch. Valuable time could be lost because of a moment of carelessness and all theatre staff had it drummed into them. Taking care was an essential part of the theatre ethos.

Nick looked at the blue drapes, wondering for an instant whether they would prove to be the little girl's shroud. He shook himself for thinking such a thing, even fleetingly. He knew his thoughts had been clouded slightly by what had been going on around him. Now, he had to concentrate on the job in hand.

The surgeon turned to the Anaesthetist, Robert McKinley.

'All right to proceed, Robert?'

He gave the thumbs up.

John Bendrix opened his hand. A scalpel appeared like magic. Nick watched, always amazed at the silent communication between the scrub nurse and the surgeon.

Very few words were exchanged between them, but every implement he needed appeared in his hand at precisely the right moment.

Silently the skin was cut open with the scalpel and blood vessels were cauterized to minimize blood loss. The acrid smell of burning flesh filled the air, and although everyone wore a face mask, the smell was so pungent it penetrated even this. The delicate task of exposing bone began. Great care was taken so as not to cut into tendons or nerves, which could lead to paralysis of vital muscular functions of the leg.

It was extremely hot under the brilliance of the operating lights and the heavy lead coats were uncomfortable. Perspiration began to appear on the surgeon's brow. Deftly a hand appeared and wiped his forehead. Once again the trusted 'dumb' scrub nurse needed no reminder. Then Mr Bendrix turned to Nick:

'We're going to need a quick flash to see what we have.'

'OK, Mr Bendrix,' Although they had the x-ray images taken during her initial examination at resus, the surgeon still wanted to know what he was dealing with, and whether the situation had changed. With a nod of his head towards the wall he pointed Nick to the images displayed on the PACS computer system in the operating theatre.

'See, the tibia is shattered. Your initial flash has confirmed what I saw earlier. I'm going to try and put a pin in it.'

John Bendrix always liked to explain his procedures to his staff. He felt it generated a team spirit in the operating theatre, and that they would work together better. Some surgeons felt that was unnecessary and barked out demands without explanation. John willingly embraced change; he wasn't one of the dinosaurs of his profession. It always annoyed him when the old adage was trooped out about surgeons seeing themselves as God. Mr Bendrix certainly did not see himself in that light, and was keen to learn new methods and procedures. He was much respected amongst surgeons, and had contributed many well-reviewed articles to the British Medical Journal.

A tall man of over six feet, he towered above everyone in theatre. His golden blond hair had now nearly disappeared and his shiny bald patch brought to mind a monk's tonsure. He spoke in a well educated English voice which could have sounded pompous, but didn't. He walked with a highly individual gait; even from behind and at a distance anyone could easily identify him.

Having being born in a time of austerity, a vitamin deficiency had resulted in bow legs and he always reminded the staff of John Wayne in a cowboy movie. They joked that he looked like a sheriff with his breeches supporting guns slung at the hips, going out to meet the bad guys for a showdown. The staff had nicknamed him affectionately 'the cowboy', and they teased that when he was created he was shaped sitting on a horse. He took all this friendly banter in good part, sometimes saying 'I've come for my horse' when he joined them, underlining the good nature and character of the man.

It was perhaps the austere years he spent on his own with his mother that had been so instrumental in developing his compassionate approach, and most staff looked forward to working with him.

He was fond of music, with eclectic tastes, which some of his colleagues found puzzling. Being Oxford educated and considered to belong to the higher echelons of society, they expected him to gravitate more to classical or operatic music. But his love of all types of music gave them something else in common, apart from the work they did together. His sessions in theatre always resulted in a musical feast and strangely, the music he chose almost always seemed to fit in with the type of operation he was performing.

'Can you give me another flash please, Nick?'

'OK.' Nick moved his C arm under the table and depressed the x-ray button on the console. Unseen to the naked eye, a chain reaction had occurred. Millions of electrons had been produced and travelling at the speed of light, had bombarded the human body, terminating their mad rush at the C-arm receiver. Showing this had taken place, the yellow light on the monitor illuminated, and simultaneously an image appeared on the screen. Nick tried to ensure a clearer picture by use of coning to minimize the radiated area.

'Thanks, Nick. Can you save the image please?'

Nick pressed another button on the console and a number '1' appeared next to the image on the screen which would be printed once the operation was over.

'Done.'

'Transfer it to next screen please.'

'OK.'

The monitor has two screens, making it possible to view two images at right angles to each other simultaneously.

'Can you give me a lateral please?'

Nick flicked a lever on the C-arm and like an obedient servant, it swivelled ninety degrees; at the same time Mr Bendrix lifted the tibia.

'Flash please.'

'OK.'

There was another flash of yellow light followed by an

image. Two pictures were now available enabling the surgeon to assess the degree of damage.
'We'll definitely need to put a pin in.' Using the plural, he always made a point of including the whole team.

'OK.'

With the skill acquired over many years, he started the procedure. Occasionally, a grunt would issue from him if he felt frustrated, but the soothing music in the background had the desired effect. He chose a selection from his own collection to play during operations. He had downloaded many recordings and no one knew what they'd hear next.

As he worked on the girl, a track by The Four Tops *When She was my Girl* started to play. Nick thought how poignant it was, echoing the way the parents must be feeling at this moment. He listened to the words and hoped the child on the operating table would not be gone as the sad and sentimental lyrics portrayed. Sadly, he knew that this song would reflect perfectly the feelings of many of the parents that day.

'Flash,' called out Mr Bendrix.

Nick pushed the button. As he did this, Robert McKinley, the anaesthetist came round to the child, injected some more anaesthesia, and returned to his control console to monitor her condition. He looked at her saline bag and replaced it.

'It's going very well,' he said.

'Why, are you surprised?' asked Nick. 'Mr Bendrix always delivers.'

'Thanks for the confidence Nick, but I've had some challenging patients in my time, and I've had my bad moments too.'

'I'm sure you have, Mr Bendrix, but those challenging patients are partly responsible for your experience,' said

Nick.

'What'd you mean?'

'Well, Mr Bendrix, to coin a phrase, smooth seas do not make experienced sailors.'

'That's some philosophical saying, Nick. Anyway - flash.'

'OK.'

Although it was a particularly sad day in the operating theatre with so many children lost, John Bendrix knew the power of maintaining a morale boosting atmosphere, and had deliberately tried to keep a spirit of togetherness amongst the team. His warm personality and gentle banter permeated the theatre, and while the staff were not their usual irrepressible selves, nor were they as low as others in the hospital.

'The guide wire is in,' he said so all could hear. 'I think we're ready for the pin. Let's get this poor wee girl's leg fixed, team.' No-one was surprised to hear the Scottish 'wee' slipping out. John Bendrix had lived in Scotland for a long time now.

With great care and dexterity which would rival a woman threading a needle, he proceeded with his reconstruction of the leg, the delicate operation punctuated by his instructions to Nick, who replied 'OK' to each command,

'Save.'

'OK.'

'Flash.'

'OK.'

'Lateral.'

'OK.'

'Back to the AP please.'

'OK.'

'Flash.'

'OK.'

The surgeon's speechless communication with his scrub nurse resumed. Out came the hand and a drill was presented to him. Once the drill stopped, the correct drill bit found its way into his open palm. This continued until the operation was over.

'Right, I'll close her up and hand her over to recovery,' Mr Bendrix said to his operating team. After stitching up the exposed flesh, he turned to Nick.

'Thank you, Nick. You know you radiographers do a sterling job too.'

'Oh we're all part of the team, Mr Bendrix,' said Nick, believing this was absolutely true.

'No, I mean it. I'm not trying to flatter your profession,' said Mr Bendrix.

'Flattery is ….' but John Bendrix didn't give Nick time to finish.

'I know what flattery is, it's giving undue or excessive praise, usually with the intention of getting something back. That's not what I mean. What I was saying is you radiographers are worthy of commendation too, because the simple fact is most orthopaedic surgery would be impossible without your input. So when you go downstairs, pass my gratitude to your colleagues.'

'Thanks, I'll do that, Mr Bendrix.'

'You know,' said the surgeon, 'It'd be so good if for once the media looked at the roles of radiographers and tried to highlight the good work they do.'

'That's a good idea, Mr Bendrix. Maybe one day, a radiographer will write a thrilling novel to grip readers' attention and weave in their roles … watch this space, Mr Bendrix, watch this space,' concluded Nick.

The operation over, the little girl was taken to theatre recovery to be monitored and to ensure she was fully awake before being transferred to the children's ward.

As soon as she'd been wheeled out, an army of cleaners suddenly appeared in the theatre. Usually, they came in at the end of the shift, but with so many casualties, the theatre had to be restored to its usual pristine condition to safeguard against any of the patients picking up an infection. As the cleaners entered, all attired in their green uniforms, Nick paused. He felt he could not pass without commending them too.

'Jean, can I speak to you and the A team.' They all laughed at the mention of the A team.

'What do you want?' said Jean, 'we're a bit busy as you can see.'

'I know. It will only take a minute or two. I wanted to congratulate you all on the important jobs you do.'

'Important? Well, it doesn't seem so.'

'No, honestly, this is not to butter you all up. I'm deadly serious. You all know about the tragic things that have happened today. We've just fixed a poor lassie's shattered leg and another kid will be coming in here straight away. Mr Bendrix is one of the top surgeons in the country and so the wee girl has had the best possible care. But you cleaners play a very important role in the operating team too, and we need your skills.'

'Och, anyone can be a cleaner,' one of the others remarked.

'Yes, but not everyone can clean to an acceptable standard,' Nick reminded her.

'What do you mean?' asked another.

'Well, just imagine you were all sloppy in your cleaning habits and any of these children caught an infection. They may have had the best surgical team operating on them, but if you haven't done your jobs properly, and they pick up an infection, they might have to have a limb amputated. The analogy….' Nick didn't get a chance to finish as Jean interrupted.

'My, that's an awful big word, analogy, what'd you mean?' said Jean.

'What I mean is if you lot are sloppy in your duties, all the efforts of everyone involved in this or any other operation would be fruitless. So, although you may feel insignificant at times, you should never, ever, underestimate the role you play in the operating theatre,' Nick told her.

'That's the nicest thing anyone has ever said to us,' said Jean in amazement. 'I must admit, when people ask me what I do for a living I always say that I'm just a cleaner. But you're right, we're not just cleaners. We are an important part of a team. It's so encouraging to all of us that, today of all days when we're all feeling so down in the dumps, you should bring a ray of light into our lives. Thanks, Nick.'

One by one the other members of the cleaning team agreed with her.

'I meant it,' said Nick. 'After all, remember TEAM' and he told them what it stood for.

'Well, Nick, here's another one for you then … DEAL. That means Divided Everyone Achieves Less.'

'Where did you learn that?' asked Nick

'From Mark, the superintendent radiographer,' said Jean, then added, 'and talking of radiographers, you know at times we feel you lot are just as invisible as us cleaners. We know you play an important role but most people know nothing about you.'

'That is so true,' said Nick, 'but' he added, 'I bet you, by the time all this shebang is over, all of us from porters to cleaners and radiographers will be seen in a new light.'

'I don't think so,' said Jean. 'No honestly, I mean it,

just you wait and see.'

'Anyway, Nick, we need to get a move on. You are stopping the workers working. The next patient is due in shortly.'

Nick moved his machine out of the way to enable the cleaners to do their essential work. Out came the tools of the trade, scrubbing machines, mops and wipes. All were colour coded to ensure the correct mop was used for the right contaminant, red for dealing with blood for example.

As he watched them, he realized his view of them was indeed correct. Here were people behaving in a similar way to Mr Bendrix and his scrub nurse. They might not have been to university or written peer-reviewed articles or use good grammar when they spoke; their knowledge of x-rays, physics or the physiology of the human body might be lacking, but there was no doubting their commitment to their jobs. He reckoned they were very lucky, here at Bonnyholly Hospital, to have them.

They showed the same enthusiasm for their work as Mr Bendrix showed for his. Was what they were doing any less important? Was a painter of Michelangelo's' standard better at his work than these humble cleaners? Could a comparison be made between their work and Shakespeare's? Many would give a resounding 'No' to those questions, but looking at their happy faces as they scurried about their duties, Nick was in no doubt they had the same love of their work as either Michelangelo or Shakespeare. The proof was what he had said earlier to them; any shortcomings in carrying out their work could undo all the skilled surgery carried out in the theatre.

Nick was about to leave the room to report back to Mark, when a song caught his attention. John Bendrix's CD was still running as no-one had had the time or the inclination to turn it off. The song now playing was *Search for the hero inside yourself* written by M People. He listened intently to the first chorus telling listeners to find the key to their life.

The parents, relatives and friends of the casualties were all going to have to do exactly that, especially the parents. Once all the mayhem had died down, and the media had found another headline grabbing story, they would be left alone to deal with their grief. The surviving children might be left traumatized, and they too would have to learn how to cope. All involved in any way with this day's tragedy would need to dig deep into their own reserves at some stage or other in their lives. It would be a miracle if they all came out of this unaffected and well-adjusted. They would indeed have to dig deep to find the hero within themselves.

Chapter 18

The walk to the mortuary was the longest journey Danielle, Graham and Sharon had ever undertaken. The couple had once holidayed in Australia and to them, the twenty-four hours' flight was a picnic compared to this. Every step was an agony and there would be no stopover or sightseeing tours on their way this time. The corridors were lined with memories of the good and bad times they'd known in the hospital.

The colourful pictures drawn by children from the local school which were hanging proudly on the walls suddenly took on a different meaning. Danielle could not bear to look at them. Her mind went back to her thirteen week scan. She'd been full of beans and walking down this same corridor, she and Graham had paused and looked at the drawings.

'You know, one day our child will draw something just like that.' She'd been absolutely right. Young David had loved drawing and painting pictures and had presented them proudly to his parents. They weren't exactly to the standards of Michelangelo or any of the modern or classical painters; they would not command fees running into thousands or perhaps into millions of pounds; art lovers wouldn't flock into galleries to gaze at them in amazement, but to Danielle and Graham, they were priceless and they wouldn't ever part with one of them, although maybe, just maybe, one day they might feel able to donate one of his pictures to the hospital in memory of David's short life.

Bonnyholly Hospital had played a pivotal part in his life; it had witnessed his arrival into the world, and now, sadly it had also taken him back into its arms. There would no more fitting a place to hang one of his paintings.

Danielle looked down so she wouldn't catch sight of the pictures, in an effort to minimize the pain. Sharon appeared unruffled by what had happened. The blitz mentality was all too evident. Here was someone who had experienced some terrible things in wartime. A teenager at the time, she'd helped air raid wardens dig relatives, friends and neighbours out of bombed houses. Nothing, she felt, could equal the gruesome sight of so many dead, dying and mutilated bodies.

If the saying 'tough as old boots' was indeed true, then it could well be applied to Sharon. The epitome of the British Bulldog, her erect posture and purposeful walk masked her reaction to the shattering news they'd been given. The only clue to the turmoil inside showed in her eyes, which lacked their usual brightness, and where tears she could no longer hide were beginning to gather. For once in her life she was silent; gone were the usual clichés and catchphrases about the blitz and the good-for-nothing cheating husband. Gone the rather bossy mother and in her place the anguished grandmother who had lost her only grandchild.

Graham was trying to keep a stiff upper lip for the sake of his wife. His arm was tightly around her, holding her up, and showing he loved her and that they were facing this together. Occasionally, Danielle's steps faltered and he held her even closer. Inside, he was screaming, but there was no hint of it in his posture. He knew one of them had to be strong, and with Danielle in bits, it had to be him. He choked back his own tears so she wouldn't see them, dreading arriving at the mortuary when they would have to formally identify their son. He tried to swallow the lump in his throat, but it refused to go away.

Liked Danielle, he didn't believe in God, preferring instead to accept whatever happened in his life. He'd studied a number of religions but none held any interest for him. He and Danielle felt they did not have to have a belief in an unseen and all powerful deity to lead good lives or to be caring people, and they treated everyone the same, irrespective of race, creed, age or sexual preferences.

Over the years, they'd both argued with Sharon over the existence of God, but now, faced with the loss of his beloved son, many questions were going through his mind. Questions he now found difficult to answer. If Danielle was feeling the same, he knew what would be in her mind. As always, there'd be a song in her head, a song that fitted the occasion and the mood; it was her way of dealing with everything, good or bad. Graham thought the Johnny Nash song *There are more questions than answers* would be the only one right for this day.

Mike Reid and John Pottinger were also silent. They led the way, just a few paces in front of the shattered family. Experience had taught Mike what would be going on in their heads, but he knew this day would prove to be the most difficult assignment he'd ever had. He didn't know if he would be able to carry on afterwards, and was now seriously considering whether to take the early retirement on offer.

One design flaw in an otherwise excellent building was the position of the mortuary which could only be reached by a corridor going right through A&E. This could sometimes cause distress to relatives. No-one knew whether this was an oversight that neither the architects nor the Health Board had picked up on, or because the designers had thought more deaths would happen there, so it would be more convenient.

Whichever it was, for the Darlings, passing through the A&E corridors had the effect of compounding their grief. Milling in the corridors were scores of anxious parents, some venting their fears on the staff as they waited impatiently for answers. At that moment, the doors of resus, which also opened into the corridor, were flung violently open as a radiographer hurried out with a bundle of cassettes for processing. With the doors open, Danielle and Graham could clearly hear the urgent sounds of the medical staff trying desperately to save the lives of their tiny patients.

The doors were quickly closed, but that brief exposure to the work going on inside had a dramatic effect on Danielle. She collapsed in tears, wailing in her grief. Her distress reminded observers of television news when it was showing a funeral cortege in Middle Eastern or African countries.

Reaction in the corridor was instantaneous. The parents arguing with staff about whether to be allowed into resus to witness the care of their children stopped, and even the radiographer rushing to process her cassettes stood still. For a brief moment everyone knew this was no ordinary cry for help, this was a woman in utter despair, and looking at the two men accompanying the family, they knew too this was just the start; there was worse to come, possibly for some of them waiting there.

They remained silent, not just out of respect, but because for an instant, it made all their problems pale into insignificance. As the group passed the crowd of relatives, some of them parents themselves, were moved to tears. They all moved aside without any prompting, and formed an unofficial guard of honour as the bereft family passed through.

'Poor thing,' was the only comment heard.

Once the party was out of hearing, the arguments began again.

The seemingly endless walk eventually reached the entrance to the mortuary. Mike and John, who had led the way, did not immediately open the doors but paused. It was Mike, the veteran of so many episodes of bad news, who spoke.

Danielle was still sobbing.

'I know this is going to be very, very, difficult for you. All I can say is your David did not suffer.'

'Did not suffer?' Danielle wanted to yell at him, 'you have a cheek, you weren't there, how can you say that with certainty?'

Tears were threatening to blind her now but the words wouldn't come out, and as she tried to speak through the sobbing, she started to hyperventilate.

'She can't breathe,' Sharon shouted. 'For goodness sake, do something man!'

John knew what to do. He grabbed a wheel chair which had been parked in the corridor and sat Danielle on it.

'Just take deep slow breaths,' he said encouragingly, 'imagine you are breathing into a paper bag.'

Slowly her erratic breathing subsided.

'Feeling a bit better?' asked John.

Danielle only nodded.

'We'll wait a few minutes then,' he said.

Danielle shook her head and pointed to the door of the mortuary. Mike needed no interpretation, her gestures plainly stated she wanted to get the whole episode over and done with.

Supporting each arm, Graham and Mike raised her from the wheelchair, and with her sandwiched between them, they walked her gently towards the mortuary door. As they neared it, she began to hyperventilate again. Mike couldn't see her face but he could hear her laboured breathing and feel her shaking.

'Do you want to have another rest?' he asked. Her answer came by starting to resist them violently and by making every effort get to the door. Mike guessed she wanted to confront the demons that waited for her behind it.

A look passed between him and John; Mike nodded and John pushed the mortuary door and held it open.

The chill of the room hit them, and Danielle became absolutely quiet. It was as if a bucket of cold water had been flung violently into her face. She shook off her escorts and went in. On a trolley was a covered body, the size and shape of a child. The group moved towards it and took up their places around it, without anyone saying a word. Mike went to the head of the trolley, Danielle and Graham stood at the right hand side with John and Sharon on the left. John went through the usual procedure of formal identification.

'Do you want to say a prayer before I begin?'

'No,' the bereft parents said quickly in unison. Neither wanted Danielle's mother hijacking this intimate moment. They knew that would have been her first instinct. Indeed, Sharon did want to say a few words but kept silent. She knew this was no time to impose her religious views on her daughter and son-in-law. She had brought Danielle up to form her own opinions, and by heck she was going to respect her today of all days. But nothing could stop her saying her own silent prayer, and she prayed they would not find her grandson in here.

'Mr and Mrs Darling, can you identify this child as your son David?' Mike removed the covers slowly and revealed just the boy's head.

Danielle merely nodded. Graham replied with no hint of emotion.

'Yes,' he said.

'I'm sorry to ask you both again, but are you quite sure? Are there any distinguishing features?' said Mike, hating what he had to do at this moment.

'Look at his mop of hair, man. Look at his dad. Are you blind?' said Sharon, in an effort to speed up the process, and her voice for the first time showing some of the emotions she was feeling.

Graham spoke as if he hadn't heard her.

'There's a scar on his left leg. He slid down the chute one year and fell off at the bottom, and this left a permanent scar on him.'

Mike moved towards David's feet. The little boy's body covered barely a third of the length of the trolley. Slowly the feet were uncovered and the tell-tale scar could be seen. The identification was complete.

'Graham, please take me home now,' said Danielle.

'Of course, dear,' he replied.

'Obviously, there'll be the usual pathologist's examination of the body, but it ….' Mike cursed himself for using the word 'it' and hoped none of them had picked the word up. He was wrong. Danielle shot him a look of pure hatred.

'I'm so sorry, Mrs Darling, I meant to say he'll be released to you shortly to enable you to make the funeral arrangements,' and as if pleading for her understanding, he added, 'it's been a long day for all of us and we're not thinking straight. Please forgive me if I've offended you in any way.'

Once the formal identification was complete, they made their way back to the car park, having to pass through A&E yet again. The same parents were still there and they could see their suspicions had proved true. Those who were sitting down stood up immediately; the others merely stopped talking. Their gestures of support were comforting to Danielle, who, because of her grief, had failed to recognize some of the faces, but as she acknowledged their concern, she knew some of them would probably have to face the same shattering news she had. She gave a half-hearted smile of appreciation and walked on toward the hospital entrance.

Sitting near reception was David the paramedic, taking a brief respite from the rigours of his hectic day. He recognized her immediately and went over to talk to her. Haltingly, she tried to tell to him what had happened.

'Whit can I say? I'm sae sairy; ye hae my deepest sympathy. I will be thinking o' youse,' he said. Danielle was unable to reply.

'Thank you,' said Graham, and then, recognising the paramedic, added, 'aren't you the guy who brought Danielle in when she was in labour?'

'Aye that's richt, and whit a mess she made of ma ambulance.' It was a half-hearted attempt to lighten the bleak mood.

'Thanks for your sympathies,' said Graham. Before they went outside, Danielle looked back and caught David's eye. There was a silent message there but David couldn't work out just what she was trying to tell him.

Chapter 19

At 8 o'clock the following day, nearly twenty-four hours since a crazed gunman had shot at a room full of children and their teacher, Mark assembled his crew for a briefing before they went off. They all looked exhausted and bedraggled. Their clothes were dirty. Patches of perspiration showed in their armpits, although those who had been assigned to theatre had changed their regulatory white tunics and black trousers for theatre blues giving them a fresher appearance. The few available seats were soon filled with weary bodies, and it did Mark's heart good to see the younger radiographers give up the seats they'd flopped into, to the older ones. He decided at least one positive thing had come out of all this, it had brought them all closer together.

'How do you all feel?' he asked them.

'Fairly whacked.'

'I'm shattered.'

'I feel knackered.'

'Completely bushed.'

'You wouldn't want to know.'

'I could sleep for a week.'

'I hope to high heavens I never, ever have to go through something like that again in my whole life. It's like being in a war zone.'

The last comment elicited a firm response and agreement all round.

'I know,' Mark continued, 'at the moment, the whole impact of what you've been through will not have fully sunk in. But once you get home and have a good kip, if you manage to, then yesterday will take on a different perspective. There will be some emotional fall-outs. Some of us, in fact, most probably all of us here will be affected one way or another.'

'Oh, by the way, how's Fatima,' asked Nick.

'I was going to come to her. Fatima's a classic example of what I am talking about. On the surface, she seemed to be coping, but you all saw how she went to pieces. She's at the other end of what happens in situations like this. Some will be in the middle hiding their feelings. Some of you will take things in your stride. To those of you in the middle, please remember we're going to have counselling sessions.' Mark paused, looking round the room as if trying to guess who'd be most affected by the terrible day they'd just experienced.

He continued. 'After Lockerbie, no one stopped to consider the effects on the mind of seeing such appalling devastation. But as soon as I got the phone call about this major incident, I arranged for everyone in this department to receive counselling.' He spotted one or two exchanging glances. 'No, it's not an option. It's mandatory. Please don't feel I'm taking over your lives or interpret this as me being a busybody that has nothing better to do. It's out of care and concern and because I don't want any of you to end up like I did. I wish the systems had been in place then.'

'Thanks for your concern, Mark, we really appreciate it. But you never answered our question. How is Fatima?' said Nick.

'Margaret?' said Mark, nodding in her direction

'I sent her home,' Margaret answered.

'When?'

'After taking her for a tea-break, I put her in a taxi and sent her home.'

'You sent her alone?' queried Mark.

'Well, yes.'

'I thought you'd put her in the rest room,' said Mark in disbelief, 'she was in no fit state to look after herself. Do you know where she lives?'

'I thought she lived with her parents,' said Margaret.

'No, Margaret, she doesn't. She moved out because she had a disagreement with them. They tried to bring her up in a strict Muslim manner, but she objected, saying she wanted to live her own life and choose the way she practised her religion. Her parents were not very happy, I can assure you.'

'So what you're saying is she has no backup at home?'

'Precisely, Margaret. You should never have sent her home in that state. Why, oh why didn't you tell me?'

'Mark, you saw what the place was like. You were running around like a headless chicken. The last thing you needed to worry about was one less staff member. I acted in good faith. I was looking after both you and the department, and, believe it or not, Fatima's welfare.'

Realising the atmosphere was turning hostile, George stepped in.

'Mark, seeing as you know her so well, why don't you give her a call to make sure she is alright. Go on, do that now.'

Mark dialled Fatima's home number. No answer.

'Try her mobile, no doubt she'll go to bed with it by her side,' said George.

Mark called her mobile phone. Still no reply.

'Maybe she's got it in silent mode.' Margaret was starting to feel guilty that she'd left the girl to go alone.

The phone went to the answering machine service. Mark left a message.

'Mark, if you get me her address from your files, I'll call on her on my way home just to see if she's all right,' said Margaret.

'I'll come with you, Margaret,' said Jenni.

'Are you sure? It's a bit out of your way,' said Margaret, reading the address Mark had jotted down for her.

'It's fine, I'll just follow you in my car. Afterwards I can use the back roads to get home, but I might just stay with her today. We get on quite well.'

'Thanks, Jenni.'

'Just before you all go,' said Mark, 'there is one last task. Forensics wants us to x-ray all the bodies for their records. They want to establish where the bullets went and also if they are still in the bodies.'

'Which bodies?' asked Nick.

'The ones in the mortuary. Some of them didn't go through resus as they were dead on arrival. They went straight to the mortuary. Others died while they were being worked on in resus'

'How many bodies are you talking about Mark?'

Was it tiredness or the sheer numbers, but somehow Mark could not bring himself to mention the figure.

'Quite a few,' he said.

Margaret picked him up on this.

'What'd you mean, quite a few?'

'Well it's more than there was at ....'

'Mark, you're not making sense,' said Margaret, 'more than what?'

Mark's reluctance to answer was based on his wish to spare his staff this final, dreadful job. He believed it would be a step too far for them to be confronted with all the dead children. Each radiographer had been in contact with several children in the past hours, but in the main they hadn't witnessed the final outcome. To be confronted with the deaths of so many all together would be too devastating. This was a task he, and only he, should shoulder. He'd been through a similar situation and was better placed to deal with it and cope with the aftermath. He wouldn't tell them the final figure. It would be better if they heard it from the media.

In Mark's mind, this way, it would be less personal and therefore would have less of an impact on them than if they were to go the mortuary and actually see an endless array of young bodies draped in black covers. He wouldn't subject any of the staff under his leadership to such an unforgettable sight.

'You've all had a hard time. Go home and rest. I'll do this last job,' he made a half-hearted attempt to smile.

'Mark, you can't run up and down with the cassettes from the mortuary. Why don't you let me come with you,' said George.

'No, it's fine, honestly. The walking will do me good, I could do with it - I need to de-stress after being cooped up in here all night.'

Nobody replied and Mark went on. 'Well done all of you. You did your profession proud. I'll not be surprised if this whole episode brings the role of radiographers into focus. Mark my words, the media will be shouting your praises. School kids won't want to play doctors and nurses any more, but nurses and radiographers. You'll see, the universities will find they're inundated with applications from talented people all wanting to be radiographers.'

Mark was confident that their role would at last be recognized and appreciated.

Margaret was more philosophical.

'You mark my words,' she said, 'there will not be single paragraph about a single radiographer. I bet you'll never read in any paper or see on any news bulletin the vital roles the radiographers played yesterday. They'll mention the police, the emergency services, the paramedics and the medical staff. I mean it, there'll not be one word about us.'

They all hugged each other and encouraged everyone to take care. One by one they shook Mark's hand as they left the room.

Mark watched them go with a feeling of pride. He was satisfied with their performance on a day like no other had ever been. Their jobs had been just as important as any of the medical teams that battled so valiantly to save those tragic children.

After they'd all left, Mark went to resus and collected one of the mobile x-ray machines. Margaret had left it charging in a corner. He unplugged it and drove it away, stopping at the x-ray department to fill the cassettes holder, before carrying on to the mortuary.

Mark lost count of the number of times he went along those corridors from mortuary to x-ray department. Working alone, he had plenty of time for reflection, and took a decision influenced by the events of that fateful day. He decided never to have any children; he would stop the adoption procedure straight away.

Mark was a suspicious man and believed in fate. He believed things happened in threes. He'd been at Lockerbie and now at Bonnyholly Hospital at times of appalling tragedy. He had suffered emotionally on both occasions. He reasoned, rightly or wrongly, that if he had any children, they would end up dead before their time, and he wasn't prepared to risk it. Such a cruel world.

Chapter 20

David, who had now realized that number one had been his namesake, became thoroughly depressed. He thought back to the morgue where he had taken him with the porter John in tow. It dawned on him that if he was feeling this way for a boy he'd hardly known, how much worse it must be for the parents, Graham and Danielle. He had to do something. He couldn't just mope around; he had to do something positive. But he could not think what; his mind was such a tangled web of emotions.

He wanted to get his hands on the madman who had committed this heinous crime. That, of course, would be wrong, even if the man wasn't already dead by his own hand, evading the law and the condemnation of the world. David couldn't even bear to mention the man's name; it was odious. He could only think of him as 'that man,' and he wondered what sort of world it would be if vigilantes were allowed to administer their own form of justice.

Turning his mind back to the question in hand, he had in idea.

'I ken whit I'll dae. I'll sit doon here and write a letter to Graham and Danielle,' and straightaway he sat down to do it. It took him some time; he had to get it right, and say exactly what was in his heart.

Danielle opened the letter and read it before calling Graham through to read it too.

Dear Graham and Danielle

Firstly, I want you both to ken that I was sae chuffed when you named your son after me. What a privilege, eh? He touched so many lives too. I remember you in the ambulance when you were in labour. My, what a puddle you left! Never mind, I got Fred with a mop and bucket to clean it up. But dinnae worry, we'll no be sending ye the bill. Seriously, I ken you've both been through a terrible time, and I was talking to my wife about you. She 'whae must obeyed' asked me to send you this wee note to encourage you, and show we're thinking aboot you.'

That was not quite true; they'd had no such conversation, but David thought if the Darlings knew another couple were thinking about them it might bring some comfort. They couldn't say 'how can anyone with no children really understand.' David continued.

I was sae looking forward to retirement and spending time with my grandson who is a similar age to yer wee David. Every time I look at him noo it will remind me o' him. Please, both of you, think of Bonnyholly Hospital. You hae been in its grounds and hae seen first haun its awesome and breath-taking scenery. There are many flowers in the hospital gardens. Hae you ever noticed the way a flower seems bowed down after weathering a storm, and then lift its head again in the sunshine. It's a touching sight isn't it? After all, that cloudburst probably sent monie animals and people - who are far tougher creations than any flower - running fir shelter. Yet, yon poor wee flower stood there, rooted, and faced the weather's full fury. It was as if it was saying 'we shall not, we shall not be moved!

Danielle paused at that point. 'What a wonderful thing to say,' she thought, remembering how she and other parents had exchanged similar remarks at the school gates. The memories came flooding back; the excitement of her first prenatal scan by Linda the Sonographer, and how she and Graham had almost danced down Bonnyholly Hospital's corridors and outside the main door, as high as kites, had stopped to look at the beautiful landscape. There'd been a thunderstorm while they were inside and they came out to an awe inspiring sight. The sun had appeared and a brilliant rainbow was gracing the sky. True, as David's letter was now saying, the delicate flowers were being awakened from sleep. It seemed as if the sun was summoning them from their downcast state just like the Queen knighting someone with two touches of her sword on their shoulder, and then uttering her proverbial 'Arise Sir ….'

Danielle carried on reading the letter, thinking what a nice guy this David was. She was so glad they'd named their son after him. She realized he was taking great care with his writing.

I know ye like singing Danielle, so ye probably know the words of the song and can quote the remaining verses. Me, I'm jist a poor uncouth excuse o' a musician. Now, efter that cloudburst, the flower stands intact and erect! Aye, it may appear bowed initially but it's unbroken. It's shown strength that contradicts its delicate appearance. Ye may wonder, as ye admire it, if it'll ever regain its vigour and lift its lovely head to the sky once more. Well, it's much the same with many of us. In these troubled times as we've seen on TV, we all face all manner of storms in our lives. Some of us face economic hardships like the credit crunch, or depression, or failing health or the most traumatic loss of all, the death of a loved one. These things that happen to us can be likened to tempests or ferocious storms, and all of us at one time or another in our lives will be affected by any of these things. Sometimes we jist can't avoid them, jist as that poor wee flower can't uproot itself and run for cover when it rains. It's so moving to see you two showing such surprising strength after such a disaster in your lives.

I want you to think about trees. Why trees, you may wonder? Because, now more than ever, you need to support each other. You see, arboriculturalists have discovered an amazing thing aboot trees. They actually survive better in pairs, which appears to be a contradiction. You'd expect twa giant trees side by side to be competing for space. But in fact they help each other survive because of their root system. Twa trees planted side by side eventually link their roots and become inter-twined and the combined strength of the twa acts as one. When you visited Bonnyholly Hospital you saw those magnificent trees in the grounds of the hospital. Think of those trees and see yourselves like them, standing proud and unbowed, and although battered, not beaten.

Well in time Graham and Danielle, consider this; jist like that poor wee flower after the storm, you too can lift your heads up from grief and find joy and fulfilment in life once again. So never give in, except to convictions of honour and good sense. Those words were Churchill's and spurred on a nation. Well, the same sentiments can also keep you strong.

So remember what we've said, even if things seem dark and hopeless and you just cannot see the way out of your despair, yes, even if you feel that you're going to collapse in a heap at any time, keep going. Never, ever, throw in the towel. Always remember 'You become a champion by fighting one more round.' I'm including a poem that I hope will be an inspiration to you both.

The poem spoke of finding sunshine behind the darkest grey clouds, telling those that were hurting to hang on and be as brave as they could be. For the sadness and sorrow of those terrible days, it was absolutely perfect.

The sunshine always remains there
Even when behind the darkest of clouds
Will soon shine with brilliant intensity
And empty the sky of those grey clouds!
For, even the darkest clouds
And the most ferocious of storms
Unwaveringly are followed
By a dazzling and delightful new sunrise
So, remain as strong as a flower in a storm -
Be as valiant 'gainst all,
For tomorrows special rainbow
Soon shall be out -
You just wait and see!

After reading David's letter, the couple's spirits were eased. The despair that had overwhelmed them lifted a little, and they both started to believe that there could still be a life after their terrible loss.

'Do you know what I'm going to do?' Danielle said.

'I'm going to copy this letter, personalize it and send it to each parent who either lost a child or was a casualty of that man. Look at the effect those words have had on us. I'm sure the other mums and dads will be encouraged to keep going.'

'That's a lovely thought,' said Graham. 'I feel it will

carry more weight coming from you. They'll all say that here's a person who's lost perhaps more than any of us, and be grateful that at least they have other children. They'll know you only had one and yet in your grief you're prepared to think of others.'

Graham took her in his arms. 'I always knew you were thoughtful and caring but this has shown me, as the lawyers always say, 'beyond reasonable doubt' that I was blessed by having you as my lifelong partner.'

'Oh, that's by Celine Dion. Are you plagiarising her songs?'

One of her favourite songs of all was *Because you loved me* by Celine Dion.

Chapter 21

Each parent, according to their religious beliefs, had arranged for a ceremony for their dead child. The area Health Board, together with the Hospital Board in Bonnyholly, decided that in the light of the special circumstances, they would sponsor a neutral memorial service in a neutral location in order to avoid offending anyone. Board Members also felt many of the parents whose children survived would like an opportunity other than at a funeral service to convey their condolences, and show their support for those who hadn't been so blessed.

Bonnyholly Conference Hall was chosen and the Health Board paid for everything, including wonderful flower arrangements in every colour imaginable. The hall was on the top floor of the hospital and had a glass roof, which the architects had designed specially to maximize the use of natural light. Tinted glass panels, which doubled up as windows, surrounded the hall, and each window pane had a removable black covering to give the occupants complete control over the amount of light needed in the room for any occasion.

Opened up in full, the views from any of the three hundred seats were stunning. Every seat had a view of the hills. The podium was the middle, and could rotate slowly, thus enabling all occupants seated in a circle around the speaker a view of his face every minute. The Board ensured the Conference Hall was adorned with some memorabilia of the children. Their drawings decorated the walls; playing softly in the background was some of the music the Primary Ones had sung. Wonderful perfume from the stunning flowers greeted the guests as they entered the hall. There was an attempt to convey a serious but joyful atmosphere in celebration of the brief lives of the little ones no longer with them.

The invitations had stipulated this was not to be a sombre occasion. The tragedy had attracted the world wide attention of the press and broadcast media, and the Health Board's Public Relations and Communications Department had circulated a press release about the service. Seating was limited in the hall itself, so arrangements had been made to relay the service to the local community hall via satellite link onto a large screen. The local hall had received some financial support from the Health Board as well and had used the money to touch up the paintwork and decorate the interior of the building with more mementos of the children and a huge floral arrangement. Broadcasters from many parts of the world planned to be present.

The day of the service came with astonishing speed. The BBC had arranged to provide live coverage from inside the Conference Hall. The other channels had set up their broadcast vans with huge satellite dishes in the car parks. They looked top-heavy, as if they could topple over at any moment. It was July, the height of the Scottish summer and the hills were resplendent in their summer dress of heather and greenery. The stunning background setting of the hospital added something very special to the occasion.

In twos and threes, the parents arrived, having to brave the gauntlet of reporters trying to get a story from them. Graham, Danielle and Sharon arrived together at 2 o'clock, an hour before the service was due to begin. Sharon was wearing an elegant blue dress with a matching hat.

'No cheap dresses this time,' she'd said, 'for once in my life, a little splashing out will do no harm.' Graham was smart in a dark grey suit, white shirt and tie, and Danielle, not wishing to attract too much attention, had bought a plain red dress and like her mother, wore a matching hat. On her wrist was a specially purchased floral band and she wore a necklace with the name 'David' worked in gold. Small diamonds filled the spaces between the letters of her son's name, reflecting light from every angle and drawing people's eyes to her slender throat. Graham had commissioned this special necklace for her, sparing no cost. He wanted her to have a permanent reminder of their beautiful boy.

As they made their way into the hospital entrance, they saw many familiar faces. Greetings were exchanged, although some of the parents were nervously anticipating the service.

'I'm dreading this.'

'I hape it does nae bring back too many sair memories.'

'I'd tae drag ma Fred here. He thinks I will nae cope.'

Others were more upbeat.

'I'm looking forward to hearing what the others are feeling.'

'Oh, there's Helen, let's go and talk to her.'

Danielle walked through reception and into the now-familiar corridors. A shiver went through her body and she suddenly felt cold.

'I wish I'd brought a coat,' she turned to Graham for support.

'Och, it's roasting. Don't tell me it's ….'

'No it's not, and before you get funny, I'm years away from the dreaded menopause.'

This was like a red rag to a bull to Sharon. 'Menopause! You wouldn't know how bad it is. I tell you it's worse than what I went through in the blitz and ….'

'And threw out that no-good cheating husband of yours,' said Danielle finishing her mother's often repeated sentence.

'Young woman, you're not too old to get a skelp from your mum, so just watch your lip,' said Sharon angrily.

'Mum, you can't skelp me, I'm ….' Sharon's words were suddenly interrupted by a tap on her shoulder. She turned round and a familiar face was smiling at her.

'Hello. Dae yer mind me?' It was David the paramedic, with his wife.

'Of course I do,' said Danielle. The sight of this kind man had a therapeutic effect and she smiled back at him. Her smile lifted all their spirits, and she stopped feeling shivery.

'Oh thank you for the lovely letter. It helped so much,' she said and planted a light kiss on David's cheek.

'Hey, you've a wife of your own,' said Graham jovially.

'Aye, and don't I ken that,' said David with a wink.

'Here's ane fir ye then, you jealous guy,' and David's wife kissed Graham's cheek.

'Dae you mind if we sit with youse?' said David.

'Of course not,' said Sharon.

'It'll be a privilege having you sitting with us,' Danielle told him warmly.

The walk to the Conference Hall now felt less threatening. Danielle's mood lifted and she pointed admiringly to some of the childish paintings gracing the corridors. Graham noticed the dramatic change in her face and instead of walking hand in hand, put his arm around her shoulder. They looked like a new couple in love, with the same joy they'd had when they were leaving the hospital after Danielle's thirteen week scan.

They took their seats in the hall.

'What stunning views eh?' said David.

'You're right, David, I don't think words can describe the mountains today,' said Sharon, enthralled.

The service began and several speakers addressed the gathered families. Some parents were interviewed about how the incident had affected them and any brothers and sisters their dead child had left behind. Then the chairman of the Health Board, Donald McIntyre, approached the podium to give the keynote speech. Danielle noticed he had very few notes; perhaps he was going to use an autocue. She looked round, but couldn't see one. Donald looked around at the waiting faces and began to speak.

'I want to say a big thank you to all of you for coming here today. I know it's been a very harrowing and unhappy time for each and every one of you. It's also been difficult for us here at the hospital. Nearly all your children were born here, and many of you felt the hospital was your second home judging by the amount of visits to the x-ray department.'

His words brought a smile to everyone. He continued:

'We've all been through emotions we've found very hard to deal with. We're a small community and the incident touched everybody in it. No-one has been left unscathed. But this isn't going to be a doom and gloom speech. I want you all to remember the happy times you had with your children and the joy they brought you that no-one can ever take away from you.

I know I speak for the Board when I say it's a good

time too to show our appreciation for the help of the police, the fire brigade, all the other ancillary workers and of course, the medical teams. The ambulance crews, the doctors, nurses and surgeons all did a sterling job. But I thought today of all days, with the world media focused on us, that this would be a pertinent moment to thank another group of staff; a group who are seldom mentioned. Because of the power of film and television, many fictional paramedics, doctors and nurses have become household names, and you all know who they are. Women have swooned over many famous doctors, and nurses are featured in every medical drama. But there's one profession you hardly hear of and yet without them you wouldn't have seen your infants before they were born; the broken bones the doctors had to fix would've been impossible without them, and most of us here at some time during our lives will come into contact with them, but we'll be ignorant of who they are, or what their function is.

Some of you refer to them as x-ray nurses, but they're the *radiographers*. They are responsible for nearly ninety per cent of all diagnostic procedures. They've x-rayed your broken bones; if you've had cancer and needed treatment, it's very likely you've encountered them; if you've needed a CT scan, they would have carried this out too. The radiographers in this hospital paid a heavy price because of the outrage that deprived you of your children. Many suffered emotionally; one, fatally.'

He was referring to Fatima who had been found at her home by Margaret and Jenni, having apparently committed suicide. 'Yes,' he continued, 'let's not forget the radiographers.'

Donald paused and took a sip from a glass of water on the podium, but before he could continue, Danielle, for no apparent reason and to this day she cannot explain why she did it, stood up and started to sing. The crowd of parents, relatives and friends were mesmerized, not just because of the singing, but because of the words of the song – *I Can See Clearly Now*. They touched everyone.

Graham began to sing with her, and then Sharon and even David the paramedic added his voice. The impromptu singing rose and swelled as one person after another joined in. Donald was so astounded he couldn't put his glass down. He made a half-hearted attempt to take another sip but he felt as if his brain and fingers had stopped communicating.

The hundreds of thousands of people watching on TV at home and abroad were treated to a very unusual sight. What those in the hall failed to see was the unscheduled entrance of the Queen and Prince Phillip. For security reasons, her protection team had not publicized the fact she was coming. Their arrival wasn't visible to all because of the design of the building, although Donald McIntyre, the Board Chairman, and Danielle's group had a full view of their entrance. With the crowd singing their hearts out, the Queen and her husband gave their obligatory wave. Donald saw them and invited them onto the podium. As it rotated everyone present had a view of the royal party. Some parents burst into tears at the thought that their nightmare had even touched the higher echelons of royalty. Then, just as the crowd reached the last verse of his famous song, Johnny Nash, the American pop singer-songwriter came into the hall and joined in.

The television commentators hastily amended their scripts.

'And now an astonishing sight. Her Majesty, the Queen is making an unscheduled entrance into the Conference Hall. It's obvious by the reaction here that no-one knew she was coming. I've just been told it was at her request, that she has come here to show the families her sympathy. The audience is still singing, and it's very moving. It was all started by one mother. We don't know who she is, or her circumstances, but judging by her song, she was probably one of those who lost a precious child. Most of us will remember where we were this day. I will say nothing more - just listen to this … oh goodness me, I thought we'd seen everything here today, but the gathered families and their guests have just been joined by Johnny Nash – yes, Johnny Nash himself, whose song they are all singing so powerfully. He's come out of retirement to take part in this very special occasion, and if Shakespeare was right when he wrote that age couldn't wither her about Cleopatra, then that is equally true about Johnny Nash. His voice is just as strong as it was in his twenties. This is truly a day everyone here will always remember, and I, for one, was privileged to witness it. And now I'm handing you back to the studio.'

The crowning moment of that day was the dramatic appearance of a brilliant rainbow over the mountains. Danielle and Graham stood hand in hand looking at it for several minutes before they left the hospital. The crowd finally dispersed, unaware there was going to be a public enquiry into the tragedy. Some parents would have to relive the whole terrible event. Would their torment never end?

The memorial service would go a long way in helping them to cope.

Oh … and it was the considerate Graham Darling that managed to get Johnny Nash there when he contacted him to say one of his songs was a favourite of Danielle's. It was his prompting that moved her to sing in the hall.

Glossary of Scottish Words

aal all
aboot about
afore before
aff off
aft often
agane again
ain own
amang among
ane one
an aw as well
anither another
auld old
aw all
awa away
awfie awful
ay yes
aye/ayeways always
bairn child
baith both
belang belong
ben mountain
bide/byde stay
blethered talk nonsensically
bodie person
bonnie beautiful
brae hill
braw fine
bricht bright
brither brother
cald cold
cannae can't
cannie careful
cauf calf
cauld cold
coo cow
couthie friendly
cuik cook
dae do
deid dead
didnae didn't
dinna/dinnae do not
dochter daughter
doon/doun down
dour sullen
drap/drappie drop
eejits idiots
efter after
efternuin afternoon
faither father
fash annoy, inconvenience

Glossary of Scottish Words

fash yersel to worry
faund found
faur far
faut fault
fess fetch, bring
forenicht early evening
foriver forever
fou full
fower four
fowk people, family
frae from
fricht fright
fur for
gab talk
gane gone
gang/gae go
gaunae going to
gie give
gither (to)gether
glaikit foolish
gomeral fool
gowk fool
guidwife goodwife
gret great
guid good
guidman husband
guidwife wife
hae have
haein having
haud had
hame home
hamework homework
hauf half
hauns hands
havers nonsense
het hot
hied/ heid head
hoo how
hoose house
howp hope
ither other
intae into
ivverie every
jist just
ken know
kenspeckle conspicuous
kent knew
kimmer young girl
kirk church
kye/kyne cows, cattle
lad/laddie boy
lang long
lass/lassie girl
lave leave
leuk loo
ma my
mair more
maist most
mak make
man/mon man, husband
maun must
maw ma
mebbe maybe
micht might
mickle small quantity
mind remember
mither mother
monie many

morra tomorrow
muckle big, great, large,
nae no, not
naethin nothing
nicht night
nivver never
nixt next
nou/noo now
o' of
och oh
onie any
oniebodie anyone
oor our
oot out
ouch describes misery or anger
ower over
ower muckle too much
pairts parts
pitting putting
puir poor
richt right
richt nou/awa immediately
sae so/say
sairie sorry
shuir sure
spak spoke
stap stop
suin soon
syne ago, then, since
tae to
tak take
telt told
morra tomorrow
the nou just now
thegither together
thae the
thocht thought
thrang busy
twa two
verra very
wad would
wark work
warld world
watter water, river
waur worse
wean child
wee little, small
wee bit a little
weel well
whae who
whan when
whaur where
wheen a few
wheesht be quiet
whit what
wi with
wrang wrong
wumman woman, wife
ye you
ye've you've
yon that

Other Titles - Mirage Publishing

A Prescription from The Love Doctor: How to find Love in 7 Easy Steps - Dr Joanne 'The Love Doctor' Coyle
Burnt: One Man's Inspiring Story of Survival - Ian Colquhoun
Cosmic Ordering Guide - Stephen Richards
Cosmic Ordering Connection - Stephen Richards
Cosmic Ordering: Chakra Clearing - Stephen Richards
Cosmic Ordering Meditation CD (The Ultimate series) – Stephen Richards
Cosmic Ordering: Rapid Chakra Clearing – Stephen Richards
Cosmic Ordering: Sex Energy - Stephen Richards
Cosmic Ordering: You Can be Successful - Stephen Richards
Die Laughing: War Humour from WW1 to Present Day - George Korankye
Hidden Secrets: Attract Everything You Want! – Carl Nagel
Internet Dating King's Diaries: Life, Dating and Love – Clive Worth
Life Without Lottie: How I survived my Daughter's Gap Year - Fiona Fridd
Mrs Darley's Moon Mysteries: A Celebration of Moon Lore and Magic – Carole Carlton
Mrs Darley's Pagan Whispers: A Celebration of Pagan Festivals, Sacred Days, Spirituality and Traditions of the Year – Carole Carlton
Rebel Diet: They Don't Want You to Have It! – Emma James
The Hell of Allegiance: My Living Nightmare of being Gang Raped and Held for Ten days by the British Army – Charmaine Maeer with Stephen Richards
The Real Office: An Uncharacteristic Gesture of Magnanimity by Management Supremo Hilary Wilson-Savage - Hilary Wilson-Savage
The Tumbler: Kassa (Košice) – Auschwitz – Sweden -Israel - Azriel Feuerstein (Holocaust survivor)
Wisdom of the Heart – Flora Rocha

Other Titles - Mirage Publishing

Releasing you from series

Releasing You From Fear CD
Releasing You From Insomnia CD
Releasing You From Social Anxiety CD

The ultimate series

The Ultimate Confidence & Ego Boost CD
The Ultimate Self Hypnosis CD
The Ultimate Stop Smoking CD
The Ultimate Success in Love CD
The Ultimate Wealth Creation CD
The Ultimate Weight Loss CD